AT BAY

An Alex Troutt Thriller

Book 1

By
John W. Mefford

AT BAY
Copyright © 2015 by John W. Mefford
All rights reserved.

Second Edition

Sugar Hill Publishing

ISBN-13: 978-1-709126-40-6

Interior book design by
Bob Houston eBook Formatting

To stay updated on John's latest releases, visit:
JohnWMefford.com

One

Even a parched mouth couldn't suppress this runaway mental sprint. Nothing could.

"More numbers," the man whispered while smacking his pasty lips.

Raucous laughter made his heart bounce, and he shot a quick glance over his shoulder. The woman in the low-cut green sweater was laughing at him. So was the man wearing the Red Sox ball cap.

Why are they laughing at me? Don't laugh at me!

He sunk lower in his booth while squeezing his eyelids until spots materialized in his vision. He gasped a single breath, then opened his eyes and went back to counting granules of salt on the wooden table of the Back Bay restaurant.

A minute passed, maybe longer, but his pulse still raced. And he could hardly swallow from the cotton mouth.

"Water?" He lifted his glass at a passing waitress, but she acted like he didn't exist.

Fear gripped his body. But something else was there. Could a hint of exhilaration be coursing through his veins? It had been a while since he'd been out in public. Yet, he couldn't draw any logical conclusions from these polar-opposite feelings. He only knew that he could taste the batter of fried catfish in the back of his throat. The mixture of these conflicting thoughts was so toxic, it took every bit of personal restraint to stop himself from jabbing a fork into his eye socket.

He panted like a dog, and his hands started to tremble…until they face-palmed the table.

Salt granules under his fingertips. Back to his counting routine.

"One, two, three, four…"

While he silently cursed himself for starting over, the man couldn't recite the numbers any faster. His verbal skills were no match for his brain's processing speed. Someway, somehow, he had to drown out the merciless anxiety.

"More numbers, more numbers, more numbers," he muttered under his breath in an auctioneer-like cadence.

He scrambled to find another source. He blinked twice and recalled one of the equations written on his white board at home. "Schrodinger's Equation," he said aloud.

Almost instantly, his mind filled with the soothing music of JS Bach's Prelude No. 1 in C Major. He took in a breath, closed his eyes, and began to methodically plug numbers into the equation that had forever changed the field of quantum physics.

Anything to cope with the scorn of public humiliation just because he was…different.

"The fuck I don't!"

The jarring voice interrupted the man's thoughts. He opened his weary eyes to see a man in a bespoke charcoal gray suit draping his coat over a chair at a neighboring table. "Do you not remember who you're talking to?" the blowhard said into his cell phone.

The man felt a headache coming on and an instant desire to walk out and ditch this social experiment. Then he noticed the blowhard's starched dress shirt had French Cuffs. He'd only seen those in high-end stores, but never up close on a real person.

French Cuffs groaned onward. "I can close the fucking deal. And you know that," he said while thumping his chest before taking a quick peek toward the front door of the restaurant. "Just give me five minutes tomorrow with that asswipe, and he'll cave on the settlement. Guaranteed, or I'll get down on my knees and suck your..." He chuckled before he could finish his vulgar comment.

The man started feeling queasy. French Cuffs wasn't just your average blowhard. He was in a league of his own. The man was ready to end this night. He set his cash on the table, hoping the waitress would soon pick it up. He went back to counting salt granules until he heard French Cuffs grunting. He looked up and saw French Cuffs tugging on his hand while juggling his cell phone under his chin. Was he trying to pull a ring off his finger?

A second later, the ring flew off his hand and skittered along the smooth concrete floor. French Cuffs snatched it up like he was the Red Sox shortstop and slipped it in his front pocket.

"Always business, huh?" A woman with wavy Raven hair sauntered up and gave French Cuffs a brief kiss on the lips.

"Gotta go," French Cuffs said before ending his call and leaning in for a follow-up kiss.

The man couldn't help but watch and wonder. As their tongues danced like a pair of wet seals, his stomach churned. But he also felt a tingle inside.

"You want to ditch this place and just go to my car?" French Cuffs popped his eyebrows.

Raven tapped his cheek. "How romantic. I'm hungry. Let's eat first and then we can play," she said with a seductive wink.

The couple sat down and their conversation became subdued as their fingers interlocked under the table.

"Peeping Tom, are ya?"

"Huh?" The man cracked his knee on the table as he glanced up at the waitress refilling his water glass.

"You know I caught you in the act," she said with a sharp cackle.

"But, I'm just... But..."

"Yeah? Look, don't worry about it. I was just bustin' your chops." She waved a dismissive hand at the man, who didn't know how to respond. She stared at him an extra second, and he jerked his attention down to the salt granules on the table. When she walked off, he chugged his water while stealing another glance at the horny couple.

A song blared from their table—was that the theme song to the original *Rocky* movie?—and French Cuffs glanced at his cell phone.

"Your ball and chain?" Raven asked him.

French Cuffs rolled his eyes and set the phone face down on the table. "She's such a frickin' nag."

"What if it's about the kids?"

"It's never about the kids. It's always about her so-called important job. Fuck that. I bring home the bacon with my—"

Raven pressed a finger against his lips. "I thought you were going to end it. Soon."

"I am, I am. Just a little more time. Hey, here's the food." A waiter arrived with a tray of food and drinks.

The man knew his social instincts were a little off, but he was aware of what was going on. And he couldn't wait to tell his friend.

Using his phone calculator to validate some equations he'd whipped together in his mind, the man walked past the table while casting a casual gaze at the giggling couple. He choked on his own saliva. French Cuff's hand was moving up Raven's thigh. The man purposely fumbled his phone until it dropped to the floor. The couple paid him no attention when he leaned over to pick up the device. Fine with him. He loathed such interactions.

From the fluttering glow of the table's candlelight, the man snagged his best mental snapshot of French Cuffs' chiseled jaw line and dapper hair.

Once outside, he turned his face into the brisk wind blowing in off the bay. He knew he'd never forget that face. Just like he never forgot a number.

As he walked down the sidewalk, one question lingered in his mind: which number would French Cuffs be?

Two

For a fleeting moment, I could feel my breath stutter against my chest. Then the smell of fear returned, choking every other sense.

Piss. And not just a passing waft. It seemed like my head had been dunked in it, with a hint of crap lingering in the damp air. But there was more. An underlying scent of stale disinfectant clawed at my nostrils.

I tried to swallow, but a sticky saliva filled my mouth. I would have hurled had I not been scared to death.

I called out. No discernible words. I think I pushed air through my voice box, but I couldn't hear a damn thing.

Where was I? Why couldn't I speak?

Other than the pungent mixture of smells, a dark fog suffocated me. Suddenly, my chest lifted faster, and I heard a rushing thump. The thunderous beating of my heart.

I tried reaching out, but I couldn't feel my arm. I wasn't even sure I had an arm. I couldn't feel a fucking thing.

Somehow I sensed tears pooling. I hoped, begged to feel water run down my face. But it didn't happen. Nothing happened.

Was I alive? Maybe…partially. But not completely.

Holding my breath, I squeezed my eyes and yelled as loudly as I could. But there was only emptiness. Loneliness.

And fear. Fear that I'd never escape. Fear that I would.

What was that? Something metallic, cold against my fingertips. It was smooth and rounded. My pulse quickened, and the hope that I was still of this world emerged from nothing.

Centering all of my focus, all of my energy on my fingers, I traced the cool metal object… Human skin.

My breath stuck in my throat, and my heart exploded. I cried out.

"Alexandra?"

A flicker of light around the voice. A man's voice. I sensed that I should know this person. But nothing immediately came to mind.

"Your beautiful eyes are finally open. Guys, Doc, she's awake. Look. She's finally awake."

I blinked several times, and I saw a man's face hovering over me. Dark, dense head of hair. Thick beard like he hadn't shaved. He brought a hand to his cheek. His eyes became moist.

Other voices filled the air, competing against my racing heart. I moved my head a few inches left and right.

"Alexandra, my darling. You're in the hospital. Can you hear me? You're in the hospital."

Why is he screaming at me? I'm not deaf.

"Who…" I didn't recognize my own voice. I tried to lick my lips.

A horde of people lunged to the side of my bed, and my chest fluttered again. I focused my sights on the man with the thick beard, on the tone and pitch of his voice. I tried to speak, but my throat felt like it was full of cracked seashells.

"God bless that woman," someone said.

I looked around, but none of the other three figures in the room were familiar to me.

"Get her some water, dammit," another voice said, this one laced with an obnoxious accent. A thought zipped through my mind. I was supposed to know that voice too. And not for the most pleasant reasons.

Something cold touched my lips, and my body quivered.

The unshaven man said, "It's okay. It's an ice chip. You should suck on the ice. Your throat will feel better."

I let the ice roll down my tongue. It tasted incredible.

"More?" I gurgled.

"Here you go, hun."

Hun? The question lingered for just a brief second, but the feeling of ice in my mouth made my body tingle all over. I motioned for more ice chips, and they were given to me. My teeth crunched the ice, which only added to the euphoria.

Amid the low rumble of noise in my hospital room, I moved my fingertips again.

"Look, she's playing with my wedding ring. She must remember our wedding," the man said with anticipation as he moved closer.

My eyes shifted, and I saw his face again, full of hope and promise.

"Who are you?" I asked.

The room went silent.

Three

"**Y**ou're kidding me, right?"

Inching up in my bed while balancing a cup full of ice water, I felt a twinge in my lower back as I peered over the extra-large set of shoulders belonging to the person who purportedly was my boss and spotted the man who earlier had claimed he was my husband, Mark. He was a good-looking guy. Broad shoulders, fit. Reminded me of a young Andy Garcia.

Mark was speaking with a doctor and some other guy who wore a fedora and green suspenders. He looked a tad familiar. Or maybe I was just hoping to remember him—or anyone for that matter.

My mind had been deluged with questions in the last two hours, ever since I'd awakened from my unconscious state, a result of a car crash from four days ago apparently. My so-called significant other had conveyed that news right after I'd delivered that hundred-mile-an-hour serve right past his shocked face: *Who are you?*

How could I recall Andy Garcia, but not my own husband? And what was up with the tennis reference?

Two beefy boss fingers snapped just in front of my eyes.

"Alex, you're not drifting back into the dark world, are you?"

"Oh, sorry, I, uh…" I rubbed my face and realized my fear had subsided, but was replaced by a sense of inadequacy.

"Don't beat yourself up, Alex. The doctor said it would take a while to get your memory back. Like a patchwork quilt."

"Right. A quilt. I'm just looking for that first square."

He chuckled.

I squinted my eyes and looked at the big man. "What did you say your name was again?"

He leaned down, his beady, green eyes staring down at me like I was a specimen. "Jerry Molloy. I'm your SSA."

"SS…what?"

"Supervisory Special Agent. FBI. Damn, Alex, you're just not the same."

"I, well…" I wasn't sure what to say or how to say it. I felt conspicuous by my own presence, lacking understanding of everyone and everything. "Sorry, Jerry."

A twinkle of lights pulled my eyes toward the window, where a sparkly skyline interrupted the darkness. I pointed in that direction while turning back to Jerry.

"Where are we?"

His face stretched upward, then he ran his fingers through a thin patch of hair on his pumpkin head. "Whoa, we've got a ways to go," he said, turning back to the others like I was nothing more than a caged animal.

The people in the room shifted around, and then the man with green suspenders appeared next to my bed. He extended his arm for a handshake.

"I think we should start from the beginning," he said.

I glanced at his hand, then moved up to his face. Not exactly an Andy Garcia. He had soft lines, seemed like a calm guy. I reached out and shook his hand. I think a smile crossed my face.

He tipped his hat. "Nick. Nick Radowski, FBI. Nice to meet

ya."

"I'd give you my name, but, uh, it doesn't seem right to use a name I don't recognize."

"No worries. I know who you are, and you will too, eventually. I'm just here for you whenever you have a question. To help you start to piece together—"

"The patchwork quilt. Same thing that Jerry said."

"See? You're remembering things already."

"Short-term, yes, but long-term? I might have a better chance at whipping Steffi Graf in a straight-set match."

A vacuum of silence fell over the room.

"Okay, guys, I'm not real fond of being the butt of everyone's joke right now. What did I say this time?"

Suddenly, Mark pushed himself between Nick and me, his hands grabbing mine. They were strong, yet gentle. But why did I want to pull away?

"This is great, Alexandra. Right, Doc? This shows she's starting to come back to life."

A regal man with silver hair framing his face cleared his throat and approached the bed. He rested his hand on my arm as he eyed Mark, then turned to address me.

I appreciated the admission of my presence.

"Alexandra, you've suffered a substantial head trauma. I'm not surprised to see you've lost part of your long-term memory."

"It's Alex," Nick interjected.

"Shut up, Nick," Mark said without turning around, his lips puckered at me like I was a cute little baby doll.

"As I was saying, you banged your head pretty badly inside that metal cage. It was probably a good thing you've been mostly unconscious the last four days. It's allowed your body to rest and recover a bit. But more is warranted," the doctor said. "The memory thing…I wouldn't worry about it. Easy for me to say, I know."

He offered up a three-second chuckle, as if it were a part of his doctoral performance. I just listened, unworried about pretense.

"It's good for you to listen to old stories, try to recognize faces of friends and family. I'd be surprised if you didn't fully recover. I'd still like you to see a speech therapist, someone who will help you with mental exercises to improve your memory. Your other injuries are minor. A few scrapes and bruises. I noticed earlier, when you tried to move, your back seemed to tug at you. We haven't identified any issues there yet. Might just be some inflammation. If you're okay for now, I can have the nurse provide you a cold compress, and I'll ask the on-call orthopedist to drop by in the morning. Any other questions for me before I go home and try to catch the last half of Jimmy Fallon?"

I looked down and puffed out a breath, wondering if I should ask the doctor the myriad of questions bouncing around my empty brain or simply wait and ask one of these other guys. Just then, I noticed my sheet was down past my hips, and my hospital gown was shoved up a bit too high. I grabbed the sheet and pulled it up to my waist.

"It's okay, I'm the only one who saw," Mark whispered with an accompanying wink.

I felt my face burn. Embarrassed.

The doctor said, "Don't stay up too late trying to piece together your memory." He rested his hand on my shoulder, and I spotted his name tag.

"Dr. James Spurlock."

"Yes, that's my name. Sorry if I didn't introduce myself properly," he said, stepping toward the door. He stopped and pointed at the others. "Let her get some rest tonight, okay?"

All three agreed, maybe a little too eagerly.

Jerry followed the good doctor toward the door, dumping a can of soda in the trash.

I stopped him with, "You can't leave yet. I have some questions for you."

A tired smile washed across his face as he moved toward the bed. "I'm all yours, Alex. Ask me anything you like."

Before I could respond, Mark yawned and reached for the ceiling. "I'm bushed. Been spending most of my days up here, working at night, tending to the kids when I can. Thank God for Sydney." He crossed himself.

"We're Catholic?" I asked.

He forced out a chuckle and shifted his eyes from Jerry to me.

"It's one of those long stories. We'll save it for another day." He patted my hand, giving me the distinct impression he was blowing me off. I felt a seed of resentment in the pit of my stomach. And it didn't settle well.

"Wait." I reached for his arm where his sleeve was rolled up. So hairy, and I thought of a baboon. I quickly removed my hand.

"Yes, hun?"

His tone sounded insincere to me. Or maybe I was just being overly sensitive.

"We have kids?"

His smile returned. "Erin and Luke. I've already spoken to them tonight. I'll have Syd drop them by in the morning."

A slow nod. "Syd."

I searched my thoughts for memories of kids. A few images flashed through my mind faster than a speeding comet, but nothing stuck.

"Right. Sydney. She's our nanny. Lots to catch up on, Alexandra. I'm sure Nick and Jerry here can bring you up to speed on some of it. Hopefully it will start to click in the next few hours for you." Mark walked to a chair and picked up a navy-blue peacoat. "I'm beat. Need to get some shut-eye if I'm going to appear in court tomorrow."

My eyes shifted to Jerry and Nick.

Jerry flipped his thumb toward Mark. "He's an attorney," he said, then stuck his thumb in the front pocket of his jeans, over which hung his commanding gut.

"Damn straight, I am. Work for the most powerful firm in the city," Mark said, leaning in and kissing my hand. He let it drop as his dark eyes looked through me, or beyond me. It was hard to say.

"So you're going to work tomorrow?"

"Hun, if you were…you," he said with a chuckle, "you would have already checked yourself out of this hospital over the objections of doctors and family, and you'd be trying to find the guy who caused you to crash. Or solving the case you were on when you crashed. Or both, all before your morning coffee."

Mark attempted to rustle some laughter from Jerry and Nick. They seemed mildly annoyed.

"I'm off. I'll try to drop by during a break tomorrow." He waved his hand over his head as he walked out the door.

"Is he for real?" I said with a serious gaze at Jerry and Nick.

The turned to look at each other, and then burst out laughing.

Four

Jerry took a step closer to my bed. "Ha! Whew, Alex, you're too much right now. Mark's been the same for the forty-one years he's been alive, that much I assure you."

I shrugged my shoulders. I'd get into that scene later, but I had other questions right now for the two FBI employees.

"Where am I?"

The pair glanced at each other again, then back at me.

"The hospital, Alex. Geez, do we need to call in the floor nurse?" Jerry's schnoz seemed to grow as his face scrunched up.

"I understand that part. I'm just looking for a state, a city or town."

"Boston, Mass., Mrs. Giordano," Nick volunteered as Jerry sat in his chair again.

I looked toward the corner and spotted a blank TV screen. I immediately saw the irony, but kept my feelings to myself. "So that's my last name. Giordano. Very Italian."

"That's Mark. His family has roots back to Sicily. At least that's what you told me before," Nick said.

I pursed my lips. "Sorry I'm not able to, uh, you know…"

"It's perfectly fine, Alex. That's why I'm here to help. Plus, he told me I had to be here." He tried to look serious as he pointed at

Jerry. But then a smile broke through.

I grinned. "Ah, sarcasm. My perceptive powers are apparently working okay," I said.

"When you were on a roll, they were the best I've ever seen. It's like you had some type of voodoo power. Able to read right through anybody's bullshit."

"I know you're joking, but why are *you* here? I mean, I know he's my boss, but...you?"

Nick ran his thumbs up his suspenders, rocking forward on his feet. "Once upon a time, we were—"

"Don't say it." I threw up my hand.

"Did you think I was going to say...?" Nick left the sentence unfinished and released another sly smile. Jerry almost bounced out of his chair he laughed so hard.

"No. Ugh, I don't know, Nick. Tell me the truth, man."

"I always have, Alex."

"Okay, waiting..." I gestured for him to keep going, my patience for receiving facts running a little thin.

"We used to be partners."

"In the FBI?"

"The one and only," Jerry interjected.

"Who's my partner now?"

Jerry belted out a single chuckle, his torso lifting a good two inches, then he scratched the back of his head. "That's the thing, Alex. You didn't really want a partner. You said partners only slowed you down."

Processing everything that had just been shared, I slurped some ice chips.

"Can I get you more water?" Nick asked.

"Sure. Thanks, Nick." I tried to lock eyes, but he simply gathered my cup and scooted out the door.

"So tell me the real scoop, Jerry. Why isn't Nick my current partner?"

"I told you the truth. You thought partners got in your way. Nick included. You have no idea how much of a ballbuster you were. That's why we're all looking at you like you have four tits."

Part of me felt offended, but a sliver of some memory pinged a small piece of gray matter. "I may not be laughing—my head still hurts a bit—but I think that's funny."

"Nick is a good agent, but he's also a nice guy. You two were polar opposites."

Nick walked back in and handed me the cup of ice water. "Thanks." I took a few healthy gulps, then set the cup on the tray in front of me.

I scratched my nose and took in another strong dose of the rank odor.

"You smell it too, huh? Shit, I thought it was just me and hospitals," Jerry said, waving a hand in front of his face. "I think I have some type of strange allergy to these places."

"It was this godawful smell that woke me up."

"What a way to come back to life," he said.

A quick thought from our earlier conversation. "So, Jerry, before Mark and the doc left, you asked me if I was kidding you about something. What did you mean? What were we talking about?"

"Figure of speech."

"I got that part. But why did you say it?"

Jerry shifted his weight and said, "I was basically stunned to hear those words come out of your mouth."

I closed an eye, hoping to recall what I'd said. Nope, no such luck. "Dammit, now my short-term memory is slipping. What words?"

"I was talking to you about the crash, and you *politely* asked if there was a way you could avoid having to drive that particular type of government-issued vehicle in the future. You didn't like the way it handled."

"Uh, okay. What's the big deal?"

"The big deal is the old Alex wouldn't have asked me anything, certainly not nicely. You would have *told* me to shove that Crown Victoria piece of shit up my ass." He guffawed. Nick and I joined in, although I realized I was essentially laughing at myself. Or my old self.

Would I be me again? I curled my lower lip in and chewed on it a bit, then reached for the water and slurped another mouthful. My eyes searched the starched sheet for answers…about me, my past, and my future.

I lifted my head in quick order. "Tell me more about my crash."

Jerry pursed his lips for a moment, then said, "Well, you were moving at a high rate of speed. The roads were slick from a light rain, middle of the night. They think you probably just lost control."

"Who's they?"

"It's being investigated by the state police."

I nodded. "Any reason why I was driving so fast on a rain-covered road?"

"Shit, I've seen you move fast when you're at the grocery, practically running through a store, throwing boxes, cans, fruits, and meats in your cart. You seemed to have your shit together, but you were always in motion, as if you were an hour behind where you needed to be," Nick said.

I studied his face, but I could see he wasn't bullshitting me.

Nick continued, "You were a super mom, juggling your career as an accomplished FBI agent while being a wife and mothering two kids."

"Are you calling me a Type A, Nick?" I raised an eyebrow.

"You've been called a lot of things, Alex. Some good, some

not so flattering, mainly because you wouldn't take shit from anyone," Jerry said.

I shook my head and glanced back at the dark TV screen.

"Sorry if this isn't easy, Alex," Nick said.

"It feels like I'm standing at the pearly gates, and I'm having my entire life replayed, one judgmental segment at a time."

"That's the other thing." Nick lifted his hat for a moment, then reset it on his square head.

"What other thing?"

Nick shifted his eyes at Jerry.

"What's all this about?" I moved a finger between them.

"We just don't want to upset you, Alex, that's all."

"I'm a grown woman. I can deal with it as long as I don't have to ask ten times and it's the fucking truth."

I stopped breathing for a brief second, and I wondered if I'd just said what I thought I'd heard.

"She's baaaack…" Jerry curled into a ball of laughter, but I waved him off. I didn't feel like I was back. I was still as lost as ever.

"You and religion, and those pearly gates you mentioned, aren't really on friendly terms," Nick said, wincing a bit.

"Damn, you're good at dancing around the facts. You act like religion is a cousin or a neighbor down the street."

"I'm just saying that Mark comes from a more, uh, traditional family. His parents are Italian and Catholic. Oh, very Catholic. You? Not so much."

I hadn't thought to ask about my side of the family. Maybe later.

"What do I have against religion?" I couldn't escape the surreal feeling of asking others about my opinions.

"It goes way back. You were raised, at least for a while, in a very strict environment. I think you've been rebelling ever since,"

Nick said, his thin lips tight against crooked teeth.

"Hmm. That couldn't have gone over well with Mark's parents," I said more to myself.

"Or Mark," Nick said, quickly bringing a hand to his mouth.

I thought more about Mark and my current feelings toward him. He was a hard one to gauge. I could recall a few snippets of our past, laughing with him, maybe on our honeymoon. Mountains in the backdrop as we lounged on beaches, drinking frozen beverages that were teal and orange. Hawaii maybe.

In some respects, he seemed enamored by me, especially when I'd first woken up from my four-day nap. But then again, he seemed like he couldn't wait to leave. I didn't feel special. More like an odd combination of suffocated and empty. Of course, I wasn't in a normal state of mind. I had no sense of self, how I was supposed to respond to anything. I felt like a nomad searching for the invisible door where all of me existed.

Recalling my earlier interaction with Mark, I realized I never heard him tell me that he loved me. Not that I would have returned the favor—I just didn't feel it yet. But with all his fawning after me at first, I would have thought he would have provided a loving comment on his way out.

A crinkling noise stole my attention from my thoughts. As I turned toward Nick, I spotted a gum wrapper falling aimlessly to the floor, as if in slow motion. Then I heard lips smacking. And one slice of memory returned, just like that.

"It's you, Nick. I remember you now," I said as the beeping sound from the heart monitor accelerated.

My former partner's face lit up, but my eyes quickly shifted to the gum wrapper on the floor.

"You litterbug prick. Stop smacking your gums and pick up your damn trash. What do you think this is, a fucking landfill?"

Jerry looked at Nick. "*Now* she's back."

Five

Hunkered in a corner wooden booth, the man slurped the foam off his beer three times, one of the forty-nine brews that the bar, located in Back Bay, claimed were handcrafted. Lifting his gaze, the collar of his peacoat brushed against his thick beard, yanking a few whiskers. It annoyed him, but he appreciated the feeling of cover. In some ways, it also excited him, although he knew his mission wasn't a jubilant matter. It was serious.

Life-or-death serious.

He took a quick glance across the room—many of the women, employees, and even a few customers were dressed in traditional garb from the colonial days: colorful hooped skirts, quilted petticoats, tall hair, and low-necked bodices. In other words, breasts were the highlight of the show. Some things never changed. A few tables over, he admired one young lady scooping up her purse from the floor next to her chair.

"You never seen a boob before?"

Startled, he nearly bit his tongue. A tall woman shaped like a lamppost hovered just to his left. He tried looking her in the eye as she started tapping her pen on her pad.

"Can you speak, man?"

Dipping his head below his coat collar, his eyes found the

greasy, plastic menu.

"I'll take some potato skins and some fried shrimp."

"Gotcha. Can I get you some breast milk with that?" She giggled.

He accidentally swallowed his saliva and began to choke until his eyes watered. He gulped down a mouthful of beer, then slammed down the mug, sloshing some of the beer on the table.

"Dammit!" he said, grabbing a handful of napkins. He scrubbed, but somehow the liquid seemed to expand, some of it dropping to his lap. "Crap."

"It's okay, dear," the woman said.

He refused to make eye contact.

She grabbed a rag from a nearby busboy and helped mop up the suds from the table, then she rested her hand on his shoulder. "Really, it's okay. I didn't mean to startle you."

"Potato skins and shrimp, please," he said through gritted teeth, disgusted at the way her bony fingers gripped his shoulder.

"Okay, okay," she said, holding up both hands as if he held a gun. "I'll have it right out to you. You must have had an anxious day at the office. Drink some more of that beer. It'll help calm your nerves."

"Whatever," he said, picking up the beer and taking a sip.

She walked away, and he mumbled a phrase to himself six times.

Finally able to see straight, he walked to the bathroom and washed his face. When he returned, his appetizers were sitting on his table. Relieved he didn't have to interact further with the waitress, he sat down and picked up one of the shrimp, inspecting it for a good five minutes.

"It's not going to bite." The curly-headed busboy snickered as he passed by with a crate full of dishes.

The man held up his hand, ready to defend his protocol. *Screw that kid*, he thought. *The guy wouldn't understand the impact of iodine on the human nervous system.* He pulled out his phone, tapped his app of choice, and began reviewing a series of numbers. They filled his entire screen.

Slowly, his breathing calmed.

He ate the shrimp, then most of the potato skins. The same skinny waitress delivered another beer. She tried to make small talk again, but he refrained from any conversation, acting as if he was enthralled by the content on his phone. He actually *was* engrossed in his ritual, something he enjoyed several times a day. He viewed it as his own version of yoga—to find a place that brought him at least a sliver of internal peace in this chaotic, fucked-up world.

Glancing up, his eyes found the same girl he'd noticed a few tables over. Her elbows were on the table, her hands propping up her chin. The net effect created an avalanche of cleavage. She batted her eyelashes. Even from twenty feet away, he could see her extensions. Despite her rather slutty appearance, she had a sweet look about her, a caring soul. Maybe she'd grow up to be a social worker or a nurse. Really contribute to society.

But he wasn't sure she'd ever get the chance.

His eyes shifted to the right about three feet, toward the guy she was admiring. Actually, she was gushing over this tool. With his red and gold tie pulled away from his neck, he tossed a couple of cashews in his mouth, letting his designer watch dangle just enough to catch the eye. Who knew how much he'd sunk into that piece? Two grand, four grand maybe?

Wearing a Gucci suit, including a vest with custom-made buttons, Gucci dress shoes, designer money clip and belt, this guy was a walking decadence machine. Not surprisingly, he made a not-so-honest living as an investment banker, focusing on hedge funds, working out of the Prudential Tower just a few blocks south of the bar.

But it was his ultra-cool demeanor that created a stir inside the man still positioned in the corner booth. The way he lured any girl of his choosing with the wink of an eye. The jackass even had dimples to give the illusion he was as innocent as a baby boy. The girls typically couldn't resist touching his face—that was when the invisible pheromone leash would be attached.

The man peered at the oblivious couple, realizing he'd seen this situation play out a million times. And it always ended the same.

Shaking his head, he nibbled at the few remaining pieces of potato skins and tried to divert his attention back to the content on his phone. Typically, that would be enough to shut out the rest of the world and all its flaws.

A few seconds ticked by, and he couldn't help but glance back over at the fox hunt. The girl patted the investment banker's knee, then began the slow crawl up his thigh. She thought she'd hooked a prize fish, maybe the biggest catch this side of Gloucester. But the man knew it was the investment banker who was pulling the levers at just the right moment. No hooks were needed. It was more of a tap-dance routine that would end up with the young girl waking up next to a cold pillow. Sure, there might be a follow-up rendezvous, possibly some words exchanged to make it seem like there was a common bond between them, maybe even a hint of a future—if this and if that occurred.

Halley's Comet had a better chance of screaming across the Boston skyline tonight.

The man could see the arrogant dick's hand. No wedding band. The girl with the push-up bra was nothing more than a part of a game. The thimble, or the car, maybe even the horse—just like the game pieces in Monopoly. Made of metal and with no soul—that was how the cheesy asshole viewed this girl, and many more before her.

But she wasn't the victim in this sexual coup. The real victim was at home as usual, busy changing the diapers of her four-month-old and spoon-feeding her three-year-old who had Down syndrome, both girls, all while dealing with decorators and architects for the new addition to the house. Her husband had already told her he expected two more kids in the next three years, with the hope that one would be a boy. The family lineage couldn't end with a complete prick. His wife had also been convinced that her partner for life would need ample freedom to socialize with potential clients.

He was the sole breadwinner and, therefore, could dictate every aspect of their relationship. Right?

"What a dipshit," the man muttered, his eyes shifting between his phone screen and the pervert, who now laughed at the girl's joke, something he surely couldn't give two shits about.

The man watched her hand reach its intended target, and then her eyes went wide. Essentially, she believed she'd landed Boardwalk and Park Place all in one bold move. And she had every intention of setting her roots down, creating a hotel or two. She'd probably already gone from envisioning a night of passionate sex to a jet-setting lifestyle that included homes on both coasts, lavish vacations to breathtaking destinations, butlers, and lawn boys.

In some respects, her naïveté was almost deserving of how she would be used like a tissue. But what the hell did she know? She was probably no more than twenty or twenty-one. That guy, Christopher Barden, was a vulture wrapped in Gucci—whether it was made of snakeskin, eel skin, or in his case, foreskin—focused on nothing more than the ego-boosting conquest of bagging another ditzy girl who couldn't resist his cute dimples and mesmerizing charm.

The man in the corner considered walking over to their table and sticking his finger down his own throat, so he could spew his rancid puke all over that loser. But it wouldn't do that guy justice. Not even close.

He took in a breath, then finally released a filter in his brain. With his eyes studying the data flashing by on his phone screen, he casually stuck his hand in the right pocket of his coat, then pried apart the coat's material until he touched the plastic encasing. It was long, thin, and for now, protected.

Ten cc of propofol would be enough to get the party started. Tonight, he was going to get some satisfaction for a change. It was difficult to hide his emerging smile.

He knew he'd make someone very proud.

Six

I flipped through the four pictures Mark had sent me, pausing on each one for a few seconds, hoping to find that emotional thread that connected me to my kids. I'd birthed them, changed their diapers, rocked them to sleep every night, and woke up in the middle of the night when they were sick, holding them in a steamy shower until their lungs opened up.

I'd done it all. At least that was how I envisioned it.

The fact was I couldn't remember a damn thing about that part of my life.

Sitting cross-legged in my hospital bed, I glanced out the window where I picked up horns beeping several floors below. The day appeared to be gray, like my mood. Sullen was more like it. I was angry at myself for having the crash, annoyed at the man who said he was my husband because he didn't seem to care much—he'd shot me a text an hour earlier with the four pictures, saying that's all he had time to find before his court appearance—but even more annoyed at myself for thinking I needed his attention and sincere love.

Come on, Alex. He's your husband, and the father of your two kids, even if you can't recall them. Cut him a break. He's been dealing with a lot of shit since you wrapped your car around a tree.

I pressed my fingers into the corners of my eyes. My head ached from the inside out. I took in a slow breath, wondering if my first session with the speech therapist later in the morning would provide that magic moment when all my memories and thoughts and feelings would flood my body, like lifting the wall of a dam. I was ready for it, even if the Alex that Jerry and Nick had described wouldn't be nominated for Miss Congeniality. That was work, I reminded myself. That had nothing to do with the kind of person I was, still was—my values, how I treated my friends, and most importantly, my family.

My kids.

My eyes gravitated back to the phone screen, and I studied the first picture. Luke had a huge grin, his thick, wavy hair parted just left of center. His prominent nose was covered with freckles…and it was adorable.

Just then, I touched my own nose. "Whew," I said out loud, then giggled quietly to myself. Luke's nose came from Mark's side of the family.

Flipping to the next picture, Erin held up red-and-white pom poms, her face coated with more makeup than I would have preferred with her being just fourteen years old. *A cheerleader for a daughter. Hmm.* Not sure what I did growing up, but picturing me, or what I knew of me, in a tight-fitting outfit, my sole purpose to cheer for the hunky, brainless football players…well, I just couldn't see it.

I must have influenced them in some way, hopefully for the better. I found another picture of Luke in a basketball uniform, then thumbed through to the last picture. I paused, allowing my eyes to take it all in. It was me, with Luke and Erin on either side. We were all soaked from head to toe. It looked like we'd just gotten off one of those log flume rides. I had an arm draped over the shoulders of each kid, drawing them close. We looked silly, but connected. We wore smiles that were indicative of a tightly knit family.

They both seemed so happy. I did too.

Where was Mark? Maybe he was the one taking the picture.

"Jesus H. Christ, woman, have you thought about taking a shower anytime soon?"

Jumping in my bed, I nearly bit my tongue as I watched a new nurse marching into the room. She carried a tablet and placed her glasses on her nose to read from it.

While she was preoccupied, I took a quick sniff under my armpits.

"It all blends in after a while," she said, her eyes still focused on whatever she was reading. She walked around to the other side of my bed and started checking the machines attached to me, then tapping the screen on her tablet.

"Uh, what blends in after a while?"

"The stench in this shithole, that's what."

I watched her punch a few buttons on my heart monitor.

"If you're talking about this morning's breakfast, I couldn't agree more. The eggs looked green on the edges."

She cackled. "The food sucks. That's a given. We're a hospital, not a bed-and-breakfast." Her eyes, surrounded by wrinkles, peered at me above the tablet, then she checked the IV bag.

"I actually woke out of my, uh, sleep and smelled the oddest combination of—"

"Rotten eggs?"

"Well…"

"I could tell you some stories," she said, glancing at me again.

"I'm game," I said, setting my phone next to me on the bed.

"Oh my. GI bleeds are the worst. Brings tears to my eyes just thinking about it." She used her coat to wipe her face. Her head bobbed from her cackling. "Colostomies aren't far behind. Especially those old farts who get really surly when you try to change them out. One guy was so rude his nurse refused to change the bag for two days. Then I had the honors. That was during my rookie year. Never again."

Scrunching my shoulders, I covered my mouth, trying to hide my laughter. I didn't want to be rude. "Go on," I said, enjoying the brief respite from forcing myself to remember who I was.

"Abdominal fold cheese that's been brewing a long time. A man rolled in here with all sorts of issues. For starters, he topped five hundred pounds. He couldn't even wipe his own ass," she said, snickering. "And apparently he'd given up trying."

"Oh, gross."

"Valerie's my name, in case you're searching for my name tag. I refuse to wear one. Patients never forget a nurse's name. They've chased me down in the parking lot before," she said, walking to the end of the bed.

"What about that man who had the, uh, underactive thyroid?"

Her brow furrowed like crumpled bacon. "He didn't have any thyroid issues. He had a Big Mac issue. Ate every meal at McDonald's. In fact, we found a cheeseburger under his left boob. I kid you not."

I snorted through my fingers. "What did that smell like?"

"Crotch rot and swamp butt, all wrapped up in soiled clothing for a year. That's the best description I can give. Want to hear more?"

I could feel this morning's eggs rumbling a bit. "That's okay. I don't want to be hugging a toilet when I see my kids."

"I understand your memory loss must be a bit frustrating. Good news is you should be out of here in the next couple of days, as long as you have the proper supervision."

I wondered if Mark would be willing to care for me until I

could care for myself. I didn't want to stay another night in this rancid place, but spending a night in a bed next to a guy I didn't know might be worse. "I'm sure we'll work out something."

"With your kids coming, you might want to cover up your va-jay-jay."

My jaw opened as she tossed the sheet over my lap just as I unfolded my legs.

"And let me tie the back of your gown. You may have small breasts, but that's nothing for a kid to see."

I looked down at my chest, taken aback by her comment. Was I that unfamiliar with my own body? *Geez.*

"Thank you" was all I could think of saying as she finished up.

Suddenly, a rumble of noise approached my room.

"I don't know why you think I care about who the Celtics trade. That's boy stuff. I'm a young woman." A teenage girl marched into my hospital room, followed by a boy almost half her height.

My kids.

"Oh yeah? Well, people actually want to know if the Celtics have a chance to upgrade their starting five before the trading deadline. It matters, unlike what you talk about with all your prissy girlfriends."

The boy, Luke, turned his head as he dragged his coat on the floor behind him. "Oh, hey, Mom." He gave me a quick wrist wave, then walked to the couch on the opposite wall and pulled out an electronic device that was twice as big as his hands.

Erin had both thumbs moving at the speed of light over her cell phone. Then she holstered it in the back pocket of a tight pair of jeans, folded her arms, and tapped her foot. Her eyes met mine. "Can you tell your son that he's a dork and he needs to grow up? Sheesh."

Nurse Valerie gave me a quick wink as she quietly shuffled out of the room.

"Hi, Erin," I said with less than great confidence.

"Yeah, hey. You doing okay and everything?" Her blue eyes inspected the room, and her nose twitched. She had a cute nose too, but in a different way than her brother's.

"I had the same reaction when I woke up. Kind of smells bad, doesn't it?" I said, waving a hand in front of my face.

Her flawless features scrunched up into a prune. "Bad isn't the word I'd use," she said, her arms still hugging her chest. She was wrapped in a colorful denim jacket that was two sizes too big.

"Are you cold? I can warm up your hands." I paused for a second, shocked that those words had crossed my lips.

"I'm good," she said, not looking me in the eye.

"I suppose your father told you about my condition?"

"He just said something about you having a tough time remembering things, kind of like Grampy."

I almost laughed, but I couldn't have picked Grampy out of a lineup. Still, something ate at me, maybe Mark's representation of what I had been going through. Then again, teenagers weren't exactly reliable sources.

"Doctor said it's good if you guys tell me things like that. I'm sure this brain of mine just needs a jump start." I kept the tone positive, thinking that teens can either provide a thirty-minute soliloquy on a topic or a one-word response.

"Uh, do I have to do this by myself?" Erin said, taking a step closer, her arms still locked together. "Doesn't Luke have to do this too? It's just not fair."

I raised a finger, my mouth half open.

"Oh. My. God. Can you believe that biyatch? She frickin' slipped him a roofie just so he'd sleep with her," said a young woman waltzing into my room, a cell phone to her ear. She gave me a quick finger-roll hello. "I'm so going to be watching the next

Bachelor. Wanna make it a face-painting party and binge drink some peppermint schnapps?"

I mouthed to Erin, *Who is that?* She said something in return, but I couldn't understand, though it was becoming clear this was Sydney, our nanny.

I watched the bubbly nanny, who looked to be close to twenty, slide off her scarf and toss her pink jacket next to Luke on the couch. She plopped down.

"I know, right? Well, given what I've seen so far, I can't say I wouldn't do the same thing. I mean, we can't all rely on our amazing brains. We girls do have other needs. What? I can't really say exactly. I'm kind of in mixed company."

While her words were enough to have me question her role in my kids' lives, I couldn't get past what she was wearing. A cropped shirt with slinky spaghetti straps. A tight stomach, including her pierced belly button, were visible for the world to see. In the winter. In Boston.

She must have noticed my gaze.

"Oh, sorry to kill the buzz, Demi, but I gotta run. I'll text you later, girl. Ciao." She blew a kiss into the phone, then tossed it onto her jacket and bounced back up.

"Oh my," I said without thinking.

"What? What's wrong, Mrs. G?" She bounced again.

I wanted to grab her coat and wrap her up to hide her lack of modesty, and maybe protect mine. Instead, I just stared at her boobs. Each were the size of both of mine combined—multiplied by five. Were they being lifted by some type of hidden pulley system? More than that, it was rather obvious to anyone who wasn't blind that it was cold. For some reason, I could recall a person from my past or present say, "It's a tit bit nipply outside," joking about someone flashing her headlights.

Damn, who'd said that? Must have been on the work side of

my life. Yeah, it sounded like a typical sexist comment in a law-enforcement setting.

I curled my greasy locks around my ear, then situated Bert and Ernie in their most prominent positions. Not that I felt deficient. Not me. "You must be Sydney," I said with little enthusiasm.

"That's me," she cooed, clapping her hands together and more jiggling ensued.

I quickly shifted my eyes to the two people who were the most impressionable. Luke was going to town on a video game, it appeared. His face changed expressions every few seconds in dramatic fashion, as if it were made of rubber. I had to remind myself that he was eleven. Probably not very interested in girls.

Then I glanced at Erin. I assumed boys were one of her main interests. She pursed and then pouted her lips while she tapped her foot like a rabbit. And her arms were still firmly pressed against her chest.

"You feeling okay, Erin?" I asked. She seemed uptight.

"I'm fine. I just can't…you know."

I glanced at Sydney, who gave me a simple nod. I figured that was a signal for something.

"What am I missing here, girls?"

Sydney raised her hand as if I were a middle-aged teacher who needed to be connected to the real world. "Mark…I mean Mr. G asked Erin not to spend her entire visit with you texting on her phone."

Mark? How old was this nanny? *Lord, please tell me I didn't hire her.*

"Can you believe it, Mom? It's so, like, unfair. Again and again, I'm asked to do things that the little runt never has to do. Just look at him over there, grunting while he's playing that silly video game. It's really kind of gross."

"Screw you, Erin," Luke said, his eyes never leaving his game.

Sydney walked over to Luke and held out her hand.

"Okayyy," he groaned, then grudgingly plopped his oversized phone in her hand.

Flipping on her heels, Sydney gave me an approving wink, as if we'd just shared some type of motherly bond.

I said, "Guys, do you mind coming over here? You can sit on these chairs or the edge of my bed. I want to ask you some questions." I really wanted to get to know them better, although I was already feeling that pull of familiarity.

Their sassy attitudes seemed authentic. I wondered how much of that I used to tolerate before I came down on them. Another dozen questions smacked me like a brick. What kind of Mom was I? What kind of punishment did I dish out? What did I tend to ignore? Where did I draw the line? Did the kids just walk all over me? Didn't seem likely, given how Jerry and Nick had described my work personality. How much different could I be at home??

"Anyone want anything from the cafeteria?" Sydney asked as she nabbed her phone. "I'm sure they must have something close to a Starbucks downstairs, right? A snack, a late breakfast, Mrs. G?"

A pang of hunger washed over me, my mouth salivating for something spicy. But I couldn't put my finger on exactly what, and I didn't feel like asking the present company what my favorite breakfast food was.

"I'm good, thanks. Kids, you want anything?"

"A candy bar?" Luke asked.

"A double espresso with whipped cream," Erin said.

"I don't know if those are the healthiest things for you two," I said, the mom coming out in me.

Luke didn't respond.

"Mother," Erin said, as if I'd just outed her in front of her best friend.

I decided not to give in, and I pressed my lips shut as something of a test.

"Uh, I get it," Sydney said, exchanging glances with Erin and me. "I'll just see what they have, guys. Something *healthy*. Erin, maybe they'll have some of those cool health juices you and your friends were talking about the other day."

"Sounds good, Syd. Thanks."

Syd disappeared through the door, and I instantly felt like a ten-foot wall—actually more like a see-through stocking—had just been removed from the room. I took in a breath and patted the bed, wondering if I was ready for the mom test.

Seven

Erin rolled her eyes, and Luke trudged over. Just before he sat on the lone chair, his big sister scooted into the chair first, and he sat on her lap.

"Get off me, dork," she said, shoving him upward like he weighed five pounds.

"Screw you. This was my seat. I was sitting in it. Mom," he said, now stiff as a board, leaning back as his sister used her knees to keep him at bay.

This was motherhood? I wondered if I'd been gone for longer than just a few days. They seemed oblivious to any type of parental oversight. With a near mutiny on my hands, I had a couple of options. I chose the calmer path.

"Luke, you get to sit next to me. Come on up."

He looked at me, then all the tubes connected to me. I patted the mattress and scooted a little to my right.

"Plenty of room. Just hop on up."

He seemed apprehensive, which was natural, given the circumstances. But it also seemed like his trepidation involved more than just the hospital setting.

"So, Erin, how's the cheerleading going?" I asked.

"What do you mean, Mother?" She crossed her legs and started a rapid kick routine with her one leg. Her arms remained folded in front of her.

"Are you…?"

She twisted her head, her face a hairball of torment. "What are you trying to say?"

I think I'd just stepped in it. "Well, with your arms crossed in front of you like that, I just wondered if you felt okay."

"I'm fine. No worries here." She looked toward the window. Maybe she was thinking about her escape route.

"Luke, so tell me what position you're playing on your team."

A strange look crossed his face as he stepped onto the metal guardrail and plopped onto the mattress. It shook the bed, and I could feel the jarring in my head.

"Are you okay, Mom?" He touched my forearm, but accidentally brushed my IV tube extending out of my arm. He flinched. "Oh, sorry."

"It's okay, Luke. I'm not made of glass. I only had a car wreck. Your dad did tell you that, right?"

"I think so," he said. His eyes made a trail toward the beeping sound of the heart monitor, then he looked into my eyes. "You're going to be okay, right?"

"Oh shit. That's just great." I turned and saw Erin's face glowing red against her dirty-blond hair, the same color as mine. I made a mental checkmark that we had one thing in common. I just prayed that, even at my worst, I wasn't nearly as dramatic.

"What's wrong, Erin?" I asked, now noticing her phone by her side.

"Nothing. You wouldn't understand."

"Boy problems. Right, big sister?" Luke snickered.

She scooted down in her chair and tried to kick Luke. "Shut up, you brat."

I leaned forward, but quickly felt the tug of the tubes tethering me to the bed. "Erin, don't kick your brother."

"He just loves rubbing my face in it." She glared at her brother, red spears of contempt shooting from her eyes.

"I can't see your face with all that crap makeup you put on. And it smells too." He rolled his eyes like a seasoned pro.

I wondered if someone was catching all this on camera. This must be a test, maybe by Child Protective Services. If I could handle this nonstop squabbling, I could put up with just about anything.

"Guys, I've missed both of you." The words spilled out before I could stop myself. They weren't completely true, but I felt something. This silenced the room so much that all I could hear over the beeps was a squeaking wheel motoring down the hallway.

The kids looked at each other, then Erin glanced at me. "Sorry, Mom. I've missed you too."

I could feel my gut untwist just a tad.

"Here's what I need from each of you. I need you to pretend this is a movie, and I just reappeared in your life after being sent to another world. You have ten minutes to tell me everything about your life. If you don't tell me everything, I disappear for another year. Ready?"

I could see Erin debating her participation in such an immature exercise. Finally she said, "Okay, I'm game."

Luke nodded.

"Cool. Each of you tell me something about your life, and then we'll go back and forth for ten minutes. Go."

And go they did. My head swiveled back and forth between the two kids as I listened to their stories, and the rubber bullets of data slowly began to penetrate my brain.

Luke's basketball career had yet to take off, I learned. Even though he was in Little League, he only played a few minutes a game. Coach said he needed more work on his dribbling and court awareness. I made a mental note to work with him on that.

Erin said her boy troubles were about some nasty rumors floating around the Internet. She'd been accused of kissing some boy at a party—a party she hadn't even attended. But someone had doctored a picture, and the rest was history. I told her we could fix it, and she believed me. At least I thought she did.

School was a bore for both of them, but I actually heard Erin mention the word *college*. Luke was all about his online games, mostly involving sports. It seemed like he knew every player from every era who'd ever played any of the professional sports. He was a brilliant young man.

Erin admitted she wasn't all that fond of being ogled while she cheered. She did it to be around her friends. She said she'd much rather be involved in a competitive sport. I agreed that it might help reduce some of her aggression toward her brother.

They both laughed. And so did I. We finished the ten minutes with funny stories about Pumpkin, our orange tabby that sounded more like a dog than a fat cat.

"It was the funniest thing when Pumpkin saw a bird just outside the kitchen window," Erin said. "He wound up those legs and scooted across the hardwood as fast he could go, then *splat*. He face-planted right into the window."

Their giggles were infectious. The next thing I knew, Luke had inched down the mattress to rest his head against my shoulder. I kissed the top of his head. I couldn't say that a lot of memories were coming back, but I did feel something inside. A connection. A responsibility for their well-being. I wondered what I was like as a mother, but I knew I couldn't straight-out ask them. Maybe I could get a real answer from Mark later.

I watched them joke around with each other, and I couldn't help but smile. While I felt bad they hadn't had a mother with them in the last few days—and no, Sydney was not an adequate replacement—there was an opportunity here that most people never got. A clean slate. No baggage. A sense of relief permeated my core, and I suddenly didn't feel the pressure to know *everything*, at least not right now. I could sense a part of me in both of them. These two *needed* me—that much was obvious.

I had a purpose.

I asked Erin to help me to the bathroom, towing the portable IV bag with me. Just as I exited, Sydney bounced back into the room. I stood a few feet in front of the bathroom, watching her interact with the kids. She appeared to do her job decently, although she seemed more like a big sister than a nanny. She didn't have on a lick of makeup, and her hair was just there, yet naturally pretty. I wondered how a person could be so hard and soft in all the right places. She had the perfect figure.

"So, Sydney, you go to school?"

She was leaning over to look at Luke's screen, revealing the bottom slope of her breasts in the process. Thankfully, Luke was eleven and not fifteen and, therefore, was more interested in strategizing how to win his basketball video game than ogling his gravity-defying nanny. I hoped.

Bouncing up to face me, she said, "Yep. Pre-law at Tufts University."

Damn, she must be fighting off the men. I began my trek over to the bed, hoping Erin would jump in to help with pushing the IV cart. But she was too busy giggling about something on her phone, which she then shared with her new *breastie*. I laughed at my internal humor.

I wondered what Mark thought of Sydney.

Shuffling along at a decent pace, I could still feel the chill of the floors through my hospital-issued socks, the ones with rubber footings on them. Out of the corner of my eye, Erin reached inside her denim jacket and scratched her stomach.

Did I just see…?

"Erin, let me see your shirt." My voice was steady as I crawled back into bed.

The giggling ceased. Both Erin and Sydney lowered their heads and appeared to be scouring the floor for lost change.

"It's not that big of a deal, Mom."

I could feel my pulse ping my temples, which only increased my brain pain. "Let me see, please."

With her baby blues pointed to the ceiling, she pulled open her coat and showed off a cropped T-shirt. Splashed across the front was a phrase: *You're halfway there*.

"Really?"

"But Mom, it's not the twentieth century anymore."

"You want to be known as *that* girl, at age fourteen even?" I could feel everything in my body tense up.

My eyes shifted over to Sydney, whose hands were clasped in front her chest, as if there were some magical way of minimizing her curvaceous body. She would not look me in the eye.

I pointed at Sydney. "Were you in on this, or is it just your mystical presence that's causing my daughter to dress like a slut?" I tried swallowing, but my throat was starting to close up.

"I, uh…" Sydney mumbled while trading stares with Erin.

"This is crazy, Mother. I'm just like every other freshman. What's the big deal? It's just a shirt."

I could feel my face turn red, possibly my neck as well. Steam would soon be shooting out of my nostrils. I moved to the edge of the bed and pinched the corners of my eyes before I said another word.

"Mom, you okay?" Luke asked.

"Go back to your game, son."

"No problem," he said.

I took in a fortifying breath, wishing I had some history of experiences with Erin to draw from. What was really going on in her head? Was this the first time she'd crossed the dress-code line? Had she actually…with a boy? I reached for my water and took a sip.

"Erin, you may not know this at your age, but your actions impact your reputation. And I don't want to see you make decisions that follow you throughout high school, and maybe beyond."

"You're actually going to feed her that crap?" Sydney said. "I know you might be my boss and everything, but the world has changed. It's all about peace, love, and take-what-you-can-get. And that includes s-e-x. Yes, I said it. Sex." She planted her hand on her hip, her mouth half open.

Words were stuck in the back of my throat, and I couldn't force them out.

"By the way, she borrowed my shirt." Her eyes narrowed, as if she were trying to throw darts at me and my parenting skills.

I rose from the bed, anchoring my weight with the IV cart, and pointed a finger that refused to sit still.

"I might be missing a good amount of my memory, and I might not understand all the cool trends, but I understand disrespect. And you, Sydney, just—"

"What are you going to do, fire me? I doubt Mark would agree to that. I've practically raised these kids the last year. Erin needs a role model she can relate to."

I almost laughed. "And you think you're a good role model? You're nothing but a two-bit—"

"Hey, everyone."

I flipped on my sock-footed heels and found my former partner walking right toward me. He put a hand on my finger, as if he were securing a weapon.

A woman could dream.

Eight

"**H**ey, Uncle Nick," both Erin and Luke muttered.

"Uncle Nick?" My eye twitched as darkness started closing in on my vision.

"Alex, are you feeling okay?" Nick said, helping me to the bed.

"I'm fine, dammit. And I'm tired of people acting like I'm sick and feeble."

No sooner had my butt hit the bed, I had something else I wanted to say to the prissy sex goddess. "Listen to me, Sydney…" I tried to push upward, but Nick pleaded with me to stay where I was.

"Why don't you take the kids home or to the mall or something?" he said to Sydney.

"Nick, what are you doing?" I growled.

"I'm just trying to calm things down a bit." He looked genuinely concerned. But I didn't give a shit about my appearance or my condition.

"Nick, get out of my way."

Sydney released a sassy breath. "I can't deal with this backward thinking. I'm out of here. Erin and Luke, the train is leaving."

Looking just beyond Nick's shoulder, I could see Sydney's milk-chocolate locks flowing behind her, as her breasts heaved up and down in slow motion. Erin paused for a second and gave me one of those looks.

"It's okay. We'll talk later. But please change that shirt," I said, my arms covering my chest.

She gave me a tight-lipped nod. "Gotta run."

With his coat cinched under his armpit and his attention still focused on his handheld game, Luke wandered over and leaned his body against mine.

"Thank you, Luke. Have a good day."

"Yeah, backatcha," he said, showing off his teeth.

"Hey, I see you're missing a tooth," I said as he walked out the door. I turned to Nick, "I guess he didn't hear me."

He put his hands at his waist and stared at me, then he paced a few steps.

"What? Am I in trouble now?"

"Alex, you're recovering from a serious injury. You can't be putting yourself in these positions."

"And what kind of position are you talking about, you know, since the world is one big sex scene and all, missionary style or up the—"

"Woah. You know what I mean. You can't lose your cool. You keep going at this pace and you'll have an aneurism on top of everything else."

"Great, now I have two neurosurgeons giving me orders." My eyes pulsated.

"Alex, are you with me?"

I could feel my chest lift at a rapid pace. "Yes."

"One-word responses. I don't recall many of those," he said.

I jerked my head up. "Tell me how I should respond. My daughter dresses like she's begging to get laid, and then my nanny not only defends the behavior but acts like *I've* got the problem."

Nick scratched his head. "I heard the whole thing from the hall. I'm sorry. It sucks, I know."

I breathed in through my nose. "I apologize for blowing my top. I shouldn't be taking it out on you." I tilted my head and looked at him. "Do you have kids?"

He released a quick chuckle, which then rolled into a full-blown laughter. His pink face turned a shade darker.

"Oh, Alex, you're cracking me up."

"I didn't know I'd made a joke. Unless the joke is on me."

"His name is Antonio," he said, his expression quickly turning serious.

"You have a son?"

"I'm gay, Alex. Shit, I have to be that blunt about it?"

I replayed the words and then slowly looked into his eyes. "Sorry if it's been about me."

"I don't care about that. I just want you healthy and back to normal. Or the new normal."

I smiled. "I guess you shared this fact with me before?"

"You're the only one in the agency. I think Jerry suspects it, but I didn't want to put him in an awkward position."

"Antonio. He's a good guy? Treats you well?"

"We each have our moments just like any couple. But he's the best thing in my life for the last twenty-three years."

For some reason, I looked at my left hand. Someone must have taken my rings after the accident.

"Thinking about Mark?"

"How did you know?"

He pursed his lips. "You shared a lot with me over the years too, you know."

I rubbed my hands together. "Cool. I need to ask you a lot more questions. Things about my personal life that I just can't ask the kids or Mark. And certainly not the *Playboy* centerfold who's pretending to be our nanny."

"I'll tell you everything I know. Remember, you spent the last eight months or so basically flying solo. So I may not have the scoop on the absolute latest information."

Glancing around the room, my eyes paused on each apparatus and tube. I took in another waft of the familiar stench.

"Nick, I need to get out of here."

"I'm sure you're eager to leave, to get home and start remembering—"

"Screw that. Well, I know I need to get there eventually, but I don't want to sit around and stare at four walls while sitting at home any more than I want to do it here."

"But it will smell better," he said with an arching eyebrow.

"A dead corpse would smell better."

"Do you want to walk over to headquarters?"

"It's that close?"

He walked to the window and pulled on the metal shade. "I can't quite see it from this angle. But it's close, and the weather is behaving for the moment. It's actually just above freezing."

I thought about walking through an office where everyone knew me and I didn't know them. "I'll pass on that, for today anyway," I said, starting to paw at the tubes attached to me. "Let's start with finding out how I ended up in here."

"You had a crash."

"Really, Einstein? I know that. But how?"

"You were traveling too fast on a wet road."

"That's what Jerry said. But…"

He narrowed his eyes again. "You're skeptical."

"Sounds like I was a bad driver or made a stupid decision. That's not me."

He chortled. "How would you know?"

"I'm not sure. But I know. Somehow."

He clapped his hands. "Okay, what's our escape plan?"

"I don't need one. Help me take this needle out of my arm."

I heard something snap, and I turned to see a man in khakis holding a clipboard. He removed a pen from behind his ear. "You're not going anywhere until you have your first therapy session, Alexandra."

I gritted my teeth, wondering what type of bribe it would take to skip the make-believe lessons.

"You're welcome to stay," he said to Nick.

"But we have important business. We're FBI agents." It sounded strange referring to myself as some type of covert operative.

"Uh-huh. And I'm Doctor Zhivago."

I could tell this was going to be a fun session.

Nine

Turning my face into the salty breeze, tears streamed from my eyes, but I didn't immediately wipe them away. I filled my lungs with the chilled air, and little tingles fired all over my body. Sparks of life.

"The stench brings tears to your eyes, doesn't it?" Nick said as he reached a gentle hand to my elbow. I had the feeling he would have normally slapped me on the back instead.

"Thanks for the restraint, and the poor joke." I wiped my face, noting my lack of makeup. While I believed we'd be clear of anyone I knew—because I knew so little anyway—I didn't want to deal with anyone else right now, at least not on my maiden voyage into the labyrinth known as Boston and all the surrounding towns.

"Any time. Why is it everywhere you go it smells like crap?"

We were standing in the trash-infested parking lot of Suffolk County's impound yard, waiting to be escorted to the vehicle I'd apparently sent to car heaven a week earlier.

"The hospital didn't just smell like crap. It was a combination odor. This place? It smells like crap."

Taking my sights off the mounds of rusted metal, I turned back to the front door as a man ambled outside, chewing the nub of a cigar. Before the door shut behind him, a Doberman barreled outside, tripping over his own leash, then righting himself and making a beeline toward the man who was approaching us. I didn't recall having anything against dogs, but the canine's wet fangs glistening in the sun caused me to tense up.

"Down, Dino!" The man jabbed a greasy hand toward his dog, who skidded to a stop on the loose gravel, then quickly crouched into a resting position, his tongue wagging, as if he were just hanging out with the gang.

I rubbed my nose to ward off another crap smell.

"Dino. He caught a rat the size of a football. And ate it."

I nodded.

"It went right through him. Laid a deuce right over there. You're downwind."

"Lucky me," I said.

He shrugged his shoulders. "Nick and Alex?"

"You must be Charlie," I said.

He smeared his hand on his blue jacket—I could see previous evidence of that behavior—then extended his hand. I didn't want to be disrespectful, so I shook it. Nick did the same.

"I was expecting a couple of dudes." He snickered, and part of his chewed-up cigar flew out of his mouth.

I dodged left. "Yeah. I was expecting you to be surrounded by three hot women with guns drawn. Instead, we get Dino the dog."

Charlie reset his smudged cap while keeping his eyes on me. "Whatever. So, FBI folks, it's over here.

Nick sidled up to me as we followed Charlie around the small, one-story building, car parts scattered everywhere.

"Charlie's Angels? You've been on a roll since we left the hospital," Nick whispered.

"I told you I needed to get out of there. I knew my neurotransmitters would start firing."

I'd survived Dr. Zhivago's initial therapy session and then four more follow-ups. After two additional days in the hospital (my version of solitary confinement)—during which time I visited more with the kids and Nick while being ignored by Mark—I was finally released. But the doctor gave me a stern warning that I would need to continue to be sedentary, as in no physical activity. And then came the real kicker: I needed to have an adult with me at all times until I could start remembering key aspects of my life, including how to get around town.

Jerry ordered Nick to be my guardian, and I think my former partner couldn't have been more at ease playing the role of tour guide and general answer man. When we left the hospital, he'd taken me to lunch at Sam LaGrassa's. "An iconic Boston sandwich shop," Nick had called it. After sinking my teeth into the chipotle pastrami, I shared the same sentiment.

I noticed Dino the dog had decided he liked Nick better. He trotted so close he rubbed against Nick's suit pants. Apparently, Nick wore a suit everywhere he went. While he had on a trench coat, earlier I'd seen his red suspenders. Maybe he was making a fashion statement, or maybe I'd traveled back in time about fifty years. I decided against making fun of the guy who had my life in his hands.

As he walked ahead of us, Charlie said, "This yard is so cramped, it's impossible to run a real business."

I almost chuckled at his saying "yad," with no "r." I'd apparently lost any recollection of a true Boston accent. None of the accented voices of the hospital staff had stood out, but Charlie's here had jogged my memory.

Nick must have heard me snicker. "Charlestown Navy Yad," he said quietly to me, purposely leaving out the "r."

I said, "We passed it on the way here. *The Town*."

"That's a movie."

"Really?" Apparently, sarcasm came naturally to me.

"Just surprised you can recall a movie set in Boston."

"I think it was his accent that got me there," I said, nodding toward Charlie. "Well, that, and I got a quick image of Ben Affleck."

"Ha. He's taken, in case you don't remember that. Well, he was at one point."

"So am I—taken, that is. I'm just making an observation," I said coyly.

"That he's a hunk," Nick said, nudging my arm.

"You said it."

"And I meant it."

"I'm glad you're gay."

"Me too. Antonio would be awfully disappointed otherwise."

We both cracked up.

I heard Charlie clear his throat, like a teacher who knew he was losing control of his classroom.

"There it is." Charlie removed his wet cigar and spit off to the side as Dino darted ahead and jumped on top of the dark-blue car, or what was left of it.

"Damn" was all I could say.

I stood in one spot, my hands buried in my coat pockets, and stared. The Crown Victoria was shaped like a taco shell. The passenger side had obviously taken the brunt of the hit, the force so strong that the front and back ends appeared to have been pulled together, forming a V. The unnatural shape had busted out most of the glass from the car.

"Is this bringing back any painful thoughts, Alex?"

I heard Nick's voice, but I was so entranced by the wreckage I couldn't respond.

"Do we need to leave?" he asked.

"No," I said quietly.

A strand of my hair that had broken free of my short ponytail blew into my face. I curled it around my ear and took three steps, then leaned forward and peered into the front cabin.

"Airbag deployed," I said.

"Just that one on the driver's side," Charlie said. "This is one of the older-model Crown Vics. They don't have all the fancy airbags that keep the driver sealed up in bubble wrap."

Dino made his way to the back of the car and plopped down on the dirt. I could hear his panting mixed in with Charlie gnawing on his cigar with the vigor of a cow chewing its cud.

"You the one who was driving the car?" Charlie asked.

"Yep." I took another step closer and glanced at the floorboard and then into the nook of the front seat. It looked like a bomb had exploded inside.

"Shit, lady, you're lucky to be alive."

I touched the fingers of my left hand, recalling that the hospital had no record of my wedding rings when I'd checked out. I was hoping, or at least wondering, if I'd see them in the wrecked car. I knew the rings might help me recall some of the reasons why I'd married Mark, what I loved about him. I had to assume I still did.

Nick moved around to the front of the car while I circled to the back. Even with the brisk gusts of wind, I could practically feel the heat from Dino's panting. He was eyeing me, but in more of a protective way. At least that was how it felt.

"So the investigator for the MSP hasn't filed his report on the cause?" I asked, looking to Nick on the other side.

"Not officially. I think it's just a formality at this point, like Jerry was saying."

Resting a hand on the trunk next to Dino's paws, I crouched lower. The government-issued license plate was crumpled, and the tires shredded. I shook my head, trying to imagine my body being tossed around the metal cage.

I heard Nick's shoes crunch closer.

"What are you thinking?"

Glancing up at Nick, my eyes were stung by the sun shining just over his shoulder, and I looked back down, but I could hear him crinkling a wrapper, then the initial lip-smacking with his first piece of gum since we'd left the hospital.

"That the Bureau gave me a crap car."

"It is one of their older models."

"I heard. Anything to save a buck, I guess." Something caught my eye, and I ran my fingers along a crease on the rear left bumper.

"They're slowly phasing out these older cars for newer ones. Chevys, even the smaller Fords, are typically what we drive now. Although the CSI teams drive the SUVs…Tahoes, I think."

"Fords and Chevys," I said softly.

"You've lost interest in what I'm saying." Nick crouched lower, then cried out and almost fell back. He hopped up to a standing position, grimacing. "Crap."

"What's wrong, Nick?"

"Damn knee. It's swollen, there just above the kneecap," he said, running his hand down the front of his leg. "Hurts like hell to bend it. But you can't tell Jerry."

He flexed his lower leg and hobbled a few steps.

"No worries, Nick. Have you gotten it checked out?"

"Yeah," he said. "Too much heavy impact over the years."

"You mean all those marathons you used to run are now catching up to you?"

He stopped and put his hand on my shoulder. "Alex, you remembered I used to be a runner."

Biting my lower lip for a second, I said, "Not sure how that memory came to mind, but I'll take it."

"Anything else?"

I chuckled. "I remember you constantly working out, always

prepping for the next big run. Didn't you travel all over the country just to participate in marathons?"

He stuck out his chest a bit. "Hell yes. I was in phenomenal shape. Body fat was right around six percent. My long-term goal was to run in a marathon in every state. Got twenty-eight states in, and then the knee started acting up. Never been the same since."

"Perhaps I'm not the only one who needs to be having therapy on a body part," I said, returning my attention to the bumper.

"Therapy. I tried it a little bit. Didn't change a thing. Then the doc started talking surgery, and that's when I bailed. I've had enough lunatics try to kill me in my day job. I don't relish a doctor cutting on me."

"Afraid of a little surgery?"

"Surgery is only little if it's happening to someone else."

"You have a point."

I heard Charlie clearing his throat. I couldn't tell if he was demanding our attention or dealing with the ramifications of smoking cigars all day. If he needed something, he could ask.

"I can't bend down to join you, at least not without lying on the ground. What do you see?" Nick asked as he joined me at the back of the car.

"Looks like chipped paint."

"From another car?"

"Possibly."

"Couldn't it be from something else you hit, like a sign, or pole, or a tree?"

"Could be, I suppose. This is a something close to a gold color. Not many signs with that color scheme."

"You're convinced you didn't wreck this car without something or someone causing you to wreck it."

Placing my hand on the trunk, I pushed myself upward as Dino licked my hand. I petted his head and scratched his ears, then turned to Nick.

"I'm assuming there are deer or other wild animals around this area that could jump across a road. That's really the only thing I can think of that would cause me to wreck."

Nick shook his head. "You sound pretty certain, even though you can't remember a thing before the crash."

"I remembered your marathon running."

"I know I'm giving you a hard time, but I, more than anyone, know you can handle yourself in just about any situation, including behind a wheel."

"There you go. More proof that I'm not crazy."

"Great. Just what I need, everything going to your head."

"Was that supposed to be a pun?"

"I'm not that smart."

I switched topics. "Take me to the scene of the wreck."

"You're not going to let this rest." He smacked his gum a few times. "Does it really matter at this point?"

I ignored him again. "On our way, I'm going to call Jerry and make him tell me what cases I was working at the time of the wreck."

Nick gave me a mocking salute. "I'm your chaperone."

"Yes, you are. Let's move." In my peripheral vision, I could see him rolling his eyes, which made me grin. I gave Dino one final pet and avoided shaking Charlie's hand. "Thanks for the help," I said to him.

Nick's new best friend escorted us back to his car and even tried to crawl into the front seat. After he was coaxed out by something stiff and hairy being tossed onto the front porch, Charlie stuck his head in the car window and said, "I got couple live ones out back, if you want one."

I told Nick to punch the gas.

Ten

As Nick pulled out of the gravel parking lot, I rubbed my nose and said, "Might need to call in an evacuation of the surrounding four-block area."

"You're just jealous that Charlie has multiple pets."

I snorted out a laugh and Nick drove onward.

After sitting through some local traffic, I tried to make note of the signs as Nick meandered through the side roads of the towns north of Boston. We skirted through the east side of Malden, cut through Saugus, and took Route 107 north into Lynn. I could see a tranquil Atlantic Ocean fluttering between trees and buildings off to the east.

"Why's the ocean so calm along here?"

"There's a peninsula a couple miles off shore—Nahant. You can barely see it through there," he said, pointing across my chest. "Lots of bays, coves, and inlets around this area. You don't even recall the geography much, huh?"

Narrowing my eyes, I could feel a sense of longing to be closer to the water. "Maybe, but nothing really specific. I have this strange feeling inside. Can't really put my finger on it."

Another minute passed. More trees impeded my view of the ocean, and we motored by a sign that read "Welcome to

Swampscott."

"Are we in Boston or Louisiana?" I asked, pointing out the sign.

Nick rubbed his chin as if he had a tuft of hair to tug on. I tried not to laugh out loud. He had a few lines on his face, but he probably didn't need to shave more than once a week.

"I think I recall you telling me you actually visited Louisiana a few years ago. College maybe?" he said.

College. My mind drew a complete blank. "Man, I'm struggling with recalling the names of my own kids. College, my life before Boston, seems like one of those dreams I'll never pull back to my conscious mind."

He nodded. "I get it. The speech therapist said it would take a while, but—"

"Not to get frustrated. Right. Easy to say when it's not your life."

We hit a string of stoplights, then moved into Salem. "Home of the witch trials. See? I remember my history classes, just not the class itself."

"Witches and bitches, you used to say," Nick said as he passed a van.

"Witches and bitches. Can't imagine what the hell I was thinking."

"This is where you live with the kids and Mark. You had some issues with a few of the other moms."

"Issues. Care to elaborate?"

He pursed his lips.

"Too uncomfortable?" I asked.

"I don't want to get you upset or thinking negative thoughts."

"Now you have to tell me. Or I'll reach inside your jacket and pull your gun on you."

He swung his head in my direction, and I responded with a

smirk and a wink.

"Suburban neighborhood pissing matches. Some of the snobby women got on your nerves, and you thought they were poor role models for their daughters. They, uh…"

Nick seemed apprehensive to tell me about my own situation.

"Spill it, Nick. I need to know if I should be looking over my shoulder when I go out to grab the mail."

"You said they dressed like hookers, which is why their teenage daughters, uh, dressed like hookers."

A tiny sting pierced the inside of my head. That quickly expanded into what felt like a metal rod ramming through my skull. I gently squeezed my temples.

"Erin. Our fight this morning. Is Erin's rebellion some type of warped payback for what I've said about my neighbors?"

"Told you I didn't want to go there."

"Maybe I had no idea what was going on with Erin."

"Probably not."

"But what does that say about me as a parent, not to notice?"

"You're a driven woman, Alex. You can't do everything yourself."

I assumed he meant the act of juggling professional accomplishment with parental responsibility.

"I need to get my arms wrapped around Erin's issues. Is it only how she's dressing, or is there more to it?"

"Your nanny hasn't helped."

Another steel rod felt like it was being shoved through my brain. "I think I need to talk to Mark first, but my gut tells me I need to get rid of her."

"And then you'll be a work-at-home mom and bake cookies."

He was implying that wasn't me. And I felt the same thing. But given what I'd experienced, my confidence wasn't very high that I could achieve a great deal as a field agent for the Bureau, at least not any time soon. I first had to master going to the grocery store and finding my way back home. Maybe then I could graduate to baking cookies.

Today's insight into Erin's life had left me with an unsettling feeling. Perhaps it was a sign that it was time to cut the umbilical cord to my job. Let Mark bring home the bacon, and I would do that cooking thing again.

My mind went idle for no more than twenty seconds, and then I got restless. I pulled out my phone and called Jerry, putting him on speaker and then sharing my idea.

"You want to do what?" he asked. For whatever reason, I could envision his nose turning lobster red.

"You know how I get when I don't have something to focus on," I said while winking at Nick, the corners of my mouth turned upward.

"Funny. What if I said you like to sit behind a desk and study terabytes of data? Would you believe me?"

"Hell no."

Jerry told me to hold on a minute. We could hear him cursing in the background, then he came back to the phone. He mumbled something—probably more curse words.

I cleared my throat then asked, "So are you going to tell me what cases I was working on or do I need to start reintroducing myself to all of my besties at the office?"

He forced out a breath. "Oh, Alex."

Sounded like something my father or mother might have said when I was younger…if I remembered them. I didn't want to create any undue worry, but part of me thought it would be somewhat therapeutic to talk to my parents on the phone. "Building connection points" was what the speech therapist called it. I made a mental note to have Mark help me reach out to them as soon as possible.

"Jer, I know I'm a ways off from taking on a real case. I'm only curious because of my crash. There's probably no link between the crash and my cases. If nothing else, it will help me build confidence in my ability to recall day-to-day details."

He blew into the phone again, then finally relented and gave me the rundown. Three main cases were at the top of my list, pre-crash. One regarding embezzlement and possible wire fraud, another involving several sexual harassment accusations across a number of global offices of a Boston-based technology corporation, and then another one regarding a series of recent thefts at Boston area museums.

I asked Jerry to email me everything that I'd compiled on each of the cases.

"Don't have much. I just checked the other day. You hadn't been syncing your laptop with the SharePoint site. So you'll find the bulk of the case data still on your laptop. By the way, waiting more than three days to update the central database with your latest case information breaks Bureau policy."

"How long had I gone without updating?"

"Think it said it had been twenty-three days."

I mouthed *ouch* to Nick.

"That's the benefit of having a new me around. You can train me the right way."

Jerry didn't respond. I could only hear him pounding on a keyboard. I looked at Nick, who was mimicking Jerry, jabbing his pointer fingers into an imaginary keyboard.

A few more seconds ticked by, but I remained patient.

"I won't get the chance. At least not with these case files," he finally said.

"Why not?"

"Apparently you had your computer out of its case when you crashed. It's basically destroyed. The IT guys are trying to recover data from your hard drive, but they said to keep our expectations low."

Gritting my teeth, I knew I'd put the Bureau in a bad spot that only became exposed when I had my wreck. I was sure my story would likely be used as a case study in the training of new agents, hopefully using a fake name.

"Sorry about that," I said.

"I know you didn't plan it. And it's difficult for me to be angry when you're not you. No offense."

"None taken."

"See what you can piece together with what I send you. Maybe something will spark a memory and help you out across the board."

"Will do." I could feel a bit of an adrenaline rush through my veins as I thought about sinking my teeth into something that had some meaning, professionally speaking.

"For the love of God, if you're able to recall anything, please write it down, even if it's on the back of a napkin. Then make sure it ends up in our case database. Can you do that for me?"

"I'm all over it."

"Hold on. I didn't ask you to be all over it. You're still on LOA. You can't officially work a case until I reissue your creds. So keep your sleuthing to your private thoughts at home while you're baking cookies."

Again with the cookies.

I ended the call, promising to avoid any physical exertion and to stay clear of any drama—for my sake as well as his.

I said to Nick, "The men in the FBI must have a thing about women baking cookies."

"At least it's not donuts," he said while executing a turn down a tree-lined road, the canopy of branches so thick it blocked out the sun.

I thumbed through the apps on my phone, wondering if I'd kept any notes on a device other than my laptop.

"You don't look like you're searching for baking recipes."

He was right. In just a few minutes, almost subconsciously, I'd gone from thinking I might be ready to stay at home and take care of the kids, to nearly begging my boss to give me work.

"I have a purpose. It's all about figuring out why I had this wreck," I said, with my eyes studying the numerous icons on the small screen.

"Yeah, sure. You can take the lady out of the FBI, but you can't take the FBI out of the lady. Or something like that," he said, laughing at his poor joke.

I heard the cadence of the blinker, and I lifted my head to see Nick pulling off the road onto a swath of grass and weeds. In front of us, yellow tape surrounded a large tree missing most of its leaves.

We exited the car and walked toward the tree. Taller pines bordered both sides of the two-lane road. A car whizzed by, blowing cooler air into my face.

"Damn, he was moving. I didn't notice the speed limit, did you?"

Nick pointed behind us. "It's on the other side of the hill, hidden by some overgrown brush. Said forty-five."

I stared at the hill, then followed the path back toward the road until I was about fifty feet in front of the tree where I'd sandwiched my Crown Vic. I spotted tread marks on the pavement. Walking closer to the road, a cement mixer motored in our direction.

Nick grabbed my arm. "Don't get too close now."

I turned back toward him with a scowl on my face. "You sure you don't have kids?"

"Pretty sure."

"Well, you're talking to me like one, and holding my arm like

I'm one." I looked down at his hand on my arm, and he let go. "I may not be able to recall much of my life, but I do know that I'm over the age of twenty-one by a long shot."

"Sorry," he said, sidling up next to me. He pointed at one group of tread marks. "This set here appears to scoot right, then turn three-hundred-sixty degrees before going off the road."

"True, but then there's this other set," I said, shuffling to my right while nudging Nick out of my way. "The two intersect near the center of the road."

I heard a whirring engine and turned to see a sports car hugging the road, moving at a fast pace. The driver, who looked to be in his mid-fifties, shot us the finger then laid on his high-pitched horn.

"That asshole must have been going eighty. Just on a joy ride." I took three steps into the middle of the road and returned the one-finger gesture, yelling, "Up yours, asswipe!"

"Up yours?" Nick laughed, leaning over at his waist and slapping his thighs. "I'm really enjoying this new and improved Alex Giordano."

Walking with more purpose, I jabbed my elbow into his rib cage as I moved toward the yellow tape. He grunted as I said, "Glad I'm so entertaining."

"I'm just messing with you," he said with limited air pushing through his lungs. "But obviously you're not."

I reached the point where my car's tires had started tearing through the turf, and I crouched down and touched the dirt before glancing back at the road.

"I'm sure the MSP did all the tread comparisons to make sure it's just one set of used tires from a government-issued Crown Victoria," Nick said from over my shoulder.

"One set," I said, following the path of torn-up dirt back out to the road.

I lifted off my knees and walked straight to the road, trying to imagine the trajectory the car had taken to end up wrapped around the enormous oak, passenger side first.

"You think this wasn't a one-car accident," Nick said, trudging my way, the fog of his breath pumping out of his mouth.

"That sounded like a statement. To me, it's more of a question which no one is asking," I said, shifting my head from the road back to the tree.

"Alex, we're not experts in this type of thing. These days, they have all sorts of analytical tools they use to help them understand the cause of a wreck, almost as if they're watching it live."

I gave him the eye, my hand planted at my waist. "I'd like to at least talk to the investigator. You know, that whole peace-of-mind thing."

"You mean you want a piece of his ass."

"Your words, not mine."

I walked over by the tree and touched it. "You realize we haven't seen any destroyed signs, which means the gold color on the back bumper came from something else."

"We drive these cars into the ground. You could have bumped another car or something else a week or more before the crash."

"Could have, yes," I said, turning to face him. "You like countering all of my theories, don't you?"

"It's my job. Someone has to do it, and when we were partners, you didn't make my life very comfortable, that much I'll say."

His eyes left mine.

I took in a breath and tried to take my foot off the mental pedal. "Sorry, Nick...you know, for anything I did or said in the past that may have hurt you."

He shuffled his scuffed shoe in the dirt as we made our way back to his car. "No harm, no foul. I'm probably a little sensitive, given you asked to ride solo a few months back."

Another regret about something I couldn't recall. "I owe you a large Dunkin' coffee, on me," I said with a sly grin.

"I'll take it."

"Over coffee, you can show me how to access my work email over this phone."

"So you're using me again, huh?" He opened the car door and stuck in a foot.

"Just taking advantage of my opportunities from those who have all the knowledge."

"Flattery will get you everywhere."

Just then his phone rang. He took the call while I studied the surrounding area. I heard him attempting to speak, but the person on the other line wouldn't give him a chance.

"Crap," he said, tossing his phone on the car seat. "They're asking me to go support a crime scene north of here. I told them I was on babysitting duty and—"

"Thanks for that description."

"Anyway, they ignored me. Running low on resources now. Lots of FBI agents are out with the flu. So I guess you'll tag along."

"What's the situation?"

"A fisherman found a man drowned to death."

"Why call us, the FBI, I mean?"

"The SSA said it was too difficult to explain. I'd have to see it to believe it."

Nick turned on the flashing lights visible on the back side of the visor, and we sped north while I tried to figure out how to access my FBI email.

Eleven

We banked right in our airboat, and the brisk wind slapped the chilled water back in my face. For the second time today, I felt my lungs clear as nature infused me with renewed vigor. If we hadn't been on our way to a murder crime scene, I would have asked for the ride to continue for another thirty minutes.

Turning to look over my shoulder, I saw a legion of airboats dip and dodge through the marshes splintering off Essex Bay. I only knew this because Nick had shown me a map on his phone while we waited on the muddy shoreline, an unsightly mosh pit of mud and weeds. FBI, MSP, local police, and a few other agencies were part of the crew headed for Choate Island.

The initial team had apparently already been working the crime scene. We were part of the second wave. Given our sheer numbers and the urgency in the way people moved, it was as if we were poised to storm the beaches of Normandy.

Another random historical fact that had zipped through my mind. But I still had no visual images of even my own home.

"We're hitting shore just ahead, around the bend." Wearing a yellow hoodie, the boat's driver pointed as he shouted above the roar of the engine.

Once my feet hit the shore, it wasn't very solid. It was a marsh, after all. Nick's first step sunk about a foot, and when he pulled up, his socked foot popped out of his leather shoe. I could see his lips fire off a few cuss words, but no one could hear regular chatter over the clapping, windmill-sized propeller.

With Nick wearing an extra ten pounds of caked-on mud, we followed the group to the southwestern side of the island.

"What's this island used for?" I whispered to Nick.

"Just random fishing, I think. Never been out here. Wish I wasn't here right now."

We trudged through waist-high weeds and sections of mud that looked more like quicksand. I heard someone call out, "Be on the lookout for snakes." The thought of a snake slithering up one of the legs of my pants didn't give me a warm-and-fuzzy, but I literally saw Nick quiver when he heard the news. Maybe nature wasn't his thing.

Led by a guy with a machete, we slowly made our way through a thicket of brush and emerged just next to the temporary hub for the crime-scene investigators.

"People, are you listening?" Some guy with an FBI jacket, mirrored sunglasses, and a mustache took charge—whether that was his role or not, I wasn't sure. He darted his head left and right, then finally put two fingers in his mouth. His whistle silenced the shore. "People, can I have your attention?"

Nick nudged me and made sure I saw him roll his eyes. Was I supposed to know this guy who looked like he belonged on a 1980s porn movie set?

"People, we have a lot of agencies with money in this game. But we must remember this is an active crime scene. We cannot and will not mess with the integrity of my crime scene."

"*His* crime scene. Eat me," Nick said in my ear.

"Do I have your full agreement on this matter?" The man used his hands as he spoke, as if he were preaching. In some respects, he was.

"If you want to jump on Facebook and chat with your friends or share a picture on Instagram, you can get a boat ride back to the mainland. Am I clear on this?"

Mumbles and a few *yes sirs* came from around me.

There must have been forty people encircling the Grand Poobah. He clapped his hands, and everyone went back to work.

Nick and I waited for the crowd to clear a bit, then made a beeline toward the lead douche bag.

Jerry had texted Nick on the way over with two explicit demands. He wanted to know what the hell type of crime had created such a stir among the law-enforcement community, and he wanted to make sure Nick kept me safe and away from anyone who hadn't received the memo that I was on LOA—even if I was at a murder crime scene.

As both of us stood next to the mustached man who was holding a one-way discussion with three guys in scuba gear, Nick was grimacing and lifting his legs, staring at the mud, which was quickly hardening into mud bricks on his shoes.

"I'm sure you can clean them off. But it might just take a chisel and a crowbar."

"I've had these shoes for ten years. They match my suits and suspenders, and they fit my feet like a glove."

"Then why aren't you wearing them on your hands?" I gave Nick a playful wink just as Mustache Man turned on his heels. He removed his mirrored glasses and eyed me, then let out a quick chuckle.

"Alex. It's been a while."

I slowly turned my torso to Nick and felt my eyes go wide.

Twelve

Had Nick forgotten to fill me in on a very important fact? The only facts I was certain of were that I didn't know this guy and I didn't feel like sharing my life story, or what I knew of it.

"Yep," I said, purposely turning my head, allowing Nick to take the lead.

"Okay, be that way," he muttered.

Just as I opened my mouth, Nick chimed in.

"How's it going, Randy?"

"Eh. Different day, different psychopath."

"How can I help with the investigation?"

"Not clear yet. I'll let you and your old-new partner here take a look at what we're dealing with, then we can divide and conquer. Capisce?"

Randy led us over to a team in amphibious gear by the muddy shoreline, where shards of cracked ice were floating in the shallow water. "We've yet to bring the body on shore since we're still trying to capture everything on film first. Of course, with a body in saltwater, we're not going to find much, if any, trace evidence. And you can blow transient evidence out your ass. There's nothing there."

I scrunched my eyes and leaned to my right to try to get a peek at the dead body. There were at least two guys in scuba gear swimming near the surface of calm water in an area about fifteen feet off the shore, taking pictures.

"Mike here will fit you with wetsuits."

Randy turned and walked away as Nick raised his hand to me in protest.

"Just need one," Nick said.

I held up two fingers and Mike nodded his head.

"Alex?" Nick moved in front of me.

"What?" I played innocent.

"Come on, Alex, you can't do this. You shouldn't do this."

"Why not? I'm an FBI agent just like you. I'm sure I can help in the investigation."

I moved toward Mike, who found a wetsuit that fit me, along with a snorkel, mask, and fins. "It's not very deep, but you'll sink into the mud unless you use the fins to stay afloat." Then he pointed at a portable tent where I could change.

"Alex, you've got to be kidding me. Jerry will have my ass for dinner if you go into that water."

"Geez, Nick, relax. It's not like I'm swimming the English Channel. I'm just getting a better view of the crime scene. Jerry said he wanted all the information, right? I'm only here to help."

"Dammit." He removed his fedora and scratched the back of his head. "This isn't my natural environment. I think I'll watch here from the shore. But if Jerry asks, I vehemently protested you going in. Hell, he might tell me I need to put you in handcuffs."

"But what would Antonio say?" I disappeared into the tent before he could respond.

As I struggled to squeeze my body into the wetsuit, I thought about the physical exertion warning I'd been given. But what was the worst thing that could happen? My head would hurt a little more? Any doctor would tell me to take two ibuprofen and get some sleep, which I hoped to do in my own unfamiliar bed this evening.

For now, though, I had to admit a few butterflies were fluttering inside. Something about the scene excited me—maybe not traipsing through mud and murky water, but the idea of studying a crime scene and then investigating all the logical questions. What was the motivation of the killer? When did it happen? And how the hell could we piece together the jigsaw puzzle to apprehend the person who committed the brutal crime?

"I'm going to lift you off the shore and set you in the water. Then start flapping your fins and you'll be fine," Mike said. He was about a foot from my face. He had a pleasant look about him.

Mike turned away for a second and used a rope to pull in one of the other divers from the water. With my finned feet planted in one spot, I leaned back to Nick, pulling down my mask.

"Having second thoughts?" he asked.

"Dude, you forgot to give me the scoop on douche-bag Randy."

"It didn't occur to me until he said something. And then it really hit me."

I could feel a knot forming in my gut. "You might want to tell me now, since I'm not in a good position to come over there and kick your ass."

He chuckled.

"What?"

"You may not remember much, or even notice the transformation, but slowly the needle on your personality is edging back to its normal state."

I tried to arch my eyebrow, but the mask had already stretched my forehead. "Are you going to answer me?"

He looked around, making sure no one was listening. "It isn't a secret that, for a while, Randy had the hots for you."

I studied his face, wondering if he was joking. Hoping he was joking. "You're joking, right?"

A strange look washed over his face, as if he felt sorry for me. "I wish I was."

"Gross. So gross." I looked into the sky, where gray clouds had now blanketed the sun, and wondered how the old me had responded to any possible overtures. "Did I reciprocate any of his advances?"

"Hell no. At least I don't think so." He brought his hand to his chin.

"Huh? Why are you waffling?"

"I'm not waffling. You just—"

"Just what?"

"Uh, well, during the last few months before your crash, you became more distant."

"You and Jerry have basically called me a bitch."

"Alex."

"It's okay. I'm a big girl. I'm just trying to figure out this world, one cheesy douche bag at a time."

We traded smiles.

"Okay, Alex, you ready for a swim?"

"Yep," I said to Mike the amphibian.

He picked me up in his arms, and I instantly understood what it felt like to be a fish thrown back into the sea.

"Did Randy tell you this was a disturbing scene?" Mike asked.

"I've been in the FBI for…" Damn, another memory gap. "…a long time." That should help him understand that I didn't need any hand-holding. Of course, at that moment, I recognized the irony of my thoughts, realizing he was holding me like a little baby.

He released me gently into the water, and I gave him a thumbs-up, then dipped my head below the surface where two divers swirled beneath me like sharks. I gave them the thumbs-up too, and I kicked my fins and veered to the right to obtain a better view of the corpse.

I glided about ten feet, ensuring that my breathing remained even. Thus far, my body had responded like a pro, which gave me more confidence. Perhaps I'd been in decent shape before the crash. I didn't feel too much flab tugging against the water.

Turning myself around, one of the divers moved out of my view, and I got my first glimpse of the floating corpse. Nothing in my life—as I knew it—had prepared me for this sight. I gasped, which forced water down my air passages, and I started to flail and gag. Kicking my fins, I lunged above the surface and ripped off my snorkel mask, gulping in large quantities of air as I continued choking and spitting up water.

"Alex!" I heard from the shore. Was it Nick?

I kicked harder to ensure I stayed above water and pinched my nose, releasing a few more gasps and then a big belch.

"Come back to the shore, Alex." Yep, that was Nick, ever my guardian angel.

"I'm…" I tried speaking but my words sounded like a raspy wheeze. "I'm…fine. No big…deal."

"Jerry will kill me if you die from drowning at the crime scene of a drowning."

I tried to bring my body into a calmer state, then I realized I could see my breath in the air. The brisk wind bit against my exposed face.

"Are you going to ignore me?"

I'd yet to give anything more than a passing glance at the shore. That would show need, or even worse, desperate need. That wasn't me.

I slipped my mask back on and torqued my body into a horizontal position, and I could hear myself breathe. Steady and even. It helped calm me. I readjusted the mask—a small amount of water had seeped in from the side—and found my vantage point. I attempted to filter out any emotion and look at the body logically.

It was a man, thick hair, stubble on his face in semi-fetal position. But what the hell was wrapped around his body? It was cone-shaped. His arms were hugging his torso, as if in a straitjacket. In further examination, the cone appeared to be made from duct tape. A lot of duct tape. Something stuck out from inside the wall of hardened gray tape. I drifted closer and looked straight down. Inside the cone were two cinderblocks.

Then I spotted two lines of string, each attached to one of the blocks and tied to something small and hollow at the other end. I wanted to dive down and inspect it, but I knew it would create a shitstorm back on shore. Plus I wasn't completely confident my body wouldn't wig out once I submerged to eight or ten feet below the surface.

The dead man wore a pair of slacks, cream-colored dress shirt, and tie. There was a watch on his wrist. Looked high-end, but I was only guessing. Could be a cheap knockoff. His skin was wrinkled, and the hue ranged from pink to red.

My eyes gravitated back to the cone, and I could see a large blotch of burgundy on his dress shirt. Maybe he hadn't drowned. Maybe he'd been shot and then the body submerged until it decomposed so badly most of his appendages would fall off.

How did I know that?

His neck seemed extra thick, which swayed the cause-of-death theory back to drowning. On top of that, he was hovering near the bottom, just at the tips of the seaweed. The gases were still trapped in his body, which made me question the idea of a gunshot wound to the chest. Maybe it was a wound of some kind, but not deep enough to tear all the way through the skin tissue.

Flapping my arms against the water, I moved backward while

keeping my vision on the body. Looking down his leg, I saw a rope tied around his ankle. The rope disappeared into the seaweed, probably tied to a heavy object of some kind, like another cinderblock. I glanced again at the cone of duct tape and wondered who had thought of this contraption and what the motivation was. Had it been premeditated or a quick reaction to an emotional killing? There were a hundred possible scenarios. Hell, probably closer to a million. I recalled somewhere in my past being taught that no two killings were the exact same, even if they were committed by the same person, for the same reasons. Too many other variables to consider.

I took another mental snapshot, then flipped around and floated toward the shore, where Mike the amphibian picked me up chest first. His hand accidentally brushed my nipple, which might have done something for me had my entire body not been frozen.

"Sorry," he said in my ear as I righted myself on the shore.

Nick covered me in a blanket. "You're going to get pneumonia, and then Jerry is going to make sure *I* get pneumonia."

I could hear my teeth rattling, and I clamped my jaw down before anyone could see.

I told Nick I wanted to change back into my dry clothes, and I shuffled into the tent, sniffling and shivering. I pulled the wetsuit down to my ankles, then paused briefly, my mind still digesting the vivid images from the dead man with a duct-tape cone wrapped around his body.

Suddenly, the tent door unzipped. My feet shifted, but I tripped on my wetsuit and tumbled to the ground. As the fabric flapped open, I spotted my clothes and threw them on top of my most vulnerable parts. I shot my eyes upward only to see Randy removing his glasses.

Thirteen

"Someone told me you had an incident in the water. Are you okay?" Randy asked, his shoulders so wide I could barely see the outline of light. I realized I still felt a bit of air...down there, and I shifted my hand six inches lower. Instantly, I was mortified from embarrassment, sending a wave of heat up my spine.

"I'm fine," I said in short order, noticing his eyes never left mine.

Then, just as quickly, he backed out of the tent and zipped it back up.

I put on my clothes, then stepped outside while roping my wet hair into its standard ponytail, thinking more about my unexpected visitor. I found Nick at a makeshift table sifting through images on a tablet. I didn't ask what he was doing.

"Did you tell Señor Douche Bag that I had trouble in the water and needed his assistance?"

"Hell no. I wouldn't do that to you, even on your bitchiest day."

"Did you see him enter the tent when I was changing?"

Nick's eyes bugged out. "He did what?"

Saying it out loud made me wonder what the hell I'd been thinking when Randy had walked in uninvited. For whatever reason, I just froze, fumbling with my words, failing to admonish him. That didn't seem like the Alex Giordano buried somewhere deep inside.

"Where is he?" I asked, turning, looking for the biggest dick I could find. Actually, the biggest asshole. He probably had the smallest dick.

I scanned the shoreline and brush, the area as active as a kicked fire-ant mound. Did Boston have fire ants? I spotted Randy, nodding his head while speaking with two guys from the CSI team. I marched in that direction as I heard Nick say from behind me, "Oh crap. Alex, please don't punch him right here at a crime scene. No reason to dip to his level, right?"

Nick was right behind me, but I couldn't have cared less. Just as I approached the three men, I overheard the older CSI agent say, "Wedding rings, Randy. They're all catalogued digitally. We just need to bring them above surface. No hope in getting any trace or transient evidence off them, although we'll go through the routine. Who knows? We could get lucky."

Taking my last step, I tripped over a stump, tumbling forward. I would have hit the ground had I not face-planted into Randy's ass. Being graceful and all, I pawed at whatever I could find—his belt loop and back pocket—and pulled myself upright. I stood at attention, then noticed a huge lock of hair dangling in front of my eyes. I curled it around my ear and returned to my authoritative position with my hands clasped behind me.

"Alex, you're not still feeling the ill effects of your freak-out in the water?" Randy asked.

"What? No, I am not," I said, sticking my chin out. I eyed the two CSI agents, realizing now may not be the best time to chide the douche bag. But I wasn't about to let him off the hook.

"So the objects attached to the cinderblocks were wedding rings?" I asked.

Three head nods.

"Were they male rings? Anything with diamonds in it?"

The gray-haired CSI agent who had a wart below his left eye—how had I not noticed that before?—bent slightly to rest a hand on his knee. "It appears to be a combination. One male ring, possibly his, since he wasn't wearing one. There were three other rings. Two had diamonds on the band. The other was a simple band, platinum maybe."

The confirmation of what I'd seen floating in the cloudy water had simmered my immediate aggression toward Randy. My eyes drifted to a couple of rocks sticking above the sand, theories scrambling in my mind that was already cluttered with scattered memories.

Nick pulled up next to me, and I realized I'd been picking at my nails. Was this an old stress habit?

"His chest. Appeared he suffered a wound," I said, looking for affirmation from the graying CSI agent.

"Yep, he did." He sounded like a Yankee version of Sam Shepherd. Kind of looked like him too.

"Do you know if it punctured his chest cavity?"

"Not likely. Looks like scrapes from the cinderblocks."

I bit my lip. "Unless there's another wound that penetrated his body, then it's almost certain that he died from the drowning itself."

"Good one, Alex," Randy said.

I gave him a stern look, then addressed the CSI guys. "I guess there could be drugs in his system."

Before they could respond, Randy chimed in with, "True. Drugs could have killed him before he was tossed in the water. This whole setup could have been put together just to throw us off." He nodded at everyone like he'd just discovered the secret to immortality.

"I'm wondering if he might have been drugged just enough to keep him unconscious until the perp was able to create the cone of duct tape and place the man in the marsh. The toxicology will tell us everything. How soon until we can see that?"

Randy chuckled. "Didn't I hear you were recently in the hospital after wrecking your car?"

"I'm here now. If you put a rush on it, how soon until we see the toxicology report?"

He checked his watch. "Preliminary, probably tomorrow morning. Full report, maybe two days later, if we're lucky."

Another agent walked up wearing nitrile gloves and holding an evidence bag. A soggy wallet was inside.

"Sir, we've got an ID on the vic." He held up a piece of paper, then lowered his eyes to look through bifocals. "A Christopher Barden, out of Beverly. From what we've been able to find out, he's thirty-eight years old and works at Transamerica Financial in Boston."

"Credit cards and cash still intact?"

"Well," the young agent pulled off his glasses and chuckled once, "I can't say how much cash he had on him. But there is cash in there, two hundred eighty bucks. I'd never seen a hundred-dollar bill before. Anyway, credit cards, license, even a soggy picture of his kids."

"No pictures of his wife?" I asked.

"Uh, no."

Randy spoke up. "Is that supposed to be strange? I mean, all of us need a break from the ball and chain occasionally."

I slowly turned my head and eyed the tall dipshit.

He held up his hands. "What did I say? You going to file a complaint? Come on, guys…and lady, let's get back to work. We need to pull the body and other evidence attached to him and make sure we bring it back without destroying a thing."

More divers arrived on the scene as they prepared to cut the body loose and bring it ashore. I heard them say they would actually conduct a preliminary autopsy report on-site, with the hopes of capturing pertinent information immediately after being exposed to air.

The sky grew a darker gray, and the temperature started to drop. With my hair still damp, I tried to keep moving so I wouldn't shiver. They pulled the body, and the medical examiner conducted the initial examination under a bank of portable lights with about ten people looking over his shoulder.

Standing there with my arms folded, my face felt frozen. Either the cold temperatures, or the tension of the scene, or an aftereffect of my head injury—or a combination of all three—had created a pulsating line of pain from both shoulder blades into my neck. I arched my neck and tried to rub the muscles. The effort seemed futile.

"You're stressed from all of this, aren't you?" Nick asked as he stepped next to me.

"Stressed isn't the right word. Keenly interested, I'd say. But I'm also a little chilly."

"You're more than a little chilly, I can plainly see that. I knew you shouldn't have gotten into the water. Doctors would probably cut my nuts off if they knew I let you do that."

"We could replace you with Randy on the nut-cutting table and make the world a better place," I said, eyeing my partner for a moment as we watched a gaggle of CSI agents analyze the cinderblocks, string, and rings.

"That guy's a piece of work," Nick said.

I shook my head. "And he actually thought he had a chance with me? Did I used to be a ditzy, bow-headed bimbo looking for her MRS degree?"

"This isn't Utah. Only one marriage at a time."

"Funny," I said, even though it wasn't.

"I'd heard he's been separated off and on. Not that I care. TMIAAA."

"What the hell does that mean?'

"Too Much Information About An Asshole."

I snorted through my hand, and one of the CSI agents turned his head in my direction. I shrugged innocently.

A few minutes passed, and the abbreviated daylight was quickly disappearing. A few domestic thoughts entered my mind: dinner, the kids, when Mark was getting home, and when our nanny would leave for good. I also felt compelled to stay at the crime scene.

But Nick started doing his big brother thing again. "It's getting late. You need to get home. This day has been far too long for you, and way too much exertion." He walked over to Randy.

I fumed a little. Okay, maybe a lot. I couldn't just stand there like a well-behaved lady, ready to take orders from a bunch of men. It didn't seem…natural.

Randy gave instructions to two guys wearing MSP hats and badges. "Okay, so we have a preliminary plan. You two will visit the Barden residence and notify his wife of the death this evening. Ask some basic questions, document anything noteworthy. Make sure you show some compassion."

I was shocked to hear Randy use that term, *compassion*. Maybe his superiors had given him that specific order during his last performance review.

Next, he turned and pointed a finger at Nick, then saw me and wagged his finger between us. "You guys can go back tomorrow and try to quiz Mrs. Barden further. I think you know how to conduct a thorough interview."

"No worries," Nick said. "We'll keep you updated, as well as my immediate boss, Jerry."

"Oh. Jerry," Randy said, rocking forward on his shoes.

Apparently, they had a history. Then again, Randy appeared to have an opinion on anyone who breathed, and a few who didn't.

Randy took a phone call and walked away.

"That's our cue. We're on the next airboat to the mainland," Nick said, walking toward the trail. "If I'm lucky, I'll get home in time to eat a warm dinner cooked by Antonio."

He turned to see if I was following, which I wasn't. "You go ahead," I said.

His arms fell against his jacket. "Don't tell me you have this sense of duty to stick around until all the work is done? If that's the case, you'll be here all night."

"No, I just need to, uh, clear up some things."

His eyes found Randy, and he nodded. "I get it. I'll take my time getting back to the airboats."

"You don't have to wait. You're not my big brother or my daddy."

"I'm barely moving now," he said, going in mock slow motion.

Just then I noticed Randy pocket his phone. I cut him off before he could join the others.

"You need something, Alex?"

"Uh..." I paused a second, wondering how our private conversations had gone in the past. I hoped I'd never led him on. The mere thought of it made me want to puke in the marsh.

He put a hand on my shoulder.

I slowly turned my head and eyed his hairy mitt. "Do you mind?"

"Feisty, aren't you?"

My body temperature shot up twenty degrees.

"Randy, that ruse you used to walk in the tent? Not cool." My hands were planted at my waist, my feet shoulder-width apart.

"Can't I show a little compassion for a colleague? Jesus,

Alex." He ran his fingers through his hair.

"You just wanted a peep show."

He chewed the inside of his cheek as he stared me down. After a few seconds, he glanced over my shoulder. "I need to get back and oversee this investigation. As you can see, this is an enormous operation. We're dealing with a real sicko here, Alex."

He'd essentially ignored me calling him out. I held up a hand. "You ever do that to me again, I'll shove your balls down your throat."

"Damn, that kind of turns me on, Alex." He winked, then moved past me while bumping his shoulder against mine.

I almost swallowed my spit. I had to stop myself from sticking out a foot, then jumping on his back and pounding the shit out of his kidney until he cried like a baby.

"Randy, don't you—"

"And thanks for the peep show," he said without turning around.

I curled my hand into a fist and raised my arm.

"Alex, it's not worth it." Nick had grabbed my fist. "You'll have ample opportunity to stick Randy in his rightful place. But wait until you can really kick his ass. I'll even buy some popcorn and watch."

He was right. As we took the chilly airboat ride back to our car, I thought about how my next confrontation might be more dramatic than the last.

Fourteen

Lifting a wood-framed picture from a built-in bookcase in the living room of our home, I touched the glass, trying to make a connection with the image. Smiling like it was the best moment in my life, my arms were wrapped around Mark's waist. We were both tan. My eyes had that raccoon look. The purple sky behind us illuminated a green mountaintop, and I could see white caps of an ocean below that. While I wondered where we were geographically, I was more curious about where we were in our relationship.

But damn, we looked happy as hell. It gave me hope.

I'd just made my way downstairs, and I could smell a homemade spaghetti sauce simmering on the stove. I wiggled my feet in my worn slippers, fluffy white and burnt orange with a Longhorn logo on the sides. I must have had a connection to Texas in my pre-crash life. How far back, I had no idea.

I could hear a game of some kind echoing throughout the house, most of which had hardwood floors. When Nick dropped me off earlier, I'd just stood in front of our three-level home in awe. It reminded me of a Norman Rockwell picture—why that image came to mind was another great mystery. In fact, the mysteries were stacking up pretty high, especially the mystery of why my brain could remember certain things and not others. I had to throw my heart in there as well. It appeared to have a say in the game.

"Get out of my room, you little twerp," Erin yelled from upstairs.

I could hear Luke's cute giggle, and then a door slammed.

And Nick thought I'd be able to ease my stress levels by hanging out at home.

I shuffled through the living room, taking in the comfortable décor. A burgundy throw was draped over a tweed, taupe couch. I noticed a couple of dark stains, and the cushions looked overused. A huge recliner hulked to the right, one that included a compartment full of remotes and two cup holders. Mark's man-cave seat, more than likely. A large flat-screen was hoisted above a fireplace, outlined with gray travertine stone. It complemented the white molding and baseboards, which were designed in the same ornate style as the exterior of the home.

We were lucky to have this jewel. I assumed Mark *really* brought home the bacon, since my government job probably didn't move the financial needle all that much.

I circled the couch, pausing at each photo or framed painting, hoping to elevate some memories. Taking in a breath, I turned my sights to the kitchen, then suddenly heard a whirring sound at my ear. I ducked while throwing up a protective arm.

Something clipped at my hand, then crashed to the floor.

"Ah, Mom, you wrecked my drone." Luke ran into the living room and snatched his machine off the floor. He jumped to his feet as I held up my hand, where blood dripped off my middle finger.

"Ouch. Did I do that?" he said while gritting his teeth. I could see a couple of gaps on the sides.

I nodded.

He took a step away from me and dipped his head. "Are you

going to punish me?"

I was taken aback. "Punish you? You didn't mean to hurt me, right?'

"Of course not, Mom. My B2000 drone lost its pitch just when I was trying to bank right. And then you know what happened from there."

"Just learn to say you're sorry, and we're good."

"Sorry."

I gave him a fist bump with my clean hand. "You want to show me where the bandages are?"

He waved me on. The floors creaked as we made our way upstairs. Walking past Erin's room, I could hear her voice, animated and speaking as if she were in a verbal sprint. Luke held his drone, making all sorts of engine noises while spraying the floor with a layer of spit. I'd heard that cute sound before, although I couldn't recall an exact memory.

Luke led me to the bathroom cabinet, then zoomed out of there while I cleaned the cut and stuck a bandage on it. With the good lighting, I noticed all the lines and blemishes on my hands, the jagged fingernails—not exactly model worthy. Maybe I could unscrew one of the lightbulbs.

I rubbed my bare ring finger, wondering how it felt to wear my wedding rings. I was mildly curious as to what Mark had bought me, guessing that years ago he probably didn't have much money. Obviously, given everything I'd seen in the home, his career had provided substantial financial rewards since then.

Regardless of how much Mark had spent, my lack of recollection about where the rings were irked me. Maybe I'd had this thing about wearing them on the job. The more I thought about it, I wasn't sure I wanted to ask Mark, thinking it might not come across too well if I said, "Do you know where I've put the loving symbol of our relationship? I've apparently not been wearing them, so they must not be that important." Or something along those lines.

I walked to Erin's door and tried turning the knob. It was locked. I knocked gently, then said, "Dinner in five." A second later, loud rap music filled the entire upstairs. I considered a response, but I wasn't up for anything emotional. I headed down the stairs, ensuring I held the rail. My legs felt like the cooked noodles Sydney was making in the kitchen.

I rubbed my face as my feet hit the first floor, my eyelids heavy. The dead man's anguished face loomed in the back of my mind. Hell, who was I kidding? It was front and center. The duct tape, cinderblocks, and wedding rings. It was all so elaborate and detail-oriented. Whoever committed the crime must have had a goal in mind. To communicate a message about this guy, Christopher Barden, or maybe about even himself. I'd already made one assumption—the killer was a man. Subduing this Barden fellow, transferring his body, restraining him in the duct-tape vest, throwing in the cinderblock weights, would take considerable physical strength and endurance. Whoever it was had to be extremely fit and motivated. Which led me back to my original thought. *Why? Why go to the trouble?*

The smell of meat sauce made my mouth water. A meal heavy on carbs might spark a possible theory, or even a probing question that I could use with Barden's wife tomorrow. That reminded me that somehow I needed to get my FBI credentials from Jerry.

"We about ready for the kids to come downstairs for dinner?" I asked Sydney as I walked into the kitchen and made a beeline for the basket of freshly baked garlic bread. Out of the corner of my eye, I saw she was wearing a Tufts University sweatshirt.

"Uh, yeah. If you'll call them down, they can go ahead and knock out their Pumpkin duties."

"Right, the cat."

I called for the kids, but quickly lowered my voice. The rattle of my own voice sounded like an internal megaphone battering my brain.

"Where is that darn cat?" I noticed the mixed salad sitting in a glass bowl, like a picture out of a home magazine. I grabbed a piece of cucumber and ate it.

"You said something?" Sydney said while leaning into the fridge.

I could see a green vein bulging from her otherwise perfect neck. She seemed stressed.

"Just wondering where to find Pumpkin."

She waved her arm. "Could be buried among the pillows in the master bedroom or hiding under the loveseat in the living room."

I didn't have the energy or desire to hunt down an animal that didn't want to be found. I snatched another piece of cucumber and noticed it was nearing eight o'clock. "Is Mark usually this late getting home?"

"It can vary. Mark works his ass off. I try to hold off dinner as late as possible, hoping he'll make it home, but the kids revolt if it gets past eight." She scooped some pasta onto a plate. "It would make things easier if he sent a text or called. But he's not unlike most men."

I was in the middle of carrying the bowl of salad to the Lazy Susan on the table, but it almost slipped through my fingers. How many red flags did I just hear from Sydney? Hell, she practically sounded like she was married to the guy. My husband.

"Sydney, you're welcome to go on home. I can take over from here."

"I'm fine. No worries. I typically stick around at least until nine, ready to warm up a meal for Mark...I mean, Mr. Giordano when he gets home, and help the kids with their homework."

I could feel a ball of emotion formulating in the pit of my

empty stomach. Wasn't she basically describing my job as a mother and wife?

"Don't you have your own studies to worry about?"

"I dropped down to six hours this semester. Nothing I can't handle in between trips to basketball or cheerleading practice."

Dammit, she was pissing me off. Or was it just our family setup? What the hell had I allowed to happen? It sounded like I'd been in a coma for years.

"Why did you drop your hours?"

She actually connected her eyes with mine for a brief second. "Honestly, you guys pay me so well it's hard to not get addicted to the money. Plus, I could see I was needed around here."

Needed to do what exactly? Blow my husband?

Fifteen

My face turned flush just letting that thought roll around in my brain, as Luke motored into the kitchen. "I'm hungry," he announced.

"Do your Pumpkin duties, and you'll have a full plate of spaghetti waiting for you," Sydney said before I could throw in my two cents.

"I've got the cat food. You have to scoop shit this week," Erin said to her brother the moment she arrived in the kitchen. I noticed she'd slipped on a sweatshirt.

"Erin, please don't cuss," I said.

She gave me the teenage "whatever" look, then shuffled over to the pantry and found a can of cat food.

"Luke, make sure you don't spill the cat litter all over the floor," Sydney said while handing me a plate full of pasta. I felt like the hired help, while the college coed appeared quite comfortable taking the role of lady of the house.

"That's for Erin," she said.

I felt defiant. "I'll give it to Luke."

"But Erin only likes a small amount of meat sauce. Luke wants a ton of it."

I was being schooled about my own children by a college kid, one who happened to have a body like a centerfold. I knew my memory loss was to blame, but I was finding it hard to figure out my role in the family. I felt like a distant relative who visited only on special holidays.

Once everyone was seated, I kicked off the meal with a generic question. "How was school today?"

"Oh, Mother, do you really want to know?" Erin asked.

I counted to five, then raised my head with noodles dangling from my mouth. I slurped them up. "I'm genuinely interested. Remember, I don't have a lot of background."

With her eyes plastered to the ceiling, Erin catalogued her day in monotone for about ten seconds.

"Is everything okay with...you know, what we discussed earlier?"

She dropped her fork and put a hand to her head. "It changes by the hour. I walk out of history class and everything is good, people are nice to me, and everything seems normal. Next period, I walk out of biology, and I hear catcalls from guys calling me a slut."

I quickly eyed Luke, who didn't have his video games, TV, or drones to distract him.

He said, "A slut? Isn't that bad?" His eyes were wide.

"Very bad, Luke. But it's not true. Someone is spreading lies about your sister. And by the way, don't ever repeat that word. Understand?"

"I'm pretty sure I know who won't let it go," Erin said before Luke could respond to me. "Julie. She's nothing but a little b—"

"You don't need to sink to her level, Erin."

Another fork clanged against a plate. Sydney, who seemed exasperated while still maintaining perfect skin tone, gestured with both arms. "Give Erin a break. She's just calling it like she sees it. Girls are mean sometimes, and this Julie bitch needs to be taught a lesson. Straight up."

If I could have shot poisonous darts out of my eyes, Sydney would have face-planted into her plate of spaghetti. Out of sight, I grabbed a handful of my sweatpants to keep from shaking. "I think we're in violent disagreement, Sydney."

She twisted her head. Apparently, I'd spoken over her head, or under her boobs. The thought made no sense, but it helped relieve a tiny bit of anger, and my eyeballs finally retreated back into their sockets.

"I think we both want the best for Erin," Sydney said.

I turned to my sassy fourteen-year-old. "After dinner, let's have a private conversation about this. Given my life experiences, I'm sure we can crack this nut."

Three blank faces stared me down.

I said to Sydney, "Supporting Erin is cool. But throwing gas on the emotional flames of a kid isn't. So please either be respectful of the tone I'm setting or keep your thoughts to yourself."

She gave me the eye while opening her mouth, as if she could really come back with a zinger. Instead, she tossed her napkin on the kitchen table and jumped out of her chair.

"Any more spaghetti for anyone?"

"Me, me, me," Luke said, extending his plate.

I brought a hand to my head and rubbed it. Then I noticed a bottle of red wine on the counter.

"You want a glass?" Sydney offered, pulling a goblet out of the glass-covered cabinet.

I was shocked she offered me anything, other than a drive back to the hospital.

"Uh, me?" I pointed at my chest.

"Yes." She'd already set one glass on the counter, and her hand was paused in the cabinet.

"Oh, well. Part of me needs it, but the doc wouldn't want me to mix wine with the pain meds."

"But the meds aren't helping, right?" she asked all too logically.

Was I going to let this bimbo dictate my health decisions? As much as I really wanted to tell her off, I knew the kids were watching. "No thanks. I'm good."

"Your life." She shrugged her shoulders, then dinged the bottle on her wine glass and filled it to the rim. She tipped her head back and gulped down half the wine. She wiped her mouth on the sleeve of her sweatshirt as she said, "Ah."

Classy.

"Wait, Sydney, how old are you?"

"A sage twenty."

I did a double-take on that comment. "Sage, huh?"

She chuckled, then leaned against the counter and sipped her remaining wine. "It's good. You sure?"

"Sydney, I don't want to sound like I'm a cop." I paused, realizing I was an FBI agent—that must count for something. "But you shouldn't be drinking alcohol. Most importantly, you shouldn't be drinking alcohol in front of my kids."

I'd purposely claimed them as mine, even if I couldn't recall holding them as babies. That had to come sooner than later.

Sydney had the audacity to down the last bit of wine, then give us another "ah," her eyes on me the whole time. I was beginning to think this perfect-bodied student had issues.

"This whole fucking country has problems, I'm telling you." She flipped her sweatshirt over her head, her cropped shirt edging up to show the bottom of her breasts.

"Amen, Sydney." Erin took off her sweatshirt. Fortunately, she didn't have the goods to give us a peep show, but her defiance screamed just as loud.

"People get their panties in a wad about a little bit of wine and boobs." Sydney then grabbed her breasts and shook them.

I put my hand over Luke's eyes.

"It's all natural. The wine is natural. My body is natural. Sex is natural." She paced the floor as she tossed pots and pans into the sink.

"Sydney, this isn't the time for a protest."

"I just need to move to Europe, where sex and alcohol aren't such taboo subjects. People are free. I need to be free."

For the first time in…ever, I guessed, Sydney had a sensible thought—moving to Europe. I wondered if I could help her pack, even pay for a one-way ticket to the French Riviera. She'd have a hell of time fending off hundreds of obese men walking around in banana hammocks.

"European babes have hairy armpits. Nasty," Luke said.

I glanced at Luke, who scrunched his nose then gave a devilish smile.

With my adrenaline nozzle completely open, I pushed the chair back and got to my feet. "Sydney, it's time for you to leave."

She paused at the sink, and her face went from pissed-off protestor to wounded animal in two seconds. She was a pro at the manipulation game.

"But I need to help Erin with her homework and make sure Luke has his shower," she said with a shaky voice.

Now she wanted to come across as the victim. Screw that shit.

"I'm fully capable of handling that."

"You usually deferred to me in the past. So I just figured…"

"I can't speak to the past because I can't recall it. No one's fault, but it's obvious the kids need their mother. A real adult figure who's not still acting like a hormonal teenager."

Her jaw opened again, more words at the edge of those damn perfect lips. A moment of silence, then finally, the words came.

"Why, I've never—"

"Actually, I think you have. Many times over." Now *that* was a verbal jab. I stuck out my chest.

Sydney stormed out of the kitchen. A minute later, I heard the back door open.

"You shouldn't drink and drive," I called out.

The door slammed shut.

"Whew," Luke said, running a hand across his forehead. "Too much drama. I'm going to let off some steam by playing the second half of my NBA 2K game. It's the 1969 Celtics with Bill Russell against the 1986 Celtics with Larry Bird. Guess who's going to win?"

I pinched the corners of my eyes, already feeling like someone pulled the plug on my tub of energy. "Uh, the '86 team with Bird?"

"You kidding me? Red Auerbach would never lose to another team, even against a future Celtics team."

He ambled out of the kitchen.

"Luke."

"What?" His feet were already clamoring up the steps.

"Where are you getting images of European ladies and their armpits?"

"Sydney, duh?"

I forced out a breath, then glanced at the bottle of wine. Damn, it looked tempting.

"She's not that bad, Mom."

I shifted my eyes to Erin.

"Now you're giving me the evil eye," she said.

"I'm giving you the tired-as-hell eye," I corrected.

"Didn't think we were supposed to cuss in this house." She stuck out what hip she had and put a hand on it—a picture of major attitude.

I bit my tongue and tried not to say another word about the T-shirt. "I'm an adult, and last I checked, I can do anything I want. But I'll make you this promise. I'll only cuss if I'm so pissed that I'm about to gouge my eyeballs with a fork."

Erin nodded slowly as she folded her arms in front of her.

"Ready?" I asked.

"What, Mother?"

I picked up the fork, held it for a second, then set it back down. "I'm beat. But I'm also fucking pissed. You're not twenty yet. You're far from it. And if you keep taking advice from the free spirit pretending to be a nanny, things will not go well for you, at school or in this house."

Erin puffed out a breath.

"Please clean up the kitchen. I've got to lie down, close my eyes for a few minutes, and ponder theories on why a man was drowned by a cone of shame."

"A what? That's disgusting, Mother. I don't want to hear about your creepy work."

I had no more fight left in me. Thirty seconds later, my head hit the pillow.

Sixteen

I woke up and stuck out my left arm—why I felt compelled to do that, I had no idea. But my hand only slapped a cold mattress. Mark had yet to come home. I'd texted him when I left the hospital earlier, so he knew not to bother going by there. Turning over, I saw it was just after midnight.

I rolled out of bed, poured myself a glass of water, and then for some reason, was drawn to our closet. I touched a few of Mark's shirts, even put one up against my cheek. I felt nothing. They all seemed so foreign. Glancing around, I noticed boxes sitting on shelves above the racks of clothes. The area made me feel restricted, so I shuffled back into the bedroom.

My leg bumped a small table next to a framed window, and I looked down and found a jewelry box and small mirror. I began sifting through the jewelry. I was alone, so for the first time all day, I was able to relax and not worry if I could recall the sentiment behind each piece.

Angling the mirror toward me, I raised a colorful brooch and held it next to my chest. It was a reindeer, complete with a red nose. Rudolph. It was a little obnoxious, but cute. I guessed the kids got this for me, maybe with a little help from Dad.

Strands of pearl necklaces were tangled with other necklaces and bracelets. I picked up the wad of jewelry, a little frustrated it wasn't better organized. When was the last time I'd worn any of this?

A small silver bracelet dropped from the hairball. Picking it up, I could see it was a charm bracelet. There were two baby heads, one for Luke and one for Erin. Other charms included a soccer ball, a basketball, a cheerleading pom-pom, and a flute. I wondered if Erin used to play. Now she was riding the popular wave, which meant there were times when the social pressure would engulf her entire life—like today.

I searched for my wedding rings. I found a couple of other rings with large colorful stones, one ruby, and another emerald. Costume jewelry. But no sign of the wedding rings. As I closed the box, I spotted a simple necklace with a heart-shaped locket at the end. I opened it and saw a picture of a plain woman. She wasn't smiling. She was just staring at the camera. I wrapped the necklace around my neck and eyed it in the mirror.

"Hi, Alex."

My heart erupted. I'd heard Mark's voice just before I felt his hands on my arms.

"Jesus, Mark. Trying to give me a heart attack?"

"Sorry."

I could see his face in the mirror just above my shoulder.

"How did you sneak up on me so easily?"

"Sock feet," he said with a smile.

I turned and saw him wiggling his toes.

"I didn't want to wake you up."

"Oh. Uh, thank you." His act of genuine kindness caught me off guard.

"What do you have there?" He placed the silver heart in the palm of his hand.

"Do you know who this woman is?"

Tight lips split his stubbly face.

"Is this a touchy subject?"

He took a step back, scratching his head. "It's your mother."

"Oh, I've been wanting to—"

"She died years ago, Alex. When you were a kid."

My eyes moved to the floor.

"I know there's still so much you don't know. I didn't want to overwhelm you, but you need to know the key facts. And this is one of them."

I looked back up, his eyes briefly catching mine. He looked tired. Maybe this was how he looked every night at midnight after a long day's work. "Do you know much about her? She looks…not sad, but just there."

Mark walked over to his dresser, took off his watch, and set it in a pewter tray. His sleeves were rolled up, his shirt wrinkled to hell.

"She died in a car crash when you were young. You were, I don't know, maybe six or seven." His back was to me. All of sudden, it felt much colder in the room.

Something occurred to me then.

"Is that the reason you were all worried about me in the hospital? Because you thought I'd end up like my mom?"

"What? Uh…no, Alex. The thought never crossed my mind."

"Why are you turning away when I'm asking about my mom?" I was becoming more comfortable with straightforward questions.

"Um, it's really nothing now."

"Now as in 'this day,' or now as in 'this time of my life,' or what?"

He glanced over his shoulder quickly, then flipped back around and stared at the dresser while he unbuttoned his shirt. "You had a rough childhood. Let's just leave it at that."

I was intrigued, but also weary. It had been a long day, and my body wasn't up for an all-night fact fest that probably wouldn't open any doors to the memories of my life.

"Maybe some other time then," I said, clasping my hands in front of me. My fingers rubbed against each other, and the absence of my rings made me feel exposed.

I kept my hands occupied, and we went about our business getting ready for bed. No words were spoken. Climbing into bed, we locked eyes momentarily, then found our positions at least an arm's length apart. Suddenly, he leaned over, kissed the top of my head.

What was I, a dog?

As he pulled away, I happened to notice his left hand. No ring. Maybe we'd both agreed not to wear our rings. What couple does that? Maybe we were going through a difficult time. I certainly wasn't feeling the mojo from Mark. But he could be feeling the same about me, even before the crash.

We exchanged cursory goodnights, and then I stared at the ceiling thinking about two stiffs and how they ended up that way— the one in the water earlier and the one lying in the bed next to me.

Seventeen

Fog pumped into the midnight air like a locomotive chugging up a mountain. The steam coiled beyond the jagged rocks and above the pines, illuminated by a moon so bright the man could probably read a good book. Stephen King's *The Shining* came to mind. In some respects, he could relate to the main character, Jack. A purpose in life that seemed to have evolved into an urge so rewarding it felt nearly uncontrollable.

Using the sleeve of his denim shirt, he wiped beads of perspiration from his forehead. Even as the temperature plummeted below the freezing mark, he'd worked up a full-on body sweat. No pain, no gain, his father had always told him. And he was just getting started.

He felt something smacking his shoe. Looking down, he spotted a hand grasping at his rubber boots. Kicking it away, he glanced back up and surveyed the uninhabited island. All that could be heard was the Atlantic Ocean calmly lapping against the tapered shore.

"Please…please help me," a quivering voice said.

The man watched the loser stretch across the muddy sand, his body shaking from lying in a foot of frigid water.

"Right on time, Rick. Thanks for joining me. We're going to

have a grand time tonight." The man moved to his right, where he had assembled all the material needed for the evening's festivities. He sat on one of the smooth boulders that protruded just above sea level, pulled twine and a plastic baggie out of his duffel bag. While eyeing the moon, he lifted the baggie close to his ear and jiggled it.

"Do you hear that, Rick? That's the sound of fornication."

When Rick didn't respond, he looked closer and saw him pawing at the sand, trying to drag his body down the shoreline one inch at a time.

"A sand turtle would have lapped you by now," the man said, noting that his prisoner had moved all of five or six feet. "Rick, I'll give you a little insight."

Rick, whose legs were hardly able to function due to the strong sedative he'd been given earlier, paused, his trembling arm falling to the sand. "What do you...w-want...with me?"

The man slapped his knees, lifted off the boulder, and walked down the shore. Passing three pines, he tapped his forefinger on each one. Then he stopped, backpedaled, and tapped each of them again in the same order.

Once he reached Rick, he crouched down while grabbing a handful of rocky sand.

"Why am I here, with you, on this island?"

Rick tried turning his head, and for a brief second, the man could see his red-rimmed eyes.

"I'm a pretty smart guy, Rick. Some might even call me a genius. That's their opinion, I suppose. But I've also learned a few things as I've grown up."

"Am I supposed to ask you what you've learned?" Rick asked with a hint of attitude in his garbled voice.

The man poured half of the sand into his other hand. "I've always seen the world as symmetrical, a perfect balancing act across a billion variables. When one of those is thrown off balance, there is an equal and opposite pull to make it even again. I've been taught that applies to more than physics. It's applicable to humans and the impact we have on each other."

"Huh?

"You're not catching on very quickly, Rick. I know a lot about you, but I never looked at your aptitude test scores. Are you not very smart?"

"Screw you."

"I take that as a no. Anyway, you've crossed the line countless times. So, for every action you've taken, it's now my job to counter that in the best way I know how."

Rick shook his head, then raised up on his elbows. "You're not making any sense. I think you have the wrong guy. Really, I do. Just put me in your boat, drop me off on the mainland, and I'll be on my way. Then you can find the person who needs to be fixed. I won't tell a soul, I swear."

The man began to chuckle.

"What's so fucking funny? I'm freezing my ass off. You drugged me with something, and I can barely hold myself up."

"You didn't know it, but you used a pun. Fixed. Get it?"

Rick rubbed his eyes, his hand still shaking. He began to breathe in heavy gasps. "Just tell me what the fuck I need to do."

"Fixed can be used to describe an animal being spayed or neutered. I thought it was applicable to our discussion." The man found specks of sand on his hand and began to count each one.

"What? You're going to castrate me? What kind of sick fuck are you?" Rick asked with more emotion creeping into his voice.

The man silently moved his lips, counting higher and higher.

"Are you chanting or what?"

The man could hear Rick speaking, but it wasn't as important as finishing his task.

"Hello. Are you even there?"

Out of the corner of his eye, the man could see Rick lunge to his left—breaking through the thin shell of undisturbed ice—then roll across the shore like a seal playing in the shallow water.

"Where are you going, Rick?" The slimeball hadn't learned that he couldn't get away even if he could use his appendages. "Rick, I owe you an answer to your question."

The man walked past Rick, touching each of the trees with his forefinger, and over to his workstation. Sitting on the boulder, he said, "You cheated on your wife, Rick. First with Kelly, then with Amber, and then again with Felicia. And that doesn't include the young college girl tonight."

"How do you know that?"

"I have my ways, Rick. I have my ways."

A few minutes ticked by as the man started piecing together his vignette.

Again, Rick apparently saw this as another opportunity to escape. He made a feeble attempt, moving about twenty feet. A little more progress on this go-round. The man noted that Rick was slowly regaining his strength.

"Rick, my man, I forgot to provide that insight."

"What the hell are you going to give me, a stock tip?"

The man didn't laugh. All numbers aside, Rick wasn't taking this seriously.

"I'm going to kill you, Rick. That much is certain."

He heard a whimper as Rick dropped his head.

"How much you suffer, though, is really up to you, my friend. So think about your life for the next few minutes as I set up our scene."

Rick's whimper morphed into a wailing cry. A minute later, he was cussing and throwing fists of pebbles and sand at him. The man simply ignored the middle-aged insurance salesman, acknowledging that even the idiots of the world had to work through the five stages of grief.

With all the pre-work completed, the man straddled Rick and picked him up.

"Do you have your sea legs yet?"

Rick wiped dirt and tears from his face. "Yeah, I do. Thanks."

"You're even speaking with some manners. You have done some soul searching. That's cool. Hold it right here while I get something."

Rick said, "You know, I've been giving this a lot of thought. Actually, I've been praying. Yeah, me and God, we're like this."

The man didn't bother looking up.

"Anyway, I'm glad you've taken me out here. I kind of feel like Scrooge being shown how he's screwed up his life and others he cared about by the Ghost of Christmas Past. It's been enlightening."

The man returned to Rick and stood behind him. "Hug yourself."

"Huh?

"You first need to love yourself before you can love anyone else."

"Right. Okay." Rick did as he was told. They all did, thinking they could slither out of their predicament as smoothly as they'd slithered into the pants of the naïve younger women.

The man found the edge of the duct tape and started wrapping it tightly around Rick's waist.

"What are you doing?"

"What I told you I was going to do."

"But I thought you wanted me to acknowledge my sins and ask for forgiveness."

"And did you?"

"Yes, I told you I said a prayer. It's all good. I'm ready for my second chance at life."

The duct tape had reached Rick's elbows.

"This is where I need your help. Can you bow your chest a bit? I'm trying to create an upside-down volcano. Can you picture it?"

"Uh, I guess. Is this some kind of prank?"

The first roll of tape ran out. He pulled out the second roll from his bag and continued the process, walking around Rick, ensuring the proper amount of overlap to build the strongest funnel possible.

"This isn't a prank, Rick. I thought I explained the law of human physics."

"But didn't you say I had to love myself first? I did, and then I asked for forgiveness."

The man circled Rick and stopped inches from his face. "You believed that bullshit?"

He tied two cinderblocks to Rick's ankles, knowing this was when the reality would start hitting.

"Please, please, please, no. You can't do this to me. I'm a good person, I swear."

"On your own grave? That would be difficult, wouldn't it?"

Jostling left and right, Rick tried to pull his arms free. A waste of energy.

"Rick, you've mocked your marriage and your family, sticking your dick into anything that moves—no offense to Kelly, Amber, or Felicia. And now you want me to pretend nothing ever happened."

The man picked up Rick, dragging him and his cinderblocks another six feet into the ocean.

"But I'll change, I promise. You know, just like Scrooge," Rick whined.

This was the part that annoyed the man the most—whining and whimpering like a baby who had just lost his pacifier. Still, he knew Rick was special. He reached for his back pocket and felt the outline of his rusted, dull switchblade. He had plans for the blade, and the body part that Rick cherished more than any other. Later, though, when Rick would be on his last breath.

Taking in a salty breath, he decided to stick to his plan—for now—and he picked up a cinderblock, waded into the water, and tossed it into Rick's duct-tape pouch. Rick nearly toppled over, screaming as the block scraped his neck and chest.

"You can't fall over. That ruins the fun far too early in the process. That's the trick, Rick. I like that. I'll call you Tricky Ricky. Kind of fits, given your propensity for using all your catchy one-liners to lure those young girls with bullshit promises. Meanwhile, Jeanne is at home trying to deal with twin teenage girls, both of whom have a learning disability, while she also has the burden of taking care of her ailing mother. It's just not right, Rick."

"And you think you have the right to judge me? You're nothing but a fucking asshole. You've probably never been laid in your life. I'm a grown man, motherfucker, and I can fuck who I want to fuck, when I want to fuck them."

Lashing out. It was all part of the process.

"By the way, there's a ring attached to that cinderblock."

Rick tried dipping his head, until his eyes found the ring. "What...who are you?"

"I'm just a guy helping make the world a better place. And that can only be done if guys like you are six feet under—the water, that is."

Rick looked around as the water lapped against his chin. "What are you planning to do?"

"We're going to play high-low. Well, it's really more low-high."

"*You're* fucking high."

The man just stared at Rick, then shook his head. "It's all about the tide. As it gets higher, you begin to drown, slowly, painfully."

Rick began to cry, his head bobbing up and down, water entering his mouth. "I'm s-sorry. Doesn't that mean anything?"

"*Sorry*. That's an interesting term. If you were going to be transparent about your intentions, you might say something like, 'To show you that I regret everything I did, I'm going to use a term that will hopefully manipulate your opinion of me.' One word, and it all goes away. Right, Rick?"

"I don't know what to say. You're judging me for making a mistake. I'm human. Shoot me."

Self-pity. Pretty much following the formula.

"Rick, do you know how old that girl was tonight?"

"Which girl?"

"Which girl, Rick? You think I'm that gullible, or even blind?"

"Okay, okay. I didn't mean to upset you. I know who you're talking about. I think her name was Amanda."

"Being a salesman and all, you have to remember names, don't you?"

"I have to be good at everything, names, numbers."

"Nineteen. Is that a number you recall?"

"Nineteen what?"

"Years. Amanda, a sophomore in college. She's almost as young as your own daughter. You were trying to screw a girl who's as young as your daughter. That's messed up, my man."

Shivering, Rick eyed the wall of duct tape, then lifted his sad eyes to the man. "I was just talking to her. No harm."

"Right. Just like the others," the man said, back at his workstation, looping the twine through the other rings and then tying them to the cinderblock.

"I'll pay you. I can see your boat over there. You need to upgrade. Wouldn't you like to have a nice yacht?," Rick asked with a forced smile. "Twin inboard engines with a maximum speed of fifty knots, three cabins, mahogany trim. It can be yours. I know just the place to get you your dream yacht."

The man stopped moving and stared blankly at Rick.

"Then again," Rick said, licking his lips with the desperate anticipation of closing the deal, "you may not want to deal with all that maintenance and overhead. What if I just paid you the money? Straight cash, homey." Rick tried to chuckle, then coughed, his lungs apparently responding to the icy water.

The man stopped in his tracks and watched the ocean water slap Rick's chin. "You think I'm your *homey*?"

"Just a figure of speech. But I can see it in your eyes. You know I have something that you want. And that's what Rick does. Rick takes care of his peeps."

"Now I'm your *peep*?"

"I don't know your name."

The man could feel the spotlight of the moon on his face. Surely, Rick could see that he wasn't falling for the cheesy sales-guy moves.

"How much do you want? I have a lot of money stashed away. You want a hundred grand? Anything. It's yours. We can take all this crap off me, jump in your boat, and take me to my car. I have a checkbook in there. I'll sign it right there. Better yet. I can have my financial advisor send it to the bank of your choice. I'd recommend an offshore account, just to keep the tax man from knocking on your door."

Finally, Rick shut his trap, and the man watched the moon shimmer off the rolling water.

"Dude, did you not hear the offer of a lifetime?"

The peaceful silence had lasted for all of thirty seconds.

"It's time to get back to work, Rick."

"Seriously? After all that?"

"You're starting to annoy me, Rick."

The man waded into the water and raised the cinderblock to his shoulder, his calloused, oversized hands maintaining a firm grip.

"What are you doing? I thought we had something going here. A deal in the making. Everything is negotiable, right?"

The man shook his head. "Character is all about doing the right thing when people aren't watching."

Rick's chin began to quiver as he raised his eyes to the cinderblock. "This isn't right."

"You were given a chance to show strong character. You failed, Rick, plain and simple. You may have thought you could walk this earth and toy with those who couldn't see the real you. But they will soon see the *real* Rick Lepino. And they will come to know what he was all about."

The man tossed the second cinderblock into the gray funnel, and Rick wailed like a million babies. "I…I don't what to die. I repent. I repent. I repent!"

"I'm sure you do. And now you will die."

The man sat back on his boulder and watched Rick struggle to crane his neck for another ten minutes. Slowly, water rose above his mouth and nose. Even under the water, eyes of terror caught the full moon's glare. His strapped torso lurched until the water filled his lungs and the last air bubble made it to the surface. And then he began to sink—a cadaver with no soul.

The man took a mental picture and stored it in his memory bank. Nothing could eclipse this kind of serenity. It was a feeling he planned to repeat over and over and over again. Just like everything else in his life.

Eighteen

Rippling ocean water rocked me back and forth as I lay on my back gazing at a clear blue sky. Two squawking seagulls gracefully glided across the sky by while crashing waves drowned out every other sound around me. Emptying my lungs, a gust of wind brushed against my wet body, keeping the summer heat at bay.

This was my serenity, the only time I could ever feel completely happy inside. It was a peace I knew would be short-lived, so I immersed myself in the moment. It was all I had, and it kept me sane.

A jab to my ribs, and I screamed out.

"Mom, Mom, you gotta check this out," Luke's arms rammed against my chest and stomach.

After an initial heart tremor to knock me out of my dream state, I took in a gulping breath and crouched into a defensive position while my eyes peeled apart.

"I figured out this thing with my drone. It's cooler than the other side of the pillow. Come on, wake up and watch me."

Had Luke already downed two shots of caffeine this morning?

"Good morning, Luke."

He gave me a funny look. I cleared my throat. "Did you think

I'd turned into a monster?"

"Yeah, Mom. You had me."

"That phrase, 'cooler than the other side of the pillow.' I actually remember hearing that before. That's pretty catchy. You're creative," I said, rustling his hair.

"Can't take credit for it. Stuart Scott from *SportsCenter* used to say it. He died from cancer, but I sometimes say it just to remember him."

"That's cool, Luke. You're honoring his memory."

"Yeah, sure. Anyway, Mom, can you come down so I can show you?" He picked up his drone and motored across the bedroom.

Propping myself up on my elbows, I touched my head. Still intact, and the pain seemed a little less intense. Wiping gunk out of my eyes, I tried to think about my dream for a couple of seconds.

"Erin, Luke, the Syd-mobile is about to take off. Can't be late for school."

She was back. Damn. Should have known to actually think ahead to the morning. I could drive the kids to school. I was their mom, for goodness sake.

Luke zoomed out of the room.

Climbing out of bed, I took two steps then stopped and grabbed the bedpost. The room wasn't spinning, but someone must have raised one corner of the house about a foot. A few seconds passed, then I gave it another attempt, reaching for the next bedpost. A few more steps, and I made it to the doorway.

"Erin," I called out.

I could hear voices downstairs. Sitting on my ass, I scooted down the steps. Luke was waiting for me at the bottom. I knew I either looked resourceful or like I'd regressed about...how old was I? Probably wasn't the right questions to ask my eleven-year-old son. He knew I had some memory issues, but he might wonder about his well-being if I went in that direction.

"You came down, Mom. Cool." He hopped into the living room, obviously excited to share his discovery with me, and that gave me a burst of energy.

"Let me see what you got," I said, using the banister to pull myself up.

The drone lifted off the floor and pitched forward. "Now I can make tight turns," he said. The drone with four propellers circled a lamp then came back to us.

"Now watch this." He pulled a switch, and a small screen came to life on his remote control panel. The drone then turned and motored out of the living room, curling into the kitchen. I leaned over his shoulder and watched it move above Erin, who was assembling her lunch.

He started giggling. "Isn't that cool?"

"Get that thing away from me before I destroy it," Erin yelled from the kitchen.

I nodded at Luke, who steered his favorite toy left and down.

"What is that?" He moved his head closer to the screen.

Momentarily distracted by looking at the living room in daylight, I looked back at the screen. My eyes bugged out.

"Luke, I hope you know you're looking at my cleavage. I don't really mind, but I think your mother might have an issue," Sydney said from the kitchen.

I snatched the control unit out of Luke's hand.

"What is cleavage?"

"Oh, nothing. It's just one of the silly terms girls use about their bodies. Ready for a good day at school?"

He ran off to the kitchen. I followed, but at a much slower pace.

"Thanks for taking them to school." I threw out the olive branch to Sydney, realizing I needed her at least temporarily until I could take care of my own business.

"Sure," she said, shutting the door to the fridge, her big, brown eyes never turning in my direction.

The kids headed out the door. "Hey, don't I get a proper goodbye?"

"Goodbye," they said in tandem.

"No. A hug."

"Really? I'm almost fifteen years old," Erin declared. She slowly walked my way, but Luke darted around her, then came up and squeezed my waist. I kissed the top of his bushy head.

"You need a haircut, fella."

"Later, Mom."

Erin put an arm around me, and I reciprocated. Short and almost sweet. "Keep your head up. And don't listen to the haters."

"Okay. Whatever," she said, shutting the door behind her.

Nineteen

Thirty minutes later, I met Nick halfway down the front sidewalk. He held out an arm.

"What did you get me, Nick?"

"Your usual."

"And what is my usual?" It was hot, but that didn't stop me from taking two sips.

"Venti non-fat mocha with whip."

"Damn good choice," I said, feeling the warm drink soothe my chest.

"Hey, can we take some time to visit a couple of the museums that were robbed?"

"Your wish is my command, my lady."

"You're so gallant, Nick, in a Brooklyn kind of way."

We shut the doors on his Impala, and Nick paused before turning the ignition. "How did you know I was from Brooklyn?"

I glanced down the street for a brief moment. "Your accent, maybe?"

He shrugged and cranked up the engine. "Your little mystery is second on our list. First up, we're heading north a bit to visit with Christopher Barden's wife. She's expecting us."

I wondered if I should bring up the fact that I wasn't carrying my FBI credentials.

"Oh, one thing." He reached into the center console, then handed me a leather fold-over wallet.

"Jerry knew you'd insist on tagging along with me, so he couldn't risk you not having your creds."

It was nice to know someone knew how I thought.

The edges were worn and bent. Opening the wallet, I saw my mug shot on an ID card. I rubbed my thumb across the brass eagle at the top of the badge.

"Thanks," I said, taking another jolt of caffeine.

"Jerry says you owe him one."

"Is he only saying that because he knows I'd have no recollection if he really owed me a bunch?"

"It's possible." After pulling away from the curb, we hit a quick light, and the brakes squeaked as we stopped. "Before you ask, Jerry said the only way you get your weapon back is when you're officially released by your doctor and speech therapist."

Oddly enough, I hadn't thought much about not having a weapon. Maybe safety wasn't a natural concern of mine, or at the least, I didn't have a propensity to be paranoid.

"Was I a decent shot?"

"You just looking to get your ego stroked?"

"It's either ask you or I steal your weapon from you and start shooting out streetlights."

He chuckled.

"So, was I?"

"Could you knock out a streetlight if we were moving forty miles per hour down the road?" Nick smacked his forehead as if I'd just asked the most outrageous question. "Actually, there was this one time. We had this kidnapper pinned behind a hotel—at least we thought we did. He took off into the woods just as the sun had set. You hit him on the run with one shot, about a hundred yards away, and all we could see was a vague outline of him."

"Impressive."

"You had a reputation."

"I hope you're not talking about the kind of reputation that involves creeps like Randy."

"Nah. Your reputation gave most people the vibe that said, 'I'll kick your ass if you don't give me the information I need.' But I knew you were soft inside, like the jelly inside of a donut."

"Jelly. Hmm. I must have a fair amount of aggression somewhere in this body."

"I think it's mainly because you're a woman. Any other guy who acted like you, said what you said, we'd just call him a damn good agent."

"And me? What did people call me?"

"To you or behind your back?"

"Wonderful."

"Hey, it's the real world out there."

I turned and stared him down. "I might not remember how old I am, but after interacting with Randy and his sexist, demeaning attitude, and then watching Sydney act like she's Mrs. Giordano, I think I've lived to experience the real world. And that's all in the last twenty-four hours. That doesn't include taking a swim with a cadaver."

"Sorry, that came out the wrong way."

"You know where you can put your real world?"

"No need to be so graphic," Nick said with a hearty smile.

I tapped my hand on the center console, and Nick flinched.

"You going to tell me?"

"You going to kill me if you don't like what I tell you?"

"Maybe. Spill it, Radowski."

He blew out a breath. "I was stupid. Nothing good can come from this. I'm supposed to be your fairy godfather."

"You got the fairy part right."

We both hollered with laughter.

While wiping tears from his eyes, Nick put a hand on my leg and said, "Some of the guys would call you rich bitch."

"Rich bitch. I'm a bit direct. I've recognized that in myself since I've come back to life. Sue me. Guys just looking to chop me down because they don't like me calling them out?"

"There's probably some of that," Nick said, turning west onto Wilson. "They see that Mark has done very well, and you guys live a pretty damn good life, if you haven't noticed. How many agents have nannies?"

"I volunteer to give her to anyone who wants her. In fact, I might pay someone to take her."

At that moment, we passed Salem High School. I said, "They're called the Witches? Can't imagine how the rival schools respond to that mascot." I gave Nick an arched eyebrow, then I glanced back at the campus, wondering if Erin was having to deal with more mean girls today.

Part of me wanted Nick to stop so I could pull the kids who'd teased or bullied Erin out of class and scare the living crap out of them with all sorts of federal threats as I flashed my FBI badge. I could even borrow Nick's Glock as a point of emphasis. But I knew that would only be a temporary fix for Erin, not to mention the lawsuits that would follow from the overprotective parents who coddled their teenage brats. She and I hadn't exactly hit it off, but I knew it had more to do with her environment, both at school and home. Resolving the nanny issue—really, the Sydney issue—had to be at the top of my list when I spoke to Mark.

"Are you wishing you could go back to high school?" Nick asked, turning north on Route 107.

I snapped my fingers. "There's another advantage to having memory issues right there. Everyone has horror stories from their high school years. I can easily convince myself that my teenage years were smooth sailing."

Releasing a quick chuckle, my words echoed in my mind, and I wondered what, if anything, was buried inside, something that might not want to escape from the memory-loss prison.

I forced my attention away from the soul-searching to the changing landscape, trees, and homes. The tires changed their sound pattern, and I saw water as we crossed a bridge.

"This leads us into Beverly." Nick pointed a finger straight ahead like a tour guide.

I nodded, thinking more about my colleagues' jealousy—my damn good life, as Nick called it. I couldn't recite many facts about my own life or anyone else's, but wealth wasn't helping the happiness factor at home. I wasn't sure what could help bridge some of the gaps that existed. I felt empty inside. It was possible I just needed more time.

Maybe Mark and I could sit down, focus on each other, and have a real conversation, not just about the facts of my life, but to try to understand what moved us in our relationship. Then I'd hopefully feel a true connection. The pictures of us around the house seemed authentic. We'd been happy at one point. At least it seemed that way. Maybe my accident and resulting memory loss was an opportunity—no, *the* opportunity—to rescue our relationship, if that was needed, for us and our family.

The blue water disappeared briefly as Nick veered right, and I saw a sign for Route 22. It only took a couple of blocks of idle time before my curiosity got the best of me, just like it had earlier when I waited for Nick to arrive. I had tried playing with the obese cat, Pumpkin, dangling feathers dipped in catnip. He'd just eaten, so he'd only managed to roll over like a beached walrus.

Pulling my phone from my purse—I'd found a simple Kate Spade bag in the top of my closet—I spotted the email Jerry sent me the night before. I thumbed through the notes again, as sparse as they were. For a reason I'd yet to specifically identify, I believed my crash was connected to one of the open cases I'd been working. Nothing else made any sense.

The embezzlement and wire fraud case piqued my interest at first glance. An asset management director at a local IT company, Netsix, had dipped his hand into the corporate coffers by skimming money from their vendors. Allegedly, he complicated his life even more by sending the money to offshore accounts.

Open-and-shut case, right? Not so fast, my friend. Leaders at Netsix became very fickle when four FBI financial analysts and I dug deeper into the company's records. Then lawyers got involved, asking for exceptions to the growing list of documents that needed to be reviewed. When we didn't agree to their conditions, we were forced to have a judge issue a search warrant. Threats ensued, and FBI lawyers tangled with Netsix lawyers, and from what I could surmise from the notes, I'd lost interest in playing nicey-nice with lawyers.

The sexual harassment case was more of a slow burner, mainly because everyone had lawyered up, either to protect themselves from being sued or to push members of the other side into a corner that would cost them millions. Apparently, working through in-house corporate lawyers required an insane amount of patience and thick skin, since lying was a required skill in that profession. I wasn't sure what I'd done to Jerry to receive that case. Or either case, for that matter.

I certainly couldn't imagine a need to be involved in a high-speed chase on a lonely, dark road in the middle of the night. Not with a lawyer and not on these two cases. It just didn't fit.

A question wiggled its way to the top of my mind: what was my beef with lawyers anyway, especially since I was married to one?

"We're in the White Collar Crime Squad?" I asked Nick with my eyes still stuck on the phone.

"Used to be in Violent Crimes, but it was time for a change. We now work both the White Collar and newly formed Art Theft squads. Jerry oversees both squads."

The Impala's brakes squeaked to a stop in front of a mammoth home surrounded by trees and at least a half-acre of land.

"Beverly Farms. One of the nicer areas in Greater Boston," Nick said.

I hopped out and paused at the sidewalk to take in the whole scene. A Queen Anne Victorian home, white with black shutters, a wraparound porch, and lots of chimneys.

"Now this is an estate worth talking about," Nick said, swishing by me.

"You got a million bucks?"

Just then the front door opened and a few people poured out, pausing to say goodbye and to hug. All of them appeared to be wiping tears.

"This won't be easy," Nick muttered under his breath as we both stood like soldiers at the bottom step.

A man and woman, along with two kids, waved one final time to the person at the front door and then walked past us, offering strained, polite smiles.

"You can come on up." A woman with her hair in a bun stood at the door, wiping mascara from under one eye.

Our shoes clapped against the wooden steps and porch.

"We're with the FBI. I'm Special Agent Radowski, and this is Special Agent Giordano."

We held up our credential, but she paid no attention, and instead caught me off-guard by reaching out and grabbing my arm.

"You've got to help me."

Twenty

"What can we do for you?" I tried to steady myself in case she dropped all her weight on me, although even in baggy jeans and a beige sweater, it was easy to see her curves carried no extra meat.

"There's a mob of people in my house, and I just..." She stopped, bringing a finger to her extra-long eyelashes.

Are those real?

"I just can't deal with all the fake pity."

"Mrs. Barden, I'm sure they genuinely care about the grief you're going through."

"Bullshit!"

I flinched, then shifted my eyes to Nick.

She squeezed my arm harder. "You don't understand!"

"It's okay, Mrs. Barden. Let's just go in, get you some water, sit down in a quiet place, and talk through everything."

Her chest heaved as tears bubbled in her eyes. She swiped her hand across her face, smearing the mascara. I would try to take care of that for her once she calmed down, but for now I rested my hand on her shoulder.

"Okay. I guess. First, we have to wade through all the crap," she said, stepping inside.

I first noticed flames in an enormous fireplace on the left side of the living room. Two women with sad eyes warmed their hands.

A quick glance around, and I saw nothing but money inside a grand, old home. High ceilings, intricate crown molding, French doors leading into a dining room, hand-scraped hardwood floors as far as the eye could see. I guessed the house dated back to the early 1900s, maybe earlier. Beautiful paintings that depicted scenes from the Revolution dotted the walls, including a library off to the right, where I also found a globe. She must have seen me look in that direction.

"Christopher always dreamed of us traveling the world as a family. We talked about it constantly. And then Dana was born and everything changed."

Tears flooded her face, but before I could take a breath, she was swarmed by four, five, six people, all offering to help, pawing at her like she was meat.

Her frustration was starting to make a little bit more sense. Nick and I stood in the entry, albeit somewhat awkwardly, waiting to see when—or if—Mrs. Barden would be able to break free.

A little girl then waddled into our space and tugged on her mother's jeans. Mrs. Barden picked her up and gave her a kiss on the cheek. The little girl responded by hugging her neck. A few smiles lit up the room, and then someone yelled from the back of the house, "Hot breakfast for everyone and special pancakes for Dana."

The little girl ran off, and the crowd followed. Mrs. Barden shuffled a few steps behind everyone for a moment, then cut back to us.

"I'm sorry. I tried being direct earlier, but they just thought I was losing it. So I've had to use alternative methods to have a little bit of 'me time.' Time to grieve."

She pressed her eyes shut. Her features were pleasant, her skin smooth and blemish-free. Even on what she might describe as her worst day, she looked damn good, although I knew her heart was broken.

"We can sit in here for at least a few minutes," she said, walking into the library, "until they hunt me down again." She gave us a forced smile. Folding her legs under her, she parked her body on the couch, her arms crossed like she might be cold.

"Do you want me to run to the kitchen and get you something to drink?" I asked.

She sat up quickly. "Please no. They'll realize I haven't joined the crowd, and I'll never get any peace. And with so many people here, they're at least watching over the kids. Finally, a break."

I crossed my legs.

"I'm rude," she said. "Would *you* like something to drink?"

"We're just fine, thank you," Nick said, glancing at me for a second then back to the wife of the deceased.

"I'm sorry we have to bother you at a time like this," I said. "We know the last day has been very difficult for you."

A single nod. "I'll do anything to find the person who murdered my husband, the father to our two young girls." She brought a hand to her face.

I spotted a box of tissues. I lifted from my seat and instantly felt dizzy. I grabbed the side of the couch, hoping neither Nick nor Mrs. Barden noticed, and I reached for the tissues, then swung around and set the box on the couch.

"Thank you." She released a choppy breath as she plucked a tissue and brought it to her face.

"Mrs. Barden, can you—"

"It's Agatha. Christopher's mother is the only Mrs. Barden I know."

"Very well, Agatha. I checked with the local police department, and they've had no reports of any calls from your home. Has anyone threatened you or your husband?"

"Actually, yes. And he's in our home at this very moment."

Nick and I both inched higher in our matching royal-blue Queen Anne chairs.

"Excuse me?" Nick said, turning his head slightly.

"On top of everyone invading my house, I have to deal with that asshole. He's nothing more than a Benedict Arnold." She pointed a finger at Nick and said, "That's who you should be investigating."

"Is anyone in imminent danger? If so, we can dispatch backup, and I can pull him aside," Nick said.

His sports coat flapped open, and I could see his holstered Glock. I felt naked.

"No, no, no. He wouldn't have the balls to do anything now. He got what he wanted, even if he didn't do it," Agatha said, her chocolate eyes glistening as she looked to the corner of the stately room.

"We need more information, Agatha. Did this person threaten your husband?"

"Yes."

"When?"

"Most recently at the company Christmas party. What they called an 'end-of-year celebration.' Political correctness and all."

"And what happened?" I asked, taking the lead in questioning. It felt natural.

"Trent got drunk as hell. What's new? And he started getting belligerent, his typical MO," she said.

"Trent?"

"Trent Kapler. He's a peer of Christopher's at Transamerica Financial. Stabbed Christopher in the back on repeated occasions, then he accused Christopher of all sorts of crazy crap."

"Let's take it a piece at a time. The Christmas, I mean, end-of-year celebration. What happened?"

"Trent, ever the show-off, had to get on the dance floor and pretend he was putting on a strip show, courtesy of downing about ten gin and tonics. Christopher said something to him, told him to stop embarrassing himself, his wife, and the firm. That just set him off."

"This is Trent you're talking about?"

"Who else? I think he's on steroids too. He went ballistic, and a bunch of guys had to hold him back. Someone actually said they needed to call the zoo so they could rush over and shoot a sedative into the asshole, just like they do elephants who need to be put under for surgery."

"Anything else go on at the party?"

"That little shit tried to act like he'd calmed down, even said he wanted to apologize. When he went to shake Christopher's hand, he took a swing at him, said he'd kill him if he had the chance. Knocked out a tooth."

I rested my elbows on my knees. "If Trent is that volatile, why is he in your house?"

"Two reasons. One, he admitted himself to alcohol rehab. Supposedly, he's clean. Second, his wife is my sister."

Nick and I exchanged a quick glance.

"Everything calm since they've been here?" I asked.

"Yes," she said, picking apart her tissue. "Maybe I am being a little emotional."

"I understand, but I'm glad you shared this with us. You mentioned other confrontations between Christopher and Trent?"

"I never witnessed anything, just heard about them. Christopher mentored Trent for two years. Two damn years! Brought him in as an intern and helped him become a certified financial planner, really showed him the ropes. Trent got promotion after promotion, but never acknowledged what Christopher had done for him. And from what Christopher said,

Trent even started spreading really wicked rumors around the office about him."

Nick gave me a strained look, as if he felt uncomfortable delving deeper into family drama. I had enough of my own, but this was an area we couldn't overlook.

"Can you share those rumors with us?"

Pressing her lips together, she pulled another tissue and dotted the corners of her eyes. It seemed like she had some difficulty in sharing this information.

"You've got to realize I love my husband. He is…was the best to me, my little girls."

I nodded, feeling like she had more to share. So I waited her out.

"Trent…" She swallowed back more tears and looked me in the eyes. "Trent claimed that Christopher was screwing around on me." She blew out a breath. "Can you believe such an outlandish thought?"

An underwater image of the floating wedding rings came to mind. I glanced at her hands, but they were now folded under a crossed leg. I knew Nick had digital images to show her, but I wondered about her mental frame of mind. Would she come completely unglued?

"Agatha, I don't want to imply anything one way or the other. As Special Agent Radowski said, we need to gather all pertinent information, even if it's a rumor or a result of a family dispute of some kind."

"What else do you want to know?"

"Did Trent mention any names?"

I knew we could ask him ourselves—and we would—but I wanted to hear what she had to say first, and then compare the information.

"I tried to forget." Her moist eyes met mine for a brief second.

"But I couldn't. And it impacted our marriage. I didn't cherish every moment."

I leaned over and put my hand on her leg. "It's okay to share with us."

"Kelsey," she said, biting her bottom lip and turning away just slightly. Nick jotted down the name on his pocket notepad.

"Thank you. I—"

"And there was Angela and Maureen too."

I ceased movement for a second. Her tone sounded like it was more fact than rumor. And now there were multiple girls. I kept my face void of emotion.

"Just so we have your statement, you're not aware of Christopher receiving any other threats, beside the one from Trent?" I asked.

She narrowed her eyes, and they appeared less soft. "What are you inferring?"

"Just capturing all the facts, Agatha," Nick said.

"Are you wondering if one of the women he *might* have interacted with killed him?"

Shifting my eyes to Nick for a moment, I decided to press a bit further. "I'm not implying anything, but do you know any of the women you mentioned?"

She pulled out another tissue, and then her eyes drifted away.

"Agatha?"

"Only from a distance. At the end-of-year party. They were huddled together. But Christopher was a good-looking guy, and we have a little money. People always sought him out. It comes with the job, you know?"

"His job?"

"Mine. The job of being married to him."

We were interrupted by the sound of tiny knuckles wrapping against the glass of the French doors, and then the little girl came in.

"Hi there," I said, holding out my hand.

The girl, Dana, climbed into Agatha's lap and sucked on her thumb, while her mom ran her fingers through her hair. "She has Down syndrome. Doing well, all in all, but it's been difficult since she was born. We have a four-month-old, Lindsey. She's napping upstairs, unless her grandmother has decided it's more important to interrupt her routine just so she can have a *moment* and rock her in the family rocking chair."

It sounded like a herd of cattle was on its way down the hall, and Nick quickly turned the conversation in a different direction.

"Have you seen anyone on your property or in the neighborhood that you didn't recognize?"

Dana jostled in her lap, but Agatha didn't seem fazed. "It's a pretty boring place. Honestly, if you're looking for possible suspects..."

"Momma, Momma," Dana said, hugging her neck.

"It's okay, honey." She kissed her little girl, but kept her eyes on us. "A few of the people Christopher worked with were absolute vultures."

"Is Trent included in that category?" Nick asked.

"Trent's more of a back-stabbing..." She stopped there, apparently not wanting her daughter to hear her cursing. "It's not just people at the firm. He was involved in deals all over the world. And they threw out threats on a routine basis."

"They threatened bodily harm?" I asked.

"They were too smart for that. But they implied a lot of things if deals went south."

I made a mental note that we would need full access to Christopher's client list, his itinerary from the last year, and colleagues he worked closely with, including the full names of the three ladies Agatha had mentioned. They would be at the top of our interview list, as well as any of their current love interests. The only thing worse than a woman scorned was her overprotective ex-boyfriend ready to gut any guy who looked at her.

The doors spilled open, and the room filled up with people of all ages, noise bouncing off the hardwoods, everyone oblivious to our private conversation. Agatha gave us one of those *help me* looks, but she was soon ferried away.

"Can you tell me which one is Trent?" I asked a gray-haired lady wearing sweats with JUICY written on the ass.

"Who's asking?" she said while chomping on a piece of gum.

My patience was about to be tested.

Twenty-One

I did a quick count to three, just to quell my jackhammer pulse a tad. Then, I addressed Juicy directly.

"FBI. I'm Special Agent Giordano. My partner's name is—"

"You think you can impress me? Not possible." Then she told us that Trent had stepped out on the back porch to have a smoke and turned her back to us.

"You kept your cool. Nice work," Nick whispered as he and I wove through the house and into the kitchen, where we saw Agatha practically pinned against the wall by four women who were pinging her with questions. Their eyes followed each step we took, which helped me understand the nature of the gossip.

Right before stepping onto the porch, I glanced at Nick. "You don't need to coddle me, Nick."

He brought a hand to his chest and his mouth opened.

"It's all good," I said, and then I led us onto the porch, where I could only see Trent's back. He flipped around with his head cocked to the side, puffing out three donuts of smoke.

"Nice trick," I said.

"Eh. I've been smoking since I was in high school. It's natural."

"Mind if we ask you some questions?"

Nick and I pulled out the credentials.

"I know who you are." His accent was classic Boston.

With all of us standing, Nick and I queried him for fifteen minutes straight. Trent went through three more cigarettes. But those questions were only softballs. I was ready to throw a ninety-five-mile-an-hour heater right under his chin.

"Is it true that you threatened to kill Christopher a few weeks ago?"

"It was stupid. I was stupid." He rocked from one foot to the other.

"Murder typically is stupid."

He hopped back a step, his eyes wide with either fear or astonishment. I couldn't tell for sure which one it was.

"Who says I murdered anyone?"

"We can only go where the evidence takes us," I said, waving smoke away from my face. "And right now, the only evidence we've got is about two hundred people hearing you threaten a man's life. Now he's dead. What are we supposed to think?"

I'd fudged on the evidence, wanting him to think we were solely focused on one path to find the killer.

"I was drunk. I said shit that I should never have said." He raised his chin, looking beyond us into the kitchen.

"How long you been sober?"

"Eighteen days, seven hours, and…twenty-three minutes." He chuckled, then looked out across the back yard. "Never thought I'd count the minutes of my life like that."

I let him contemplate his life for a moment.

"Trent, we need to clarify a couple of things, and then we'll leave you alone."

"Shoot."

"You've reportedly mentioned three names that Christopher had supposedly…" I chose to leave out the verb. "Kelsey, Angela, and Maureen. First of all, any truth to the rumors?"

"I never saw anything with my own two eyes, but I'm almost certain. Angela had been looking to sleep her way to the top."

This guy sounded like he pegged women in one of two categories—those who slept their way into whatever situation they sought, and those who were about to.

"And you would know this because…"

He craned his neck over my head, maybe looking for his wife.

"Because she first tried me."

"And because you've got this strong moral fiber, you withheld her advances. How gallant of you."

Nick nudged my arm.

"Look, I'm no saint, but my vice is beer and booze. Not women. I knew I hit pay dirt with Nora. I'm damn lucky she's in my life." His eyes became glassy, and he bit his lip. "That's why I…"

I tilted my head, waiting for words that never came. He swallowed hard, and I could see him holding back a swell of emotion.

"Anything else? I want to get back to my family. Try to figure out a way to undo all the crap I said about Christopher."

Nick jumped in. "One more thing. I understand you guys work in a pretty hostile environment. Did you ever hear of anyone threatening to kill Christopher, people he worked with, maybe his clients?"

"The environment is cut-throat, but not in the literal sense. It helped drive me to the bottle a little faster than I was going without it. But murder? I don't know. Never heard of that in any workplace I've been a part of."

With one hand already on the back door, Trent took a card from Nick and then hightailed it back inside, leaving us alone on the deck.

"Seems troubled," Nick said, turning to look across the back of the estate.

"We've all got demons, right? Some are just more obvious, or I guess I should say more exposed."

"Just like Trent's at the end-of-the-year celebration," Nick said with both hands on his waist.

I tried to imagine the raucous scene at the party that Agatha had described. "Trent made an ass of himself. He said as much. But when there's even a hint of truth, I would think the shelf life of the womanizer accusations would be longer than a near fight. Because those accusations involve people working at the firm and who were at the party. Trent admitted that one of the girls even tried her moves on him."

"And you believe him?"

Our eyes met for a quick moment.

"He sounded believable for many reasons. But he's an alcoholic, which translates into someone who could lie while asking the Pope for absolution."

Suddenly I was an authority on the personality traits of an addict? Damn, I was either good at pulling shit out of my ass or maybe I'd watched too many daytime talk shows in my past. Who knew? I certainly didn't.

Nick shrugged. "He's got a lot on his mind. It appears he's regretting that party incident even more now that Christopher was murdered."

"I think it's eating him up. He couldn't suck in the nicotine fast enough, and he looks like he could fall off the wagon any moment," I said, anchoring my weight on the back of a wicker chair.

"You need to rest. Your brain is working overtime. Here, sit." Nick put a hand on my back.

"I know how to put one foot in front of the other. And I'm not tired."

He immediately raised both arms. "I should have known you'd take a shot. I know how much you love for people to tell you what to do."

"I appreciate your love of my sarcasm. See? I was nice then."

"Your version of nice is warped."

"Hey, I should be offended."

He shrugged his shoulders. "Okay, everyone except your kids. You're nice to them."

I felt the urge to pick my fingernails. "I'm not sure Erin would agree with you on that. I haven't been bashful with my opinions on what she's doing with her life."

"Bashful hasn't been your MO before or after the crash. But she might be a little surprised by your interest. Maybe she was doing this crap before, but you just didn't see it."

"Eh." I shrugged my shoulders this time, wondering again about the real me. Who was the woman who'd walked in my shoes before the crash? How are we similar now? And how are we different?

"Just remember that parents aren't there to be best friends, and you only get one shot when they're young. You could just take the easy way out, sit back, and let the world raise your child."

"You mean the Internet world."

He nodded. "Or you could feel confident in who you are and help her grow without suffocating her."

"Shit, Nick, you're quite the armchair psychologist." I slapped him on the back, and he lurched forward.

"I've got three sisters and a total of nine nieces and nephews, just in case you didn't remember."

"I didn't, sorry."

"Being an uncle is pretty cool, but let's just say I've seen things. Sometimes being a parent is difficult and ugly."

Maybe Nick had been watching my family through the windows of our house using his own fleet of drones.

"I guess whenever you think you have it hard in the parenting department, you can remember what Agatha will be dealing with, alone," Nick said.

"Yeah, sure looks like her world has fallen apart." I picked at the wicker chair.

"She's rather protective of Christopher, at least a fairytale version of him."

"Or she just has a lot of hate for her brother-in-law."

"Public humiliation. I'm sure she was mortified," Nick said, scratching the side of his face.

I closed my eyes and let the information process a bit more. "Remember her tone? She sounded like a woman who knew that her husband was screwing around on her."

"Sounded like it, but never outright said it."

"So why wouldn't she admit it, especially if she's truly interested in helping us find the killer?"

He shook his head. "Because she doesn't want to believe it's true. Maybe her fantasy is the only thing keeping her from having a complete nervous breakdown. That's the only thing that makes sense to me."

"We need to interview those three, like, yesterday," I said.

"I'll talk to Randy, make sure he's cool with us taking this angle and playing it out to see if there's any tread on the evidence path."

"Cool," I said, thinking more. "I know we both feel sorry for Agatha. She's left with two kids, one with Down syndrome. She's not loving the support she's getting right now. We know she had to be mortified by her husband's cheating, right?"

"I'm following you, I think."

"So pretend that Trent never threatened Christopher's life. I know that's a big leap, but just roll with it."

Nick slowly raised his finger. "A scorned, bitter woman."

"Rightfully so. But if she's cunning and opportunistic, she might have seen a way out."

"To kill her husband."

"In the most humiliating way possible."

"We need to see the will." I glanced across the beautiful back porch. "A family rolling in it this much must have a will."

"And lots of lawyers."

"Let's hope not. While she seemed like she was in good shape, it's hard to imagine she'd be strong enough to pull this one off alone."

"A partner," Nick said with his finger raised again.

"Or more than a partner."

Nick and I nodded at the same time.

I said, "These are all just theories though."

"I like working with you. You're naughty…and then some."

I gave him a wink. "Let's get out of here, do our research, and then make a return visit."

We walked through the kitchen and waved to Agatha to join us. She waltzed over holding a casserole dish filled with something red and heavy.

"Please take this lasagna with you," she said, walking us to the edge of the foyer, her guests still within hearing distance.

"That's okay, thanks," I said.

"No, I insist. Just doing my best to help the FBI." She leaned in and whispered, "If I have to eat lasagna again, I think I might just explode." She shoved the dish into my hands. And that was when I noticed hers.

"Surprised you're not wearing your wedding rings."

She rubbed her fingers. "I get skin rashes easily, so sometimes I take them off. Honestly, I lost them a few weeks ago. But

Christopher was so understanding, knowing what I'm juggling with the children and everything. He said he'd find the right time to get me a new set, an even nicer set."

Her eyes widened for a second, and she gave us a smile—one that didn't seem nearly as authentic as during our earlier conversation.

After a few awkward seconds, she was sucked back into the vortex of visitors. Nick told her we'd be in touch, and we walked out the front door.

Once inside the car, I turned to my partner. "This hunt for the killer…I think it's the best therapy I could have. My brain is firing on all cylinders, and I feel like I've found a groove. When you update Randy, tell him we're taking the lead."

Nick's jaw opened.

"Just do it. And tell him I told you to do it. If he has an issue, he can talk to me."

At which time I'd gladly lead with my knee to his crotch.

Twenty-Two

Two kids hurdled a bench right in front of the stunned tour guide just as a third jumped in front of his classmates, spit a wad of gum into his hand, and chucked the gooey blob at his buddies. Or were they his enemies? I couldn't tell. Laughter and high-pitched shrills, mixed with generic threats, sliced the subdued tones of the Boston Revolutionary Museum.

"Fourth-grade little shits." Bartholomew Trow, the elderly curator wearing a patriotic bow tie, raised his brass-handled cane to the ceiling as if it held a special power to freeze the youngsters midstride. But no one noticed, other than Nick and me. The man darted off with the quickness of a cheetah—one that had just been sedated.

It wasn't even a race. The kids disappeared around the dark corner as their classmates cheered them on from back in the gallery. With panic covering the tour guide's face, she took a single step after the little terrorists, then apparently thought better of it, likely realizing that it wouldn't be a good idea to leave the majority of the kids to chase after a few.

"Look at those heathens," Nick said as we watched the kids jump up and down like wild monkeys.

"I have one of those. He's a bit uncontrollable, but at this age, they're still nice."

"Define nice."

"Don't confuse that with listening or behaving. I just mean not nasty."

"Where are the damn teachers?" he asked, taking a few steps to his right to look beyond a wall that held a historic painting at least fifty-feet wide.

"I think I heard them in the bathroom complaining about their jobs. One of them talked about smoking a joint while the brats were being spoon-fed information about the Revolutionary War. They both sounded stressed."

"I can see why," Nick said. "Maybe the school district should provide them some help."

"And they ought to throw in a full supply of Valium to keep the animals tamed." I couldn't help but release a smile. Easy to do when your child isn't leading the insurrection.

Nick reached in his coat pocket. "Hey, I gotta take this," he said, stepping to the side and putting his cell phone to his ear. I hoped it was Randy, the lame SSA ultimately responsible for the Barden murder investigation.

Keeping one eye on Nick, I looked around and noticed a few of the more elderly patrons holding their hands to their mouths. They'd probably forgotten what it was like to have kids. I could sympathize, but on a different scale.

"I...I..." The tour guide waved her hands, but the kids had tuned her out.

I blew out a breath and contemplated stepping in to squelch the riot.

She pulled her long, black hair off her neck and then tried again. "Kids, I have candy bars in my office."

That got their attention. They whooped and hollered and lunged at her like...wild animals. I saw panic in her eyes as she searched the room for help.

I looked over at Nick, who was still on the phone, his face turning red. Didn't look like a fun conversation. Walking over to the tour guide, I stepped up on a bench. I knew my doctor would be having a cow if he could see me. But he couldn't.

Clearing my throat, I pulled out my badge and barked, "Hey! Everyone get down on the floor. Now!"

About eighty legs crumpled to the carpet quicker than sand crabs scampering across the beach. Scanning the Lilliputian crowd with my badge tilted down so they could see it, I could hear the soft murmur of the furnace kicking on. No one moved.

"I want one person to stand up and tell everyone what it's like to have good manners in a museum."

A little girl with coke-bottle glasses inched her hand above her shoulder.

"What's your name?"

"Madeleine, but my friends call me Maddy."

"Stand up, Maddy, and tell everyone in your class," I said while oscillating my badge as if it could control their spastic outbursts.

"My mom taught me I should always listen and do what the adults tell me."

"Good, Maddy. I'm sure—"

She then blurted out, "Unless we know the guy is a pervert, and then we should scream and yell, 'Stranger Danger, Stranger Danger, Stranger—'"

"Okay, Maddy, we get the picture. You guys have a choice to make. Get back on the bus and go back to school, or don't say a word and listen to your tour guide…"

I turned to the woman, who said her name with a defeated smile, "Miss Lori."

"And listen to Miss Lori as she teaches you cool things about the Revolutionary War."

"I hate school," a voice said from the crowd.

"Let me see hands. Who wants to go back to school?" All hands stayed down, and I noticed a few of the rug rats shaking their heads, their eyes pleading not to be sent back to kid prison.

"Who wants to continue the museum tour using your best manners?"

I sea of arms shot upward.

"My partner and I will be watching from over there. If anyone gets out of line, then that person will have the FBI to deal with."

"Ah crap," some kid said under his breath. Cool, my act was working.

I held out my arm as a signal for Miss Lori to take over.

The little girl, Maddy, took a step toward me. "My mom also told me never to pick my nose, especially in public."

"Nice. Always listen to your mom."

"Can I touch your badge?"

"Uh, not right now," I said. "You guys go have fun."

I heard Miss Lori start her speech about Paul Revere's ride as I met up with Nick and Mr. Trow, who'd just returned.

"What happened to the kids who ran off?" I asked the man.

He leaned in closer. "Those three little shits? They can't be reformed like the others. They've already determined their life's course."

I glanced at Nick, then back to the man, who was shaking his head.

"I put them to work." His lips turned upward, and a few more lines appeared on his face—his version of a smirk. "In our learning center, we have about thirty desks, under which there is a plethora of decades-old gum stuck to the bottom."

"You've got them cleaning gum off the desks?"

"Sure do. I recognized two of those kids. They're out of

control. To them, work is nothing but a four-letter word."

"You're a brave man. One of those kids is bound to have a lawyer parent who will threaten to put the museum out of business."

"Bring 'em on," he said with a toothy grin, holding up his cane. He turned and started walking. He got about twenty feet away, then flicked his hand. "You want to see what the bastard stole from my museum, or what?"

Nick and I started to follow him.

"You're still showing your love for lawyers," Nick said to me, raising his eyebrows.

"You'd think I'd be a little more open-minded, given I'm married to one," I said.

Nick gave me a quizzical look, then he chuckled. "Alex, *you are* a lawyer. Well, you used to play one on TV."

He could have told me I'd been an astronaut and I wouldn't have been more shocked. I realized I'd stopped in my tracks.

"Come on. We'll talk about it later," Nick said.

We caught up to Mr. Trow as he turned into a small room filled with wartime weapons, either hanging on the wall or contained in glass display boxes.

"Impressive," I said.

"That's not what you said the first time you were here." He opened a drawer and then pulled out his glasses, scanning a piece of paper.

We'd already had the discussion about my crash and loss of memory—I admitted as much the moment Nick and I arrived. And I even confessed that I'd failed to take proper notes. Among the files Jerry had sent over, I'd found one measly note about my previous visit, which only included the basics: Boston Revolutionary Museum, Bartholomew Trow, and the date, January 12th.

I didn't spend much time on note-taking back in the day, it seemed. It was becoming increasingly apparent that, in my pre-crash life, my memory was one of my greater assets. So, what would Superman do if he lost his strength?

"Call Wonder Woman, of course," I muttered to myself as I leaned down and eyed a two-hundred-forty-year-old dagger.

"I heard that," Nick whispered. "You need to break out the magic rope to get people to tell the truth. I'm sure we'll need it on the Barden murder investigation."

"I don't know how I know this, but I think it's called the Lasso of Truth. Were you talking to Randy earlier?"

"No. Antonio. We had a little disagreement."

"Everything cool?" I asked, recalling his agitated expression.

"Bumps in the road are part of life. But it's been cool for twenty-three years."

I grimaced, trying to remember how long Mark and I had been married.

Twenty-Three

"**H**ere's the list of everything that was stolen." Mr. Trow tossed the paper on the glass container holding a number of different knives. "But showing you will tell you more, or maybe less. That's for you to decide."

Withholding the urge to fire off a zinger, I grabbed the paper and followed the curator to the far side of the room, where rifles hung from the wall.

"Brown Bess flintlock musket with the bayonet, the first on that list. Stolen. Normally it goes here." His wrinkled hand gestured to an empty space, and then he started walking horizontally to the wall.

Pausing about ten feet later, he lifted his hand again, saying, "Kentucky flintlock rifle, forty-five inches. Stolen."

Another six feet. "French flintlock musket from 1763 with a removable bayonet. Stolen."

"So you're wondering why this thief stole nothing but rifles?" I asked, but he quickly held up a finger and continued walking, rounding the corner and stopping at a glass encasing.

"Look at the sheet of paper."

I glanced at the list and said, "Scrimshaw powder horn, worth over ten thousand dollars. Stolen."

My eyebrows raised, I looked at Mr. Trow and whistled. He held my gaze for a moment, then continued his trek. Nick and I stayed right on his heels. "Dog head hunting sword, worth almost eight thousand dollars. The design on that dog head was meticulous. It was a true gem in this museum." He shook his head, somber, as if he'd been dealt a personal tragedy.

He picked up his pace, as best he could, and wound his way through a number of displays.

"Mr. Trow, do you need this list to find the next item?"

He ignored me and continued his seemingly unpredictable path. "Here." He scooted to one side of a display. "It's hard to see, but a Bugbear coconut gun powder flask used to hang on this mannequin dressed like a Patriot Army soldier."

"What's the value?" Nick asked.

"Value?" Mr. Trow chuckled just once, then gave us a stern look, his forehead folding into a horizontal accordion. "I can quote monetary amounts until my eyeballs fall out, but that's not the point."

"Then why were you telling us the value of each item before this one?" Nick asked.

Mr. Trow made some type of noise, and then he pressed his lips together so hard they almost turned blue. "I apologize, but I'm just a little frustrated with the Federal Bureau of Investigation. I've reviewed all of this with Agent Giordano in her previous visit."

"Again, Mr. Trow, I'm sorry about the circumstance." *Just rub it in my face, why don't you?*

He held up a hand. "I'm sorry. I'm trying to get past it. Well, I'll have to." He turned back to Nick. "To answer your question, I'll ask you one. What is the point of any of these stolen items?"

Nick scanned the room, while focused on Mr. Trow as he folded his hands together in front of his gray suit, his cane now resting against a display case next to him. Neither Nick nor I had an answer.

Trow helped us along. "The person or team of people stole seventeen items. And I guess I'm trying to say—"

"There's no pattern to any of it," I said.

He pointed a finger at me and winked. "Spot on. I can't figure it out."

"But what's the value…I mean, what's the total monetary cost of all the items combined?" Nick asked, spinning back around.

"It's north of a hundred thousand dollars. But as you know, these items are irreplaceable. I assure you, these are not knockoffs."

"I'm thinking more about what a thief could get for this stuff—"

"Stuff?"

I thought Mr. Trow's eyeballs were actually going to pop out.

"Sorry, precious artifacts." Nick arched an eyebrow at me when Mr. Trow looked down momentarily. "I'm wondering how much money a person could make by selling these items on the black market? You know through the Dark Web."

"The Dark Web?" The curator frowned, causing a plethora of creases to scatter across his face. "That sounds diabolical, whatever it is."

"It's the part of the Internet where bad people do bad things. No one good knows much about it, which is why you've never heard of it," I pointed out.

"You're fully aware that a black market exists for items like these," Nick said.

"Of course."

"That's all I'm saying. Whoever stole these *precious artifacts* will likely try to sell them. We have a cyber squad within the FBI that can start scouring the Dark Web and other sources that might appear to be more legitimate. Sooner or later, I'm guessing they'll come up for sale. That's when we'll be able to identify who has the stolen items, or at least a trail to who stole them."

Nick wrapped a thumb around one of his suspenders, apparently proud of his explanation of how everything would come together in the end.

Mr. Trow's line of sight went from the opposite wall back to Nick. "I might be old, but I'm not stupid."

"Sorry, I didn't mean to imply—"

"I never got my central point across."

"Which is?" I asked.

"Some of these items have a price tag that is rather high, which I've pointed out. But there are a few of these items that, individually, wouldn't go for more than a hundred dollars, maybe less. Is that worth the risk of being caught?"

"I admit, it sounds random," I said. "Maybe they thought they were stealing only the expensive items, but instead grabbed the wrong ones."

Nick and Mr. Trow pondered that thought as I began to retrace our steps, putting myself in the mind of the thief. Or, as Mr. Trow had suggested, this could involve more than one perp. A team of thieves would make more sense, just because of the sheer volume of items that had been hauled out of the place.

"What are you doing, Alex?" Nick asked.

"Just thinking." I followed the same path back to our starting point, then looked back across the room, trying to imagine the outline of my steps. The shape wasn't consistent. At one point, it appeared I'd made a figure eight, but then the path went haywire after that.

"It's possible we're dealing with a person, or set of people, who are great admirers of these relics," I said, walking back to the pair, the room still void of any patrons. "And therefore would not be looking at the Dark Web to sell the stolen artifacts to the highest bidder."

I could see Mr. Troy freeze for a second.

"What is it?"

He pursed his lips.

"Care to share your thought?"

"It's just that…" He began to pat his pants pockets as Nick and I exchanged glances.

"What are you looking for? I have the list of stolen items right here."

"It got me thinking," he said, now reaching inside his suit-coat pockets.

"About?" Nick leaned in closer.

"Ah, there it is." He pulled out a rolled-up paper program.

"Is this pertinent to our investigation?" I asked.

"Of course. Well, it's just a theory, mind you. But your thought about the thief just got me thinking." He popped the rolled-up paper off the opposite hand, as if he were an old coach from the 1950s, complete with the bow tie.

"And that is?" Nick said.

Mr. Trow licked his lips and took in a breath. "I'm part of a select group of people related to those who played significant roles in the American Revolution."

I nodded, trying to understand where this was going.

"My great-great-uncle, Bartholomew Trow, actually took part in what became known as the Boston Tea Party. My family takes great pride in this association with one of our nation's most important times. He was born just across the Charles River in Charlestown."

I narrowed my eyes. Something about the name of the town didn't sit right with me.

"My great-great-uncle became one of the infamous minutemen in the battles of Lexington and Concord, and eventually rose to the rank of lieutenant under Colonel Thomas Gardner's command at Bunker Hill. Eventually, he became second lieutenant of the frigate named *Boston*."

"Impressive," Nick said.

"I realize I'm no Revere or Franklin or Hancock, but there were only one hundred sixteen people who participated in the Boston Tea Party. That took a tremendous amount of courage and conviction. I'd like to think a little bit of that blood is still running through these old veins." He chuckled.

"That's a nice story." I paused, hoping he'd take the cue to get back to business, but his eyes seemed to bore holes through a painting off to my right. It showed a tattered American flag standing tall amid smoke and haze from cannon explosions in the field of battle. Perhaps Mr. Trow was transporting himself back in time.

"And so…" I gestured to the rolled-up program.

"Ah, yes. There are two organizations in this area that meet, hold fundraisers, and bring awareness to the glory of our nation's history through museums like this. One of those is called the Daughters of the Revolution. The women in that group have tremendous passion for the cause, and most of them I respect greatly. This highlights one of their fundraisers." He uncurled the program and popped it twice with a stiff finger.

I looked at Nick, then said, "Mr. Trow, you kinda implied there are a few of the women you don't respect."

He seemed to growl, or maybe he was just clearing his throat. "Some women…" He looked at me. "Don't get me wrong, I'm no sexist."

We'd soon find out. "I'm not offended. Go on," I said.

He opened his lips, then paused.

"Is there a problem?"

"Uh, no. I just…well, I'm the curator of this museum. And I'm a lover of these old artifacts."

"What are you trying to say?" Nick asked.

"There is a new faction of women in the Daughters of the Revolution that has voiced strong opinions about these artifacts. They believe that most of these artifacts should be on display in the homes of the people who sacrificed so much for the country."

"A faction, huh?" I found that an interesting term to use.

"They're loud and obnoxious." He pointed the program at me. "And they have no respect."

"I thought you said they respected all of these old artifacts a great deal."

"I'm talking about people in their organization. You see, the Sons of the Revolution, the group I'm a part of, routinely holds social events with our counterparts. And there are a few, dare I say, *ladies* in that group who are nothing more than…" He turned his head.

"Were you going to say thieves?"

"No, I was not. That's something I can't prove. But their behavior is abhorrent." His face lit up like a fire hydrant.

An older couple had just walked into the room. Mr. Trow instantly turned into the welcoming curator. He waved and said, "I apologize. Please, come in and enjoy the artifacts and information."

Mr. Trow gave us the eye, and we followed him out of the weapons room, but not before I made another quick visual sweep of the space, allowing me to mull over everything I'd seen and heard.

That triggered an internal question: could our snooty curator be tossing out wild theories just to throw the focus of the investigation off one party in particular? Himself.

Twenty-Four

$$\text{\textemdash}\!\!\!\!\text{—} \; \textbf{\textit{0/0/0}} \; \text{—}\!\!\!\!\text{\textemdash}$$

We passed a corridor and approached a dark room, where we found the same set of school kids sitting on the floor. Every set of eyes was glued to a huge screen where a video was playing. I paused a second and could see it was a documentary on the events that led up to the start of the Revolutionary War. I noticed Miss Lori off to the left. We locked eyes. She smiled and mouthed, *Thank you.* I nodded, mouthing, *No problem,* in return and then caught up with the two men.

Mr. Trow was saying something to Nick about security and technology at the museum. I cut in with, "So, what about these IT operations?"

"I was telling your partner new information, something I didn't know when you were here last," he said as he swung open the door to a room with the word *Security* on it.

There was a tall, thin man sitting in front of a bank of monitors. He jumped up and shook our hands with too much energy, then went back to his monitors.

"Phil just started two days ago," Mr. Trow said. "He's having to learn on the fly, since our previous director left with no notice."

Nick gave me the eye. I knew what he was thinking.

"You have new information for us?" I asked Mr. Trow, the

three of us standing at the back of the security room.

"Our IT vendor, a local group called TakeFive, let us know that we had a security breech."

"Say again? Why wasn't that the *first* thing you told us today?" I knew I sounded annoyed. I was.

"Well, we had to deal with the crazy kids, and then I had to explain the entire crime to you for the second time. And now here we are," he said, extending an arm to the rest of the room.

"What did they report?"

"Someone hacked into our computer profile where we maintain all of our codes and passwords."

"So, if someone had that information, what would they be able to do?"

"Oh my. Enter the building after hours, gain access to each room. And if they knew what they were doing, they could disarm the security for each exhibit so they could steal whatever they wanted. I recognize this is not a good development."

"It's better than the alternative."

"What's that?"

"No trail whatsoever. But we know they at least made a technical footprint. It might take a while to understand how they did it and to find them. Our cyber squad will contact TakeFive. We'll need access to all servers to continue the technical aspect of this investigation," I said.

"Fine. No problem on my end," he said.

"I believe you mentioned there was no visible forced entry, correct?"

"That's correct."

"Anything on video?"

"Nothing. Zilch. Although…"

"What?"

"TakeFive also handles the storage and backup of our video.

And they said they'd been hacked just after our theft. The video files were apparently corrupted. All you see is a blue screen."

"Damn, these guys were good," Nick said.

I nodded. "It does sound like a professional operation."

We all walked toward the front door of the museum as Nick received another call. I peeked through the window. The skies had turned gray, and I could see quarter-sized flurries swirling in a gusty wind. I could feel my shoulders tense a bit, which instantly gave me a headache.

Turning to Mr. Trow, I said, "We'll need names and contact information for everyone you mentioned in our conversation, and the full list of stolen artifacts."

He nodded.

"That includes the names of the women—the faction from the Daughters of the Revolution."

He tugged at his rubbery face.

"Any issues with that?" I asked while eyeing Nick, who was off in the corner talking on his phone again.

"Oh no. I guess not."

"Guess not," I repeated in monotone.

"I just know how much grief they've caused."

"Okay. But I'm assuming you have some reason to believe they would be motivated to steal these artifacts, no?"

"I do think they have motivation, and they're young, smart, athletic. They could probably pull it off." His face hardened into a scowl, and he punched his fist into his bare hand, his cane tucked under his arm. "Who am I joking? Three of them are just rude bitches. Plain and simple. They think the world revolves around them."

"Okay. We'll need their names, please."

Mr. Trow nodded, and we stood there in silence for a moment, waiting for Nick to finish his phone call.

I wondered how any of these scenarios would have led me to being in a high-speed chase the night of my crash—unless I'd made much more progress than it appeared, possibly confronting a suspect. But Mr. Trow had admitted he didn't find out about the breadth of the security breach until recently, after my first visit with him.

Nick walked up, interrupting my train of thought, shaking his head at me while holding the phone in front of his face.

"What?" I asked.

"Yes sir. I understand," Nick said while pointing at the phone.

We stepped away from Mr. Trow.

I whispered in Nick's ear, "What's up?"

Before he could respond, I heard another voice.

"To answer your first question, I'm okay with you and Alex taking the lead on this. But you better get your asses to this island, and quickly."

The line went dead.

"Randy?"

"Yep. We got what we want. I think," Nick said.

"Good."

"But there's more."

I tilted my head.

"Another murder. Same MO, but a different location. And I think you heard the urgency in Randy's voice."

Mr. Trow stepped between us and said, "I can send you all the information you requested within the hour. Everything you need. When can I expect to have the stolen artifacts returned?"

Nick opened the front door, and a blast of cold air stopped Mr. Trow from following us. "No promises on the timeline. We'll be in touch," Nick said as the curator waved a hand and disappeared back inside the bowels of the museum.

I took two steps outside, and a bank of snowflakes peppered

my face. "Damn winter. Who needs it?"

At that instant, I heard a car backfire, and then the glass wall to the museum just behind me exploded.

Twenty-Five

"**D**own. Get down now!" Nick yelled while jumping behind a stone planter. A little slow on the take, I finally spotted another stone planter on the opposite side of the doorway. But even those two seconds made a difference. As I planted my left foot, I heard two more shots split the air around me, and then I felt a jolt in my shoulder. I hit the unforgiving concrete on the same shoulder and skidded to a stop behind the planter.

"You okay?" Nick called out.

Still peeling myself off the concrete, I could see his head peeking just above the planter, searching for the sniper, his Glock ready at his shoulder.

"Fine," I said, even though my upper arm was on fire. To make matters worse, my brain felt like it had been thrown into a blender. "Any idea where the shots came from?"

"Across the street, I'm thinking."

I could see Mr. Trow poke his head through the gaping hole in the front window. I shouted, "Get your ass back. Call nine-one-one and keep everyone away." He scrambled off, his feet shuffling in triple time.

Just like my pulse.

I peeked around the edge of the planter. Two buildings and a bunch of parked cars, a few trees dotting the parking lot. And more snow. I had no clue where the sniper was. He could be a hundred yards away, or fifty feet and closing, knowing he had us cornered.

"You carrying an extra piece?" I asked.

"How did you know?"

"Just figured."

Without taking his eyes off the scene, Nick pulled a gun from an ankle holster then slid it across the pavement. It stopped about six feet shy.

"Fuck!" Nick yelled. "Leave it there, Alex. If I see anything moving, I'll shoot it. Otherwise, we play defense and wait until the cavalry shows up."

I heard him, but I still felt exposed. I looked around for a stick, something to pull the gun closer. Seconds ticked by. My shoulder stung like hell, but somewhere inside I knew we had to act. Not sit, wait, and hope.

Without another thought, I pushed off my back foot and reached for the gun. Just as my hand touched the grip, a shot rang out. It bit the concrete just an inch in front of my wrist, concrete dust spitting in my face.

I cried out and fell back behind the planter, the gun now in my possession.

"What the hell, Alex?"

Water flooded from my eyes, and I couldn't help but rub them. They stung, but I was almost certain nothing more than dust had invaded my eyes. "All good," I said, lifting to my knees.

The weight of the gun felt natural as I coiled my fingers around the polymer grip. It was a Sig Sauer, a P238 came to mind. Held only six rounds though. I had to be selective.

"Any better idea where they are?" I yelled to Nick, my heart still pounding fast, my breathing at a rapid-fire pace of its own.

"Didn't see exactly, but I'm thinking it's coming from that

three-story building somewhere." Snowflakes had started to coat Nick's head, his crumpled hat in the corner.

I peeked an eye around the corner, exposing just enough for me to check out the building across the street, if for no other reason than to see if the sniper had his sights set on just me. Then again, I didn't want to play target practice. Not when I was the target.

With a gray façade, the rectangular building was somewhat camouflaged by the worsening weather conditions. While a few cars sprinkled the front lot, it didn't appear to be fully occupied. No pedestrians in sight.

Starting on the left side, I eyed each window, searching for a gun barrel or any movement. The first three were dark, revealing no clues. Shifting to the fourth, my eyes paused. Was that a random shadow or the outline of a person? Hard to determine.

"Hey, lady, can I see your cool FBI badge?"

I jerked my head around and spotted one of the kids who'd been creating havoc earlier.

"What the hell are you doing? Get down." I waved an arm as I took another look into the snowy abyss.

Turning back around, I saw the kid with the curly red hair standing in a pile of glass just inside the building. He giggled and turned to look to his right, saying something to someone nearby.

"Kid!"

He ignored me. Another kid, wearing a number twelve Tom Brady Patriots jersey, sidled up next to Red, showing him something.

Was that a pistol? Surely it was a toy from the gift shop.

"What the fuck is that?" Nick barked.

The kids were in their own world, giggling, screwing around, and they had no idea their lives were on the line. I realized I'd scooted out another foot.

Out of nowhere, Red grabbed the toy gun and pointed it at me.

"Hey, lady, I bet my gun is better than yours."

My instinct was to bring up my gun in self-defense, but I forced my arm down. Red puffed his cheeks, releasing gun sounds as he pretended to fire at me. I knew they were clueless and had no respect for authority or rules, but I couldn't let them stand in the line of fire.

"Kids, listen to me, dammit. Get out of here. Run back into the museum and hide. Now!" I yelled with everything I had.

Tom Brady looked up at me with his mouth open, then he appeared to finally notice the broken glass and my gun. He nudged his buddy's shoulder, but Red was too busy trying to shoot me down to notice or care. He just kept giggling.

"Alex," Nick called out.

I had no idea what he wanted. It didn't matter.

"Nick, cover me."

I bolted out of my stance, and gunshots immediately rang out. One shot just missed my foot. The next one tore a hole through my coat sleeve, just missing my arm. My breath caught in my throat as I lunged forward. I heard the boom of a Glock—Nick responding with three shots of his own. That had probably bought me a few seconds.

I landed on my knees just in front of the boys—glass knifing through my skin—but my feet never stopped. My low-heel shoes slipped on the glass-covered carpet as I grabbed the boys' arms, nearly bringing them down to the ground with me.

One of them began to cry, and the other yelled out, "Help, help me. I'm being kidnapped!"

I didn't have the time or energy to respond. My shoes finally gripped enough of the surface to push out of my crouch, and I shoved the boys to the left. Before we reached safe haven in the corner, a bullet ripped through another plate of glass at eye level, and I swore I could feel the breeze as it missed me by the width of a hair.

I heard the wails of Tom Brady, then Red called out, "This bitch is crazy. Help me!"

If he only knew.

The three of us rammed into the corner, then I forced the kids down.

"Lady, what are you doing to us? My dad's going to sue your ass," Red said.

I was tempted to force his trap shut, but staying alive took priority. I cautiously moved a few steps toward the front door again, all senses on high alert, and looked for Nick. He had his back against the planter, throwing in another magazine. I couldn't leave my partner out there.

Looking back into the museum, there wasn't a soul to be seen, except for the two kids huddled in the corner.

"Where in the hell do you think you're going, lady?"

It was Red.

I got your lady right here. I growled, "Stay in the corner and don't move a muscle. Got it?"

I could hear Tom Brady gasping through sniffles.

"But what if I want to move, huh?" Red had to be the King of Brats.

I ignored him, then set my feet, ready to make a run back into the courtyard.

But the boy wouldn't shut up. "This is a free country, and I don't have to do a damn thing, even if you're with the FBI. My dad says the FBI is secretly trying to take over the country anyway. The whole government is part of a massive conspiracy, and they're going to turn our country into a slave state just like in the *Hunger Games.*"

If I'd had more time, I would have laughed my ass off, then called up his dad to suggest some parenting lessons—although this kid seemed beyond repair at this point.

"Red, if you don't shut the fuck up, I'm going to throw your ass into the courtyard and beg the sniper to shoot you."

"FBI brutality! FBI brutality! Did you hear this bitch? She's fuckin' psycho."

And this kid was in the fourth grade? Sounded more like a street punk I'd seen slapping a prostitute a few weeks back. His balls had become very friendly with my knee.

Did I just have another pre-crash memory?

"This place sucks. You suck. I'm going to find my friend who's not a little pussy about everything." Red shoved Tom Brady aside and started walking.

I threw out my hand and stopped him in his tracks.

"Get back, kid."

He tried to move my arm away, but it hardly budged. I glanced at his face, and he seemed perplexed by my strength. I was too.

"Screw you." He tried to scoot under my arm, but I snagged the back of his sweatshirt, shoving him back against his friend.

"You just won't stop until you get one of us killed, will you?" I yelled as I slid my gun into my pants. I slid my scarf off my neck, turned the kid around, and tied his hands together, then around a metal pole that extended from the wall.

Red started screaming bloody murder, kicking his legs. Basically, he was having a tantrum.

Turning to Tom Brady, I stuck a finger in his face. "You stay here unless I tell you otherwise. Got it?"

He sat frozen, except for his nod, his eyes glued to my face as he ignored the yelps from Red.

"Alex, can you see the shooter from your vantage point?"

Flipping back around, I saw Nick still pressed against the planter, and this time I noticed a trail of blood snaking down the side of his face.

"Nick, are you okay?"

"Flesh wound. It's nothing."

But it was something. I could see him sweating like a pig in a bacon factory. Peering over at the building, my eyes locked in on the same window, fourth from the left. No more movement. The shadow I saw earlier could have been the shooter, or just an office worker. Or no person at all.

One final look at Tom Brady and Red, whose face had finally matched his hair from his two-year-old fit, and I dashed toward the gaping hole in the glass wall. Shards crunched under my shoes. My gun was raised, two hands on the pistol, and my sights set for the fourth window from the left, ready to fire, almost itching to fire, the moment I saw anything suspicious. I made it to the planter unscathed, with no shots fired.

"Alex, you should have stayed inside," Nick said.

"I love the weather too much."

"Now I know you're full of shit."

The snow was coming down in full force, making visibility difficult. Maybe that was why the shooter hadn't fired any more rounds. Or had he taken off?

I could hear sirens in the distance. Nick's eyes met mine. "They'll be here soon," he said. "Let's just keep everyone alive for another two minutes."

I nodded and allowed myself to breathe. My upper arm stung, but it was functional. The bullet must have sliced off a couple of layers of skin. I could feel a cool trickle of blood down my leg, courtesy of the glass jabbed into my knees.

I wanted one good look at this guy—I assumed it was a guy, maybe ex-military, with some type of live sniper experience. Just as I flipped around with my gun and sights aimed at the third-floor window, I heard a man's whistle. Off to the right.

Whipping my Sig right, I held my breath, hoping to steady my aim. A patch of orange bobbled just above the snow-covered shrubs, moving closer. I could feel my finger against the cold, metal trigger.

As the man became visible, I could see he was looking down as he whistled. He was wearing a pair of Beats headphones—orange. Unless this was all a ruse.

"Get down on the ground. Now!"

He jumped three feet in the air, landing on his knees. He grimaced, then planted his face in the snow piled up on the concrete walkway.

I ran toward him.

"Don't shoot. Don't shoot," the guy said.

A foot before I reached him, another shot ricocheted off the shrubs just past my shoulder. I almost swallowed my spit as I lunged and landed on top of the man.

He groaned as I struggled to bring up my gun. That shot had come from a different angle. Was there another shooter, or had the original shooter changed positions?

Another shot plowed into the ground, spraying me with cold dirt and snow. I dropped my head.

"What the hell's going on, lady?" the guy beneath me asked.

"FBI. We're under attack," I said, scooting off him, trying like hell to keep my body down but my neck arched, searching for anything moving.

"Are you armed?" I asked him, as my eyes scanned the landscape.

"With a gun? Not allowed," he said. "Not until I get inside."

"Inside what?"

"I'm a security guard in the museum. What the hell happened? Looks like a war zone." He lifted his head.

"It is. Stay down." I pushed his head back to the ground.

His story sounded plausible, but I couldn't be sure he wasn't connected to the sniper.

"Nick, cover me."

"Alex, just wait for the good guys."

I heard Nick's shoes crunch against the concrete behind me as I slid off the so-called security guard and rose to standing, but I couldn't see the street and sidewalk. With the front yard on a slight decline, I had to move higher. The fear of a bullet piercing my skull was only surpassed by my level of unbridled fury. A chickenshit sniper just meant he didn't have the balls to confront his own issues.

Was I his issue? It seemed that way. When exposed, I'd been the target of his bullets. Or was I being paranoid?

Regardless, I wanted to hunt him down and take him out.

I walked three steps, moving in the direction where I'd heard the last shot—a guesstimate. I spotted a family walking toward us. Likely museum visitors. Beyond them, a few cars on the street, which was now wet from the snow.

I heard tires screech, and I flipped my sights back to the left. A dark-colored sedan tore out of a distant parking lot and headed south on Commercial.

Seconds later, a fleet of Boston cops screamed to a stop in front of the museum. One uniformed officer jumped from his car so fast his hat fell off. He grabbed for it, but it hit the muddy snow. His arm was shaking as he said, "Down on the ground. Now!"

Nick and the security guard were already there, so I knew he was talking to me. I couldn't debate him. And with his shaky stature, I didn't want to risk it.

Twenty-Six

Twenty minutes later, Jerry arrived on the scene, and we huddled just inside the museum.

"I give you a babysitting job, and this is what you let happen?" He crossed his arms over his Buddha belly and rubbed his chin while staring down Nick.

My partner shrugged.

"Stop moving," a medic said, attempting to clean the wound on Nick's temple. Apparently, a pebble had imbedded in the side of his head.

I sat on the edge of a gurney with my own medic trying to remove glass from my knee.

"Ow!"

The medic, a woman with short, thick curls and a prominent jaw, lifted her head. "This would be a helluva lot easier if we could take you to Massachusetts General."

"I'm not going anywhere, at least not the hospital. I'm fine. Why does everyone think I'm made out of fine china?"

"China that bleeds," Jerry added, scratching his whiskers. "Seriously, I need some answers. A shootout at the doors of a quiet little museum in downtown Boston?"

"We need a team of agents to search that building." I pointed across the street. "Check out the room behind the fourth window from the left, third floor. I might have seen the perp."

"Might have."

"Sorry, I didn't have time to draw a painting."

Jerry turned away and spoke on his phone. His opposite hand moved like a hand on a clock. Constant motion. The movement seemed vaguely familiar.

"Thanks for having my back out there," Nick said, wincing a bit as his medic applied an antiseptic.

"No problem. I think you saved my ass a couple of times."

Jerry turned back to us just as Nick added, "So, I know you were taking all the stupid risks…"

I gave Jerry a quick faux smile, and Nick continued with, "But it certainly seemed like they were aiming for your ass specifically, not just an FBI agent in general."

"Why would a sniper be after either one of you?" Jerry wagged a beefy finger between the two gurneys. "You're not on any high-profile cases. Shit, you should barely be working at all. Right, Alex?"

"Who are you? I don't recognize you at all. Stranger danger!" I said, holding up a hand to a passing Boston cop. He paused for a second, wondering if I was talking to him, then got nervous or something and continued walking.

"Very funny, Alex." Jerry just nodded, his hands buried in his trousers, which were forced to hang far too low because of the basketball hidden under his shirt.

"I'm as stunned as you. This museum heist is intriguing on a number of angles, but all in all, it seems rather harmless from a life-or-death perspective."

"Not if you ask Bartholomew Trow. He's the curator," Nick said. "And he's a descendant of a guy who spilled all the tea in the harbor."

"The Boston Tea Party. No shit?"

"Shit," I deadpanned, then added, "We need the cyber squad heavily engaged in this case."

"I thought you were just casually trying to figure out how you crashed your car," Jerry said with his arms spread wide.

"I was. I am. And by the way, I didn't crash my car. Someone forced me off the road."

He exhaled. "Can you prove it?"

"I will." I looked him right in the eye.

"This mess here have anything to do with it?" he asked.

I glanced down at the medic who was still pulling glass from my knees. I tried rotating my bandaged upper arm. Felt like the worst charley horse of all time.

"There are really only two angles I can think of. We either have someone getting his jollies by trying to take out a random FBI agent—"

"Although we both know he was aiming at you," Nick added as he pulled a piece of gum from his sports coat and tossed it into his mouth.

I nodded and continued, "Maybe the sniper hates female FBI agents? Regardless, it was either a random dude just having some fun, or he feels like I'm a threat. For what reason, I don't know. Pieces of my life are coming back into focus, slowly, but as of now, I can't imagine how this museum heist, or those other two cases I was working on, would lead to a car chase, and certainly not attempted murder."

Smirking, Nick said to Jerry, "By 'the other two cases,' she's referring to the ones stuck in lawyer hell, as she basically described them earlier."

For whatever reason, maybe because a sniper's bullets had tried to make me look like Swiss cheese, I'd let Nick's earlier comment about me being a lawyer slip between the cracks of my memory. A sieve. That was what my mind felt like. A few things stuck, then others would drop down an endless drain.

"You were joking about my former life as an attorney, I assume? I can't imagine even having the patience for law school, let alone dealing with stuffy, political types and poring over mounds of paperwork only meant to confuse a normal person…which, of course, would be used against them later in a court of law."

Nick and Jerry shook their heads.

"You may not recall your life working in the Suffolk County DA's office—which was before Erin was born, by the way—but your attitude toward lawyers hasn't changed a bit since before the crash. You must be allergic," Nick said.

"But she's married to one." Jerry apparently felt like he had to remind us…me.

I set my jaw, ready to fire off another retort. It was all fact. I just had no clue where all of this anti-lawyer emotion had come from. Maybe Mark could fill me in later.

I watched a horde of loud, demanding parents rush past us, which momentarily took my eyes off my boss.

"The Barden murder investigation. I know you two asked Randy if you could take the lead," Jerry said.

"Are you tapping our phones?" Nick asked in jest.

"I know people," Jerry said, a hint of a smile crossing his lips. "Anyway, could this sniper be connected to that investigation?"

I felt a tug on my knee. Glancing down, the medic was wrapping my leg with bandages. Apparently the other leg was fine in comparison. No bandages there. "How? We were two of two dozen FBI personnel at that crime scene yesterday."

"I don't want to sound sexist, but maybe someone—the perp— was watching all the action go down in response to what he did. It might have excited him in some sick way. And then he turned his obsession to you, Alex."

I scrunched my eyes closed. "The only things observing us were rats and squirrels. And by rats, I'm not just talking about the ones with long, slithering tails."

I eyed Nick. He knew whom I was talking about.

Jerry looked at Nick, then back at me. "Is there something I should know?"

The medic stood up and snapped off her rubber glove. "Good as new."

I pushed the legs of my pants down and eased off the gurney. My body was telling me that the surge of adrenaline to survive the brush with death might have depleted every core resource. Even my brain had started hurting. But I wasn't about to share that information.

"Nick and I are late. We need to get to this small island where they've found another body. Same MO supposedly."

For some reason, my mind started grinding on our previous theories involving Agatha Barden. The resentment and betrayal she must have felt from her philandering husband, Christopher. But now with another victim in the mix, I wondered if this sick ritual might have been repeated because the love-sex spider web had somehow snared another man.

"Unless someone threw the Harry Potter magic cloak over my head, I didn't disappear, did I?" Jerry asked as his nose lit up.

"Jerry, if something was wrong and you could fix it, you'd be the first person I'd ask. Right, Nick?"

Pausing as he was slipping his sports coat over his shoulders, Nick opened his jaw but no words came out.

"Nick agrees." I shot him a quick wink, then found my own coat with a hole in the arm. It would have to work for now.

"Alex, are you ready for all of this? Your doctor hasn't cleared you, and here you are getting in shootouts, diving into ice cold water," Jerry said, raising an eyebrow.

I pointed a finger in his direction, my mouth open.

"Yes, I heard about all of it. I know people, remember?"

Someone was a snitch. I glared at Nick over Jerry's shoulder.

"It wasn't me. I'm just the babysitter." He pretended to turn a key at his lips then throw it over his shoulder.

"I'm not a hundred percent, but I'm good enough to be on the playing field. Getting better with every hour that passes," I said to Jerry, knowing full well that I'd just taken two giant leaps backward, at least on the physical side of my health.

"Good." He raised a hand and nearly popped my bandaged shoulder before catching himself and lightly patting the opposite one.

"So can I have my own gun back?" I held out my hand and tried to smile through the pain.

"Don't have it on me." He scratched the back of his head. "Listen, I just need you to talk to your doc and get a note saying it's safe for you to carry."

"And use," I added.

Jerry closed his eyes and slowly rubbed his forehead. I'd probably given him a migraine.

I suddenly felt hungry. The only food that came to mind was something spicy, Mexican perhaps. Nick moved next to me, and I said, "Do you know a place where we can grab a quick bite on our way out to the crime scene? I'm dying for Mexican food."

He twisted his lips. "I know just the place."

"You always do."

Twenty-Seven

"You call this Mexican food?" I spit out a bite of burrito into the wrapper.

"The best in Boston," Nick said, reaching forward to wipe at the fogged-up window as the windshield wipers flapped away wet snowflakes.

"This is disgusting, Nick. Really, this is the best we've got?"

"If there is better, I haven't heard about it. Antonio cooks up a mean dish of homemade cheese enchiladas, so I'm spoiled."

I stuffed the rest of my food in the bag, my stomach still longing for something to fill the void.

"Still hungry?" he said, cramming another taco in his mouth.

"I thought you loved Antonio's homemade enchiladas."

"I do. But a man's got to eat, and we're not making it home in time for dinner. But it's okay; I'll get home in time to watch Jimmy Fallon. I think Tom Cruise and Jimmy are supposed to battle each other in Nonsense Karaoke."

"Ah," I said, not the least bit intrigued. Out of nowhere, another fact flew into my brain. "Fallon is from Boston?"

"You have a mind like a trap." Nick laughed, and I followed suit.

We motored up Route 1, making decent time as the snowflakes

grew bigger and the snow began to stick. Taking Highway 128 East, we cut across Beverly. I imagined the Barden estate with a couple of inches of snow. Befitting a postcard, no doubt. But I knew inside the home, Agatha was a boiling pot of emotions. Her husband had died, suffering a brutal death, leaving her with a kid with Down syndrome and a four-month-old baby. Her grief made sense, so I shouldn't be surprised. Then again, my internal alarm had sounded. Why? Was it the drama with her brother-in-law's accusations? Trent had seemed like he was barely able to keep it together, living life one minute to the next.

A family hairball. We all had one.

I fired off a group text to Mark, Sydney, Erin, and Luke, letting them know I'd be home after dinner and to go ahead and eat without me.

My family seemed equally tangled, but in a different way. I didn't pretend to be above it all. In fact, I was probably a major component of the complication. It just felt as if the people in the house were constantly on edge, me included. Shit had happened, most of which I couldn't recall, although flashes of images had begun to reach my frontal lobe. And they weren't all cheerful pictures. To some degree, I supposed having a teenage daughter brought out the claws in all of us. I'd seen it up close the last two days.

I thought more about my relationship with Mark. I longed to feel a connection with him…for us and the family. It felt strange to think of our group as a family if Mark and I didn't have a rock-solid foundation.

"What are you thinking about over there?"

I gazed at the white-trimmed trees as the area became more rural. "How scenic it is driving up the coast with the light snow."

"I know that mind of yours. You sure that's it?"

"Sure." I spotted a green and a sand trap just off the road—a golf course. "Do you play golf?"

"Negative."

"You don't belong to the fancy club in Beverly?"

"We live in Manchester-by-the-Sea. And we don't do clubs. A little too snobby for our taste."

"Says the man who drinks fine wine."

He took his eyes off the road and shot me a quick look. "How did you know that?"

"It's a recent development. I have this odd picture in my mind of you holding the stem of a wine glass, giving a toast."

"Huh. Could be foreshadowing."

"Or something like that."

I saw signs for Ipswich Bay. "I forgot to ask if the crime scene is in the same place—Choate Island?"

"No, but it's close. Just to the east of Halibut Point State Park, in Sandy Bay. Randy said he has two operation units set up. One on the mainland in Gull Cove, near where the boats are ferrying equipment and resources back and forth to the tiny island. And then the island itself."

Twenty minutes and a million trees later, we pulled into the parking lot at Gull Cove, although I'd seen the globe of portable lights for the last half mile. We checked in with the mainland agent in charge and learned they were about to pull the body from the ocean.

"You can't do that. Not until I see it."

About ten heads turned in my direction.

It took a little coaxing and an animated phone conversation between the agent and Randy, who was on the island, but in five minutes, Nick and I were on an open-air motor boat zipping across the bay toward an island no bigger than a comma.

"Watch your step," a young kid said, helping me off the boat. "The rocks are slippery from the snow."

We hiked about fifty yards, navigating through not only the rocky terrain and clusters of splintered trees but also people, many who had the standard FBI lettering on their shirts or jackets. A smaller number of uniforms and plainclothes detectives from the local Rockport police were mostly hovering near the heels of the Feds. Twenty or more personnel were combing every inch of the land, looking for evidence. I wasn't sure they'd find any, not left by someone as meticulous as what I'd seen at the Barden crime scene—if I were to believe these two crimes were committed by the same person.

Pushing through a thicket of trees, I hopped off a boulder and found myself three feet from the man in charge.

"Nick, Alex, glad you could finally make it." Randy pumped out foggy breaths, while resting a hand at his waist as if he'd just conquered the island.

My brain registered one thing: a dipshit alert.

Twenty-Eight

I could already feel my pulse pinging a little faster. And it wasn't because Randy was tall and reasonably attractive. Our last interaction had left me wanting to give him a piece of my mind, if not a fist to the jaw. Now after surviving the sniper shooting, pushing my body beyond its already reduced capacity, and dealing with the brat pack, my nerves were on edge, ready to take down the first person who pissed me off. Probably just my natural instinct to survive.

"We had a little jam we had to get out of first," I said, noticing each of us had a single foot on the thin strip of shoreline, the other resting on a rock.

Nick continued my thought with a few more details. "Sniper shooting in downtown. We were pinned against the front of the Boston Revolutionary Museum. They almost got us, and two kids."

"Did you take them out?" Randy asked, his eyes pausing on the tattered hole in my coat and then turning to notice Nick's butterfly bandage on his temple.

I could feel wet flakes sticking to the side of my face as I tried to look around Randy for a glimpse of the dead body. Spotlights illuminated two divers swimming in the ocean, but I couldn't see the victim.

"Take them out?" Nick sounded annoyed, and I shifted my eyes back to my partner.

Pointing a defiant finger, Nick shuffled his foot, slipping on a rock and falling to the rough surface, but not before instinctively reaching out and grabbing for something. His hand snagged Randy's belt loop, thrusting Randy's hips forward into me.

Nick landed with an audible thud, while I was forced to scramble over uneven ground to rid myself of the leech, Randy. We looked like the three stooges. It took a few seconds before we'd gathered ourselves, gotten back on our feet, and allocated the proper amount of personal space. Each of us took a quick glance around, ensuring no one had noticed.

"You guys can give me a full debrief on your interview with Barden's wife in a minute. You insisted on seeing the body in its full glory," Randy said, pointing a finger directly at my face. I imagined breaking his finger, and I had to hold back a smile.

I gave a simple nod, and Randy turned to walk down the pebbled shoreline to reach the closest point to the body. We followed.

"Technically, we're still in Sandy Bay, but since we're on the east side, facing the Atlantic, the elements are harsh on the body and anyone working the scene, especially in this shitty weather."

I spotted the submerged body about twenty feet from where we stood. Straining my eyes, I could see the familiar gray funnel circling the man's torso, a green-and-blue tie waving in front of his face for a quick moment. I thought I noticed something gold and shiny hovering just above his head. Those could be the rings being pulled in the strong current.

A pair of underwater lights illuminated salmon-colored stains across his chest and neck. Like Nick said earlier, we were looking at the same MO, which meant the same guy had killed another person. Unless it was a copycat. I didn't want to go there.

My eyes were drawn deeper, where the shimmering water played with my vision. I inched my feet down the bank until the miniature waves lapped over my shoes, instantly sending a chill up my spine. I paused for a second, my sights questioning my earlier assessment of the crime scene.

Pointing out toward the body, I turned my head to Randy. "What happened to the vic's clothes?"

He chuckled, then stroked his mustache as if it were a pet. Leaning his hands on his knees, he faced the ocean.

"He was stripped from the waist down."

"Damn, I wonder if hypothermia killed him before he drowned," Nick said, moving up to my right side, his hands on his knees as well. "Are we assuming the COD is the exact same as the other guy, Barden?"

I nodded and said, "Toxicology could show something different. By the way, did we ever get back the toxicology reports on Barden?"

"Focus," Randy said to me, wagging his finger at the dead body in front of us.

I decided not to tell him where to stuff it.

"This guy suffered like few vics I've ever seen." He turned his head to me. "If it happened before he died."

"If what happened? And has anyone ascertained why he was stripped? Someone just wanted to see how much shrinkage could actually occur?"

"Do you breathe when you talk?" Randy asked.

A stench of fish passed by my nose. Rotten fish. I immediately ruled out my surroundings and pinned it on the asshole staring at me.

I didn't blink. "I'm ignoring your ignorant comment. Are you going to answer the question, or keep your divers in the freezing water that much longer?"

He snickered, still staring at the crime scene.

I took in a shaky breath, telling myself not to be baited by his behavior or his lack of intelligence. A quick count to five, and I arched both eyebrows, proud of my ability to blow off his childish antics.

He finally returned to the matter at hand.

"Poor fella got his sausage torn off. Makes me gag just thinking about it."

"Ouch," I said.

Randy turned his head suddenly, starting to retch. He looked like a cat preparing to throw up a fur ball. I didn't realize how lucky I had it with Pumpkin—no hairballs yet, anyway.

I looked at Nick, who was wincing, and said, "Can you believe Mr. Tough Man over here?"

"There's not a man alive who wouldn't feel some pain just by looking at that gory scene. But to gag…geez, kind of makes me wonder what else he's had in his mouth."

I snorted a snotty giggle.

A few seconds later, Randy had finished his business and resumed the position, hands on knees, like a college kid who'd just regretted a night of binge-drinking.

"Was it cut off?" I asked.

He gritted his teeth. "It's hard to determine in the water and with the type of fleshy skin involved."

He paused for a second, obviously not comfortable with the discussion.

"If it wasn't cut off, then what are they thinking?"

He opened and shut his mouth, as if he didn't want to say the words. Then he did. "They think it was bitten off."

"By what?"

He raised a finger. "Or by whom?" Randy acted as if he'd just asked the key question to the entire case.

"So you think the perp did this?"

He swallowed hard. "The flesh is so mangled, there's no way to determine if it was man or animal who'd done it. That's another reason we want to pull the body—to preserve the wound as best as possible."

"A shark. Had to be a shark, right?" I turned back to Nick, who seemed less shook up than our fearless leader.

Nick shrugged. "Makes sense to me."

"Have there been any shark sightings in this area?"

"A detective from the Rockport PD is chasing that down right now."

"Where's the team lead for the diving unit?"

"Why?" Randy asked.

"I want to go in, just like with Barden. Do we have an ID on the vic yet?" I pulled off my coat and handed it to Nick, then blew warm air into my hands.

"Are you smoking something, Alex?" Nick said.

"You know I'm serious. Where is he, or she?"

"He's in the water. Had to minimize personnel on the island, given the terrain and bad weather."

"Before you pull him, I need to see the victim in his natural state. Do you have a name or anything on the vic yet?"

Five minutes later, the dive-team lead was handing me a wetsuit, saying, "You'll never get this suit on over your clothes. Not in a million years."

I heard Randy whinny like a horse. "You got two options, Alex. Drop this nonsense and let us remove the body, or give us all a little peep show."

The last thing I wanted to do was give Randy a peep of anything. I turned to the illuminated ocean and tried to imagine the victim's final thoughts. Had he been focused solely on trying to breathe or had he been in agony from the castration? "Nick, over here please."

Without saying a word, he followed me across the bed of rocks and boulders. Two tree trunks had seemingly merged into one enormous tree.

"Hold up my coat, and I'll change inside your little cave."

Putting all modesty aside, I stripped off my clothes in about twenty seconds. The laborious part was tugging the wetsuit over my thighs and hips. I grunted and growled with each tug.

I noticed Nick squeezing his eyes shut.

"What are you doing, freak?"

"Trying not to look."

His face was all wrinkled up like a Chinese Shar-Pei.

"Nick, no need to give yourself an aneurism. I trust you," I said with my breasts still exposed and very aware of the cold weather.

"We've known each other for, what, twelve, thirteen years?" he said. "But we've never seen each other naked."

"No offense," I said, pushing one arm into the suit with an extra grunt, "but I doubt seeing you full Monty was ever, nor will ever be, on my bucket list."

He started laughing, shaking his head. I peeked past Nick to make sure Randy, about fifty feet away, wasn't looking. He lifted his head my way for a quick second, then got on his phone and faced the ocean. Good. I didn't need any more bullshit from him.

Nick released another chortle.

"What's...so...damn...funny?" I said, shoving my other arm into the suit.

"The irony of it all. Here I am in this position, where every other guy in the Bureau would rather be, or at least ninety-five percent of them."

"Are you saying I'm hot, even at age—" I grunted as I pulled up the zipper, creating at least a small wave of cleavage. "How the hell old am I?"

"You're thirty-nine. And I'm not saying you're hot. You're fit. That's the PC thing to say." Then he added under his breath, "Even if I am gay."

"Thanks for being my curtain rod." I gave Nick a wink and rejoined the boys under the heavy lights as snow began to fall in buckets.

"Three minutes in the water. That's all I'm giving you," the dive-team lead said. "You're not equipped to handle these conditions."

"The moment you're out, we're cutting off the ankle weights and pulling the body," Randy said as I waded into the water. "I've got two examiners from the ME's office landing on the other side of the island right now."

Wasting no more time, I pulled the snorkel over my head and dipped my body into the churning water. I could feel the rush of the current almost immediately. I kicked my flippers three times and moved closer to the body, fully illuminated by the underwater lights. The setting seemed otherworldly. The current tried to pull the man out to sea, but then the twine around his ankles suddenly reached its limit and whipped the body back toward the shore.

That was when I got the view of a lifetime. His gnawed nads.

I couldn't help but stare at the mangled flesh. Any body part in that condition would make a person, even a law-enforcement veteran, flinch. But when the body part was the male sex organ, it meant a whole other level of something, assuming it wasn't a shark doing the chewing.

A human performing this act of brutality wasn't just barbaric. It was an act of passion or pain, or maybe both. And not necessarily toward the victim, although we couldn't rule it out.

I heard a garbled voice and turned to see a diver holding up one finger. *One minute.*

I nodded, giving him the thumbs-up.

Peeling my eyes off the remaining flesh, I circled the floating cadaver, looking at the craftsmanship of the funnel made from duct tape. Whoever made this was a DIY guy, or girl, if I were to keep the perp pool completely open at this point. And that person had a specific purpose in dumping this body here, at this exact location. Why else choose this location?

One more quick look, and I found the rings dangling near his face. Three of them. Even in the water, I could see a single emerald-cut diamond on one ring as big as a car headlight. Another ring sparkled against the lights, diamonds surrounding it entirely. The last one was a simple band, probably platinum, but much larger. A man's ring.

I felt a bump on my wounded shoulder and let out a gasp. The diver didn't know what he'd done. I nodded and followed him to the surface.

Twenty-Nine

Once out of the water, I asked Nick to serve as my cover again, and I changed back into my dry clothes in record time. Then he and Randy kicked their shoes against a tree to remove the caked mud, saying they didn't want their toes to get frostbitten. Despite being wrapped in my coat, I stood on some rocks, my teeth chattering, watching the divers sever the twine and carry the body to a makeshift table.

Randy got another up-close view of the mangled male parts. He turned and put a hand to his mouth.

"Did you ever find out who this was?" I asked over his shoulder.

Macho Man held up a finger without turning around. Then it hit me—he looked like one of the Village People. I decided to keep that comment in my back pocket and pull it out when I needed a verbal trump card.

Nick stumbled over a few rocks and made his way next to me.

"Move closer," I said.

He nestled against my good shoulder. "You cold?"

"And you're not?"

I noticed the buildup of snow had formed a tuft on the top of his head. I would have chuckled if my face wasn't frozen.

I reached up and messed his hair. "You were starting to look like a snowman."

"Happy New Year," he said in a strange, high-pitched voice.

He could see my confused expression.

"You know, Frosty? Oh, I forgot, you don't watch those annual Christmas specials."

I paused, then decided I had nothing to lose. "Why don't I?"

"All work and no play."

Even at Christmastime, I'd apparently put work in front of the kids. I wondered what they thought of my choices. Something else to deal with. An anxious feeling was growing in the pit of my stomach as I came to grips with the aftershock of my crash, trying to understand the decisions I'd made in my previous life while still living my current life. Thus far, the regrets were piling up faster than a mountain of Boston snow.

I blew warm air into my hands and watched the MEs hover over the body, and my inquisitive mindset quickly returned. I turned and found Macho Man spitting into the ocean.

"Gross. You actually tossed your cookies again?"

"Yeah. Whatever," he said, wiping his mouth while moving up next to Nick. He looked at the ME's table, then turned to face us, or more importantly, to face away from the naked man with his dick bitten off. Randy set his feet while staring down Nick and me, then flipped a thumb over his shoulder. "We're dealing with a sick motherfucker. I don't want to see this kind of crazy shit again."

I wanted to ask if his declaration was as much personal as professional, but again, I kept my thoughts to myself.

"Ditto," Nick said.

Randy put a hand on Nick's shoulder and started to put one on mine, but he apparently thought better of it and dropped his hand to his side. "If this kind of thing leaks to the press, shit will hit the fan, and once it does, it will spray everyone within range. I'll have everyone in DC up my ass."

"No one wants to go there…uh, I mean, no one wants it to get that far." I glanced down as I shuffled my shoes in the rocks, feeling the searing heat from a pair of eyes. I prepared myself for a verbal jab. But it never came.

Randy cleared his throat. "We've got two dead guys in two days. Same basic MO, but there are some differences. One big, obvious difference."

I couldn't hold back. "Not sure how big it was."

Randy paused his movement, but didn't bother responding to my snide comment. Probably for the best. "So what do we have to work with here?" he asked.

"For one, Barden's wife," I said. "She's not your normal grieving widow. I can see resentment under there, and for good reason."

"But that's an opinion. What evidence do you have to support it?"

"Nothing yet. Need to verify her alibi, check her social-media posts, talk to her close friends. And it would be easier if we could inspect her cell phone and her records with her provider."

"You need a warrant. I'll get it. Next," Randy said, tapping a finger on the opposite hand.

I paused for a moment, shocked to hear his helpful input. Then I said, "Need the final toxicology report on Barden."

He looked over his shoulder for a brief second then turned back to us. "You'll have it by tomorrow morning. Using the local resources, since we have to wait for official feedback from Quantico. Okay…next." He rolled his arm like a movie director.

"For now, if we're to assume the same perp is responsible for Barden and this guy, then we need to look for possible connections," Nick offered.

I stepped in. "Or similar routines or behaviors…or

personalities even. This killer has a grudge. Now, why he, or she, escalated the violence on this one here, who knows? It's disturbing. I'm wondering about their mental state right now. But that may not be a bad thing."

"What the hell are you thinking, Alex?" Randy said.

"If they're active in society and not a complete recluse, their behavior might be bizarre enough to stand out. People remember that kind of thing. But to narrow down the pool of suspects and who they touch on a daily basis, that could take time. Right now we're not close. Need the details on vic number two first."

My nearly frozen mouth had affected my speaking ability. "I said vic, with a *v*," I clarified.

Both guys nodded, and we moved on.

"Name is Rick Lepino, an insurance salesman, and get this, he's from Weston." Randy shifted his eyes between Nick and me.

Obviously this was important, but I had no idea why. "Sorry, but that's one fact that hasn't been reloaded into my memory bank."

"Weston is where the rich folks live," Nick said.

"I thought that was Beverly."

"Beverly has money, but not like Weston. Highest per-capita income in the greater Boston area."

"Barden was loaded as well," I said as much to myself as the others. I took another glimpse back to the illuminated portion of the ocean, hoping more theories would float to the top of my mind.

"Married, I'm assuming?" Nick asked.

"According to county records, yes. Wife Jeanne and two sixteen-year-old daughters."

I winced. "Twins. Shit. He's probably aged a bit in the last few years."

"If he's like Barden, he's a player. May not have spent much time at home. Put everything on his wife," Nick said.

"That's what you need to verify," Randy said. "But very quickly you need to start building a suspect list. If you need any help on research, any manpower at all, I'll give it to you. I'm no mind reader. You have to ask."

I said, "I have no problem asking."

"You'll visit with Lepino's wife first thing tomorrow?"

"We're on it." Nick said.

More movement behind Randy as the MEs began to bag the body.

Randy kept his eyes on us. "I'm thinking we've got twenty-four hours, thirty-six max, before we get pushed to the side and the boys from DC come in and start doing our jobs. After that, all bets are off."

"Like Nick said, we're on it." I could sense a natural competitive instinct somewhere inside me, coupled with an almost insatiable desire to find the sick prick who was flaunting his dirty business. But Randy was playing political chess, trying to predict the next move so he could ultimately cash in. I guessed a hefty promotion was within his sights.

We made our way back to the western shore and waited to board a boat for the mainland.

I rattled off a number of tasks that needed to be completed over the next twenty-four hours. Just saying them out loud made them seem impossible to accomplish. Nick pulled out his phone and tapped a contact.

"Who you calling?"

"Your go-to guy."

"I have a go-to guy?"

"Yeah, an intelligence analyst who's eager as hell to learn, but doesn't mind doing the dirty work. He's smart. Jerry will let us use him, even if he's on another case."

"But Jerry's technically not our SSA for this investigation."

"True, but he'll let it go through. He'll avoid any pissing match he might have with Randy. The case is too high profile, and he knows you're running on about two-and-a-half cylinders."

I didn't know it was that obvious, but I kept my mouth shut on that topic.

"Phone signal isn't worth a crap. I'll put the kid on speakerphone once we're in my car. Then we should be able to make some headway."

The roar of the outboard motor grew louder as the boat arrived at our location. I touched my wet hair. It felt like an enormous icicle. My fingers tried to pry through the matted mess, but part of me wondered if it might crack into a million pieces.

Once on board, I huddled behind the driver, and Nick huddled against me.

Raising my voice over the engine noise, I said, "I'm guessing this young agent either looks like Shrek or has the social skills of a three-year-old."

"Hardly. Think Brad Pitt, but when he was younger and had longer hair."

I turned to look at Nick, and my frozen hair actually slapped my face. "We've got a hippie posing as a federal agent?"

"The Bureau knows we're in the twenty-first century."

I was intrigued.

Thirty

After eating a cold plate of spaghetti—during which time I replayed the sniper shooting and the second ring-murder crime scene, and even managed to start developing a mental profile of the killer—I pulled myself up the stairs.

I was bone tired, but when I'd walked in the door earlier, Mark had agreed to have a conversation this evening. For the first time since I'd awakened from my crash, he'd also given me an indication that we had a bond. Without me saying a word, he'd noticed my bandaged arm. He asked me questions, sounding legitimately concerned. Then a caring hug, followed by an authentic wink, and a promise for us to chill and talk in our bedroom.

My body responded in a freakish way. Despite the physical exertion and mental fatigue, I sensed a building desire for Mark, the need for a release. The kind shared with an intimate partner.

Shuffling down the second-floor hallway, I noticed under the crack of the door that Luke's room was dark. No surprise since the grandfather clock in the living room would soon strike midnight. I crossed to the other side of the hall and saw light seeping out from Erin's room. I put a hand on the doorknob, but I didn't turn it. I was curious how her day had gone, if she'd been able to stay above the fray of teenage social drama. Uncertain if she'd be receptive to my questions, especially if she was in one of her infamous moods, I lifted my hand from the knob as if it were on fire.

My confidence as a mother was obviously still a work in progress.

Ambling into the bedroom, I expected to see Mark lying on the bed, waiting for me. But he wasn't. Then his head popped up from the other side of the bed frame. "Hey," he said with a breathy tone.

I angled past the bed and saw him doing push-ups, his chest bare. Was he actually pumping up his muscles in anticipation of our expected roll in the hay?

"Need to get ready for bed," I said as a burst of energy flooded my veins, and I pranced into the closet looking for something sexy to slip on.

I tapped a finger to my lips while eyeing my choices. Apparently, sexy lingerie had not been a priority before my crash. Maybe I'd stashed something alluring in a private place, where he couldn't see it, waiting for just the right moment to surprise him.

That would only work if I could recall where I'd hidden it. If it actually existed, of course.

I found a long, white T-shirt with "Georgetown University" written on the front. Possibly another connection, but it didn't mean much to me. I ran my hand inside the shirt. It was so worn and tattered I could see my skin through it. I bit my lower lip and decided against it. Cheap and trashy wasn't the look I was going for.

I didn't need him falling asleep at the wheel, so to speak, so I called out to the bedroom. "I'll be out there in just a minute."

Was that a grunt in return?

"Crap," I said, shoving aside hanger after hanger. Out of the corner of my eye, I spotted a burnt-orange nightshirt with little slits up the sides.

"Has promise," I murmured, holding it up. Another college logo—the Longhorns. There was the University of Texas again. The shirt was sleeveless and had a decent V-neck. I slid the bottom part of the V between my teeth and yanked. It ripped just enough. Then I grabbed both sides and pulled the V apart, ripping it down the middle another three or four inches.

"Just enough for my perky puppies." I giggled and slipped it on. Sneaking into the bathroom, I added just a bit of mousse to my hair and walked through a mist of perfume. "Hey there," I said, walking out of the bathroom.

"Hey," he grunted back, not lifting his eyes.

Wearing metal-rimmed glasses, he was sitting in bed, reading through a pile of papers held together by a paper clip. An open laptop purred off to his side. He was still shirtless, and I took a moment to ogle his chest and shoulders.

I cleared my throat as I leaned down to grab a pillow off the floor, pausing for a second at the optimal peek-at-my-cleavage moment. His eyes only stayed focused on the paperwork. With a sigh, I threw the pillow on the bed.

"Can you get the light?" he asked.

"Of course." *Ah, he wants the mood to be just right.* I looked around for a candle and a lighter, and even opened my nightstand, but only found a worn Lisa Gardner paperback, pens, a notepad, and a set of keys. I turned off my bedside lamp and plopped a leg on the bed.

"No, I need you to turn on the floor lamp over in the corner." He held up his glasses. "My eyes aren't quite as good as they used to be," he said with a chuckle, apparently still not noticing my sultriness.

I did as he asked then plopped onto the bed, pulled out the

book, and read a few pages of the Gardner tome. A few seconds later, the grandfather chime echoed throughout the house. I let out an exhaustive breath.

"Something on your mind?" he asked.

"I thought we were going to talk. We haven't had an adult conversation since my crash. I'm just trying to piece together my life and those who meant something to me," I said, staring at the ceiling.

His hand touched my bare shoulder. I reached for it, but he took it away.

"Okay, let's talk." He tossed the paperwork toward the end of the bed.

For a moment, I felt like the sophomore who'd just been asked to Homecoming by the senior quarterback. It was nice to be noticed by my husband of...

"How long have we been married?" I sat facing him, cross-legged, my pulse showing a bit of life.

He gave me a genuine smile. "Fifteen years and three months." He pushed his laptop farther away, tossed the packet of paper on the bedside table, removed his glasses, and faced me, also cross-legged.

I was drawn to his deep eyes, a chestnut brown that showed depth and resilience, but there was also a mystery about them. His thick head of hair pushed across his forehead in a casual way. He wore a day-long beard, which highlighted a chiseled chin. Following the slope of his neck to his well-shaped shoulders and down to his chest, I could see he either had a strong workout regimen or good DNA. Maybe both.

I wanted to grip his shoulders, then pull myself closer and touch his lips without saying another word. But something held me back—something inside me that said I couldn't just bed a man I found attractive without knowing if he felt something for me. Or was there more to why I felt apprehensive, even a bit anxious?

Turning away for a second, my sights found a framed picture of the two of us at a game.

"Did we go to a Red Sox game?"

"Yeah," he said, chuckling when he glanced at the picture. "Just after the bombing at the Boston Marathon, I got tickets through the firm. Everyone rallied together. Neil Diamond led everyone in singing 'Sweet Caroline.' It was one of the coolest things I've been a part of...we've been a part of. Boston Strong, you know."

I kept my gaze on the picture. Unsure if it was out of sheer want, images and sounds of that day fired off in my brain.

"Big Papi," I said.

"Yeah, you're getting it." He touched my knee for a quick second, and I flinched.

He noticed more bandages. "Another result of your incident, I see."

"Surprised?" I asked.

"Not in the least. You've always been a tough son of a gun. A hell of a tennis player back in the day."

I nodded, now connecting the dots on how at least part of my brain functioned. I could have delved further into all of my athletic glory, but tonight wasn't about me. Not in that sense. "You were talking about the Red Sox game..." I prompted, wanting to get back on track.

"Yeah, Ortiz had a big game, the Red Sox won. But it was one of those times when you could just feel the support and camaraderie of people you didn't even know. And you believed the world still had something good to offer."

He stared at the picture for an extra moment, and I wondered if he was trying to recapture something.

I swallowed back a hint of emotion. "Were we happy?"

He rocked back a bit and released another chuckle, this one slightly less authentic. "Why do you say it like you're talking about a previous life?"

"Well, it kind of is for me."

"I get it. I know this transition back to your old life can't be easy."

"Working with Nick again has helped not only to jog some memories, but to make me feel comfortable. It helps being around people I know and trust, even if I don't have a ton of memories."

"Sure."

"This helps too," I said, pointing at him then me. "I mean, I definitely feel something for the kids, our family, and while it's foreign on some levels, it also seems natural, at least in some ways. It's kind of difficult to explain, I guess."

"Dealing with kids can be foreign to me too," he said, looking down at the comforter. "Don't beat yourself up. Your memory seems to be coming back slowly."

"Just not fast enough."

"Patience isn't exactly your strong suit," he said while raising one of his eyebrows in a playful way. It enhanced his sexiness but also his emotional distance from me. I felt like he was trying to point out a flaw that he'd secretly never liked about me, but now he was able to let it out while he hid behind the cloak of my memory loss. I tried to brush it off. Maybe my radar was in oversensitive mode.

More and more questions were starting to come to mind. Then I realized he'd never answered my happiness question. I took another angle. "What did we do for fun?"

"Well, when it snows, the whole family goes outside and builds a snowman...you know, when it's not a work or school day."

I nodded. "Sounds cold, but fun. What else?"

"We try to see the kids do their things—Erin's cheerleading and Luke's basketball games—then we might go get an ice cream afterward. Oh, we saw a movie a few weeks ago. It was Luke's first PG-13 movie. It was one of those 3-D, in-your-face dinosaur movies. He loved it."

I wondered if he'd understood my question. It was nice hearing about family events, but I wanted to know more about the two of us, the foundation of our family. "That's cool. So, what did you and I do for fun?"

"Oh, us?" He looked off in the corner, as if he were trying to come up with a viable story. After a few seconds, he tapped my leg then pointed at me. "Just a few weeks ago, we went to a nice dinner. Took out a client and his wife. Real nice Italian place in Back Bay. It was a great evening. You seemed to really hit it off with Amy."

I picked at my nails, thinking he was either avoiding the topic, or the bucket of fun was basically empty.

"Sorry, but that night isn't coming back to me. What did I like about Amy?"

"She's a driven woman, a bit of a ballbuster, like you."

"Ballbuster. In what way?"

"Amy has worked her way up the corporate ladder. You guys traded a lot of stories about breaking through the glass ceiling. She's one of those super moms. An executive by day, then hits the gym, takes taekwondo classes. She said it helps her feel more confident that she can kick the ass of the guy stabbing her in the back at work. She also has two kids."

A buzzing sound. Mark reached over to his bedside table and grabbed his cell phone from under his stack of papers. He looked at the screen, then clicked it dark and set it aside. "Just work stuff."

"Are you full-blooded Italian?"

"Wasn't expecting that question, but yes, Mom and Dad are

from Sicily."

"Part of the Mafioso?"

"Not exactly. They moved here when they were still young, teenagers, I think. Settled in DC, opened a pizza place. I went to Georgetown, both undergrad and law school. That's where we met."

He got my attention. "All the Georgetown shirts."

"Right. I can still remember the day I first saw you." He shifted his eyes to me and held his gaze without saying a word.

"I'm all ears," I said.

"It's actually pretty simple. You caught my eye from across the bar."

"You actually picked me up in a bar? Nice."

"No, it wasn't like that. I heard you laughing with your friends at this tavern called the Tombs. It was this big hangout place where people just chill. I was up at the bar ordering a beer, and I turned when I heard you laugh. Your smile just lit up the room. And your eyes…" He shook his head and again stared right at me. "Those blue eyes melted me right then and there."

"You're serious?"

"Why wouldn't I be?"

"What happened next? Did you ask to carry my books to class?"

He smirked. "I was smitten, but I wasn't clueless."

I could see he wasn't fond of being ribbed. "So when did I notice you?"

"When I invited you and your friends to a party that night. Later at the party, you and I sat on the back porch and drank from a bottle of Goldschlager. We talked about everything, including who was better, Bon Jovi or Bruce Springsteen."

"It's the Boss all the way."

"That's what you said back then. It was wrong then, and it's wrong now." He laughed, touching my leg again. I put my hand on top of his before he could take it away, and then I lifted my eyes to his. He gave me a tight smile, then scooted his hand away and ran his fingers through his hair.

What the hell?

Looking down, I touched my left hand.

"You're wondering about your rings, aren't you?"

"I just wasn't sure if..."

"If I gave you a ring? What kind of guy do you think I am? You put them in a little jewelry box in your dresser, top one on the left."

I lifted off the bed, walked over, and pulled open the drawer, spotting a tiny container. "It's silver and red?"

"That's the one."

I opened the jewelry box, which was lined with satin. I took the two rings from the box and held them to the light. "Platinum bands, and look at that puppy," I said, admiring the emerald-cut diamond on the engagement ring. "Wow, how big is it?"

"I think it's—"

"No, don't tell me. I don't want to know. It's amazing." I glanced over at Mark. "Stupid question: why do I put my rings in here?"

"Your job mostly. You said the rings are so big you knew they'd catch on something or someone. Plus, you didn't want people thinking you were loaded."

"And you didn't have a problem with that?"

"Didn't love it at first when you took the job at the FBI, but I got used to it. Plus, you'd take them out and wear them around the house and whenever we went out."

I nodded, set the rings on the top of the dresser, and rejoined Mark on the bed. A yawn escaped my lips.

"I think you need your sleep," he said.

"Yeah, I've got an early meeting with Nick and this intelligence analyst named Brad."

"You're really pushing hard with your new cases. I guess I shouldn't be surprised. And I'm sure you don't want to hear that you should slow down, or even take some more time off."

Part of me just wanted to know that he cared, although it sounded like he knew my core personality trait, which I was becoming reacquainted with. "I'm not taking on anything that will hurt me. We can't waste any time with this one. Lives are on the line."

He nodded and stared at me. "I know, I know. Lives are always on the line. I won't ask about the details of the case. You won't tell me, and my brain can't begin to process everything in your world on top of my crazy work life." He blew out a tired breath, so I decided not to delve further into his work issues. After a moment, he said, "Listen, Alex—"

But I interrupted him. "Where did we go on our honeymoon?"

"That came out of nowhere."

"I've just seen the pictures around. Looks amazing, fun...even, dare I say, romantic." I felt a tingle in my body.

"Oh..." His lips turned up at the corners, then he looked away.

"What?"

"We had a blast. Went to Italy. Spent most of our time on the Amalfi Coast." Bringing a hand to his mouth, he released a chuckle. Was he blushing?

"Mark..."

"We did something naughty."

I could see his dark eyes looking me up and down. "Naughty. Oookay..."

"We..."

"Yes?"

"We went skinny dipping in the middle of the night in the hotel pool."

We both howled, then quickly shushed ourselves to not wake up the kids, at least not Luke.

"That trip must have cost a ton, Mark."

"Mom and Dad picked up the bill. They wanted to give us something nice and let you see my family's roots."

"They play a big role in our lives?"

"You know, they like to express their opinions."

I wondered if I'd locked horns with them, but I wanted to avoid a drama discussion.

"Luke, after all, is named after Dad," he added.

"What about Erin?"

He looked down and tugged on the comforter, then said. "That was your mother's middle name." His voice softened with the words.

"My family. Sounds like a taboo subject."

"It's hard," he said. "Your childhood had some bumps. Your mom died, and your dad..."

"Is he alive?"

"Yes. Donald Troutt is his name."

"Troutt?"

"Apparently your mom teased you with the name when you would sulk. Pouty Troutty is what she called you."

"Pouty Troutty," I repeated. I tried to move on. "Where did I grow up?"

"Moved around some, but you spent your last few pre-college years in South Texas. On the coast. Port Isabel."

I thought about my longing for the ocean and warmer weather. "That actually makes sense," I said. A quick flash of me riding a jet ski—laughing, screaming—popped in my mind. Was my dad on it with me?

"What are my dad's issues? From your tone, I can tell

something is not right."

"Mainly alcohol-related. That's why I didn't rush and call him about your accident. He's up and down and not really reliable. Last you told me, he was living with some woman he'd just met at the local Walmart."

I could feel my stomach tighten a bit. "I guess I need to call him at some point. Just to reconnect, try to remember more of my younger life. But now may not be the best time. I need to feel a bit more comfortable with who I am and with everything here at home first, before I jump into that moat."

"It will be okay. We'll be okay," he said, touching my leg and holding it there an extra second.

"Thank you."

Another unexpected yawn escaped my lips, and without saying another word, we both crawled under the covers. A slight wedge in the middle of the bed funneled us closer, and within seconds, we were joined at the hip. My eyes grew heavy, despite my mind swirling about everything I'd just learned and even felt from Mark.

"Alex," he said softly, breaking the silence. "I love you."

My eyes popped open for a second, as I replayed his words. "Love you too, Mark."

For the first time I could recall, a sense of calm relaxed every muscle in my tired body. And then my eyes shut.

Thirty-One

Gazing out windows through bubbles of condensation at the Starbucks at Harvard Square, I watched fellow Bostonians execute their early-morning ritual, some moving much faster than others. Most of the overnight snow had been shoveled into piles on the side of the street and sidewalk—Nick had said we picked up about six inches. But the biggest hazard at the moment was the blustery wind as temperatures hovered in the low twenties.

Pockets of frozen snow dust danced across the square, spraying the prickly specks of snowflakes across the landscape, smacking unsuspecting men, women, and college students in the face. I brushed the slivers of ice off my coat—a red trench coat to replace the one with a bullet hole in it—and draped it over the chair next to me while I waited for Nick to bring my coffee.

A *ding*, and I turned to see the front door push open. An older man with a pipe lumbered inside. His eyes were watering from the cold, his weathered cheeks a bright red. He wasn't who we were waiting on. The man put his shoulder against the door and leaned, trying to counter the force of the howling winds. His slick dress shoes slipped a few times as a blast of ice shot through the crack. The door finally shut, and he removed his pipe and blew out an exhaustive breath.

I could relate.

"Piping hot," Nick said, extending the smoky cup just under my nose.

"Thanks." I took a sip of my non-fat mocha with whip and felt the liquid warm my chest from the inside out. My eyes gravitated back outside. At that moment, a man's green Celtics cap blew off his head and smacked a lady in the nose. She grabbed the cap in midair and threw it to the ground while screaming something—a profanity was my guess, though I couldn't hear it—in his direction. Tapping my phone, I noted the time. Ten minutes after eight.

"I know he talked a good game last night during our quick call, but your man Brad isn't proving to be very reliable. He's ten minutes late."

Nick slurped in a shot of caffeine. "First of all, he's not my guy. If anything, he's your guy."

I scrunched my eyes. "The only person I'd call 'my guy' is at work, probably buried in paperwork. The kind that would bore me to sleep, if not death."

Setting down his coffee, Nick leaned on his elbows. "Has someone finally hit paradise on the home front?"

"Not sure I'd call it paradise, but last night was… It was nice."

"Nice." He just stared at me.

"Yeah, nice."

"That's what you're going to call it? Sounds very pedestrian and boring. I guess he's not that good."

I poked his hand. "Don't go there, Nick. It's not like that. We never got that far. But we did bond a little. It was…nice."

"Right. Nice." He smiled and took another slurp of his coffee.

I heard the front door open again and glanced over Nick's shoulder. A young couple wearing Harvard jackets walked in mid-giggle, acting as if it were a fifty-degree day.

"Fifteen minutes late and counting." I raised an eyebrow.

"Dammit, Alex, don't be such a drill sergeant. He'll be here, and then he'll blow your socks off."

I recalled our conversation from late last night. Lots of *yes ma'ams* and *no ma'ams*. It seemed as if Brad was trying to show me some respect, but it only made me feel like a grandmother.

Someone bumped the back of my chair, and I spilled my coffee on the table.

"Hey…" I said, flipping around, only to see a massive belly about two inches from my face.

"Quit taking up all the space, lady. It's a fuckin' free country, even for those of us who are weight challenged," a man with four chins said.

I reached for the badge in my purse, but was stopped stone-cold by a stench I didn't know existed. Puffing out my cheeks to hold my breath, I turned back to Nick, who was rolling his eyes.

"Hey, Alex."

Lifting my eyes slowly, a man stood on the other side of the table. He was shedding his overcoat, revealing a stylish beige sweater, which matched his straw-colored locks perfectly. A wisp of hair fell across his gunmetal-gray eyes. He extended his hand.

I gave him a firm shake, letting him know I was all business. At least on the outside.

"Brad, nice to meet you, in person at least."

"Oh, we've met several times. Let's just say it's good to see you again." His warm smile revealed a pair of dimples.

"Wish I could say the same." Truly, I did.

"I understand. But Jerry tells me your memory is slowly coming back."

"Not fast enough."

A young lady approached our table, grinning ear to ear while batting her eyelashes. She had skills.

"Here you go, Brad. Your usual coffee," she said, placing her hands on her hips. It was hard not to stare at the huge metal hoop piercing her nose. "Anything else I can get you?"

"I'm good. Thanks, Summer."

She eyed Nick and me. "Are these your parents from Richmond?"

I glanced over my shoulder to see who she was talking about. When I turned back, Nick was shaking his head, smirking. "You're talking about us?" I pointed at Nick, then myself.

Brad brought a hand to his cheek. "These are my colleagues. My mentors, Alex and Nick."

"Oh, sorry. Bad lighting and all," she said, failing at recovery.

I nodded and sipped my coffee, giving her the signal we needed to speak in private

"Are you guys, like, undercover agents or something?"

In addition to her many issues, she had no volume control.

"If we were, you would have just blown our cover."

"Oh, I—"

"That's okay. We're not undercover. Thank you," I said.

She brushed her hand across Brad's shoulder as she turned and walked off.

"You have quite an admirer there," Nick said.

"It's nothing. I've been a regular the last four years, and I attended school here."

I was reminded of our age difference. Not that it mattered, unless people were going to assume I was Brad's mother. After being dissed by Mark and now feeling like an ancient relic, it might be worth my time this weekend to try to fit in half a day at the spa. Skin rejuvenation and the whole works.

"Not a lot of time," I said. "We've got an appointment with the wife of the second victim, Jeanne Lepino, in forty-five minutes."

"Sorry I was late. My landlord needed some help scraping off her windshield."

I tried not to be impressed. "Okay, have you had any time to dig into the tasks we gave you last night?"

Holding up a finger, he pulled a tablet out of his leather bag. It kind of looked like a man purse, but I wasn't going to use that term. Did Mark have one? Another missing piece of my mental jigsaw puzzle. Brad tapped the screen a few times, then ran his finger down the side. He seemed organized, if nothing else.

"Okay, we've got a preliminary ballistics report back on the sniper shooting at the museum." He looked up briefly, and I only nodded. "Shooter was most likely a professional. Bullets were .308 Winchester fired out of either a Remington 700 or the military version of that, an M24 SWS—their Sniper Weapon System. The M24 has been used extensively by snipers in the war in Afghanistan. Standard issue for the Army."

"Shit," Nick said, running his fingers through his thinning hair.

"Did the CSI unit verify the shooter's location?" I asked.

"Third floor, fourth window from the left. Just like you thought," Brad said with a quick wink.

"I wish that win would lead us to the actual perp," I said. "I'm guessing the office wasn't being used at the time?"

"The entire west wing was going through a refurbishment, removing asbestos, apparently."

I pondered that nugget of information. "Any other trace evidence found in the room, or even trailing from the room to the outside?"

Brad shook his head. "Not even a bit of gun residue. Shooter must have draped a blanket through the open window and on the floor. They were clean. That's why I used the term 'professional.'"

"Next logical step is to start looking at—"

"Already there. In cross-checking against all local law-enforcement agencies, we've found no credible threats against any agent or agency."

"So, we're not even sure if this person is ex-military with a beef against the FBI, or just your average Joe with a beef against the FBI."

Nick cleared his throat. "You forgot about the option of the beef against you."

"I'm not that popular."

"You've already admitted that you thought this sniper was aiming at you."

"Because I was dumb enough to try to save that little brat's life."

"And the security guard's."

I nodded. "I was a moving target. The sniper was probably salivating when he saw me jumping around—and not very nimbly, I might add."

"Eh. Maybe," Nick said, sitting back while cupping his coffee.

Shifting my eyes over to Brad, I said, "I'm assuming we're looking for all registered owners of a Remington 700?"

Brad smirked. "Right. Not expecting a hit on that, but we have to check the box. Cyber unit is also scraping the Internet looking for anyone bragging about pinning two FBI agents."

"I think the person who did this has a screw loose, or two," I said, motioning my cup toward Brad. "The crazy ones don't stay quiet forever. Keep us in the loop, please."

"Will do."

"Also, we'll need a rundown of all former military personnel living in the area who have sniper experience. It won't be easy to get, but don't let that stop you."

He tapped his tablet a few times. "Got it."

"Over to the ring killer, did we get toxicology—"

"I pulled it this morning. Another reason I was late." He flashed another quick smile then tapped his screen and scrolled a bit.

The kid was predicting everything I was about to say. Nick had said we'd worked together previously, that Brad was my "go-to" guy. He seemed damn efficient, his dimples notwithstanding. But for some odd reason, my memory radar was coming up empty.

"Okay, Barden's system had a BAC of point twelve."

"So, he was a drinker. We need to check the bars. We know there are no bars near where he was killed at Choate Island. We'll have to start with a wide net, circulate his picture. Anything else?"

"Propofol."

"To drug him," I said quietly, pondering more about what type of person was at the root of this murder, possibly more. "Had to be given intravenously. Did—"

"Yes, MEs found a needle hole on his neck."

I nodded. "Official COD in yet?"

"Respiratory impairment."

"Drowning. The worst death imaginable." I shifted my eyes to a spilled package of sugar on the table, thinking about this connection I felt to the ocean, a sense of freedom. Pulling together some thoughts, I said, "This perp is very comfortable in the water—in the ocean, in particular. Might have a job working as a fisherman, or his main hobby is fishing or ocean research. Would be familiar with the tide flow in particular. I know that would take us in two different socio-economic directions, but it's a start."

"But he also knows about drugging people. Medical background?" Nick offered.

"You can find that on the Internet right next to date-rape drugs." I sipped my coffee, thinking more about what I'd just heard. My eyes went to Nick. "You said he."

"Just an assumption. But you're right, with the use of propofol, it leaves the door open to a woman. A strong woman maybe."

"Could be a team," I surmised while strumming my fingers on

the table.

I could feel two sets of male eyes on me.

"Think about it. We're probably fooling ourselves into thinking that a woman, by herself, could get a body from, let's say, the parking lot of a bar, out to BFE, and then set up the murder machine—cinderblocks, the duct-tape funnel—all with no help."

Two head nods. At least they were following my line of thinking.

"But a couple, a man and a woman. The woman makes sense because she was the one who was jilted."

Nick snapped his fingers. "Enter stage right, Agatha Barden."

"Perhaps. She, or maybe a woman the vic didn't know, but someone with a great deal of motivation, whatever that is, could be the ring leader." I raised a quick eyebrow.

"That's an awful pun, Alex," Nick said, chuckling under his breath.

"Glad you caught it. Tells me you're listening. Not sure about you." I gestured to Brad.

"Who, me? I'm just the dumb kid taking notes." He kept a straight face.

My breath caught in my throat.

"Just joking with you, Alex." He reached out and patted my hand.

"Nice one, kid."

"By the way, in the past you kind of gave me permission to bust your chops occasionally. So, I'm not overstepping my ground, am I, since you're the senior special agent and I'm…well, not?"

An awkward guttural chuckle from Nick.

"It's fine, Brad. Just getting used to the playing field." I tipped back my head and downed the last few drops of my mocha. "So, the couple angle. We have the woman over here who calls the shots. She's either pissed or demented."

"Or both," Nick chimed in.

"Or both, right. And then she needs a person to implement the plan. Could be a boyfriend, maybe somebody she hooked up with initially just to get payback at her cheating husband. Then, as things at home dissolve, her mind spirals more and more out of control, and she comes up with this plan. She's already manipulated this guy to be her side dish. Is it a stretch to think she could convince him to participate in a murder plot?"

The men looked away, pondering my theory. A few seconds ticked by as I waited for some type of feedback.

Finally, Nick leaned forward and said, "It's plausible, I guess, but we have two couples, two murders. Not sure what motivation an Agatha Barden would have against Rick Lepino. But we're talking about some extreme personalities on both sides of the aisle."

"You talking politics, Nick?" I joked, then gave him a wink. "But I understand why you're questioning my theory. Something about Agatha didn't sit right with me."

"Going on what you said, though, what kind of woman comes up with this crazy shit? And then to find another person, a man, naïve enough to believe her bullshit promises," he said.

I bounced a knuckle off the table. "That's it. What motivates people more than anything?"

"Greed. Straight up," Brad said.

"Okay, what's second?"

"Love?" Nick tilted his head.

"Or," I said, "the *promise* of love."

"She's brainwashing him," Nick said.

"Must be a kid, you know, like my age," Brad said.

"I'm thinking the same thing. The man is younger, maybe less educated and definitely more naïve."

"So, uh, just for the record, I'm willing to give a polygraph on whether I know Agatha Barden and my whereabouts the night her husband was murdered." Brad tried not to smile, but his dimples eventually made an appearance.

"You don't like being chased by a cougar?"

For just a second, I wondered if the guys were thinking I was subtly referring to myself, and I could feel my cheeks warming up.

Thirty-Two

A few seconds passed and neither of them went there, thankfully.

"I hardly interact with women at all, given the hours the FBI has me working," Brad said with a shrug.

"We can always say something to your boss, you know, about lowering your hours to nothing," Nick said.

"I'm good. I'm not bitching, just stating the facts."

I shook my cup, hoping to steal a few more drops of flavored caffeine. "Get all that to our assigned profiler. What's his name?"

"Roy. He's one of the best," Brad said while his fingers danced across his tablet.

Another name that didn't ring the memory bell.

"All of this talk makes me go back to Agatha Barden, although we have no solid evidence pointing in that direction," I said.

"Oh, Randy sent me an email, copying both of you, by the way, saying the warrant was approved overnight. I should have access to Agatha's phone and her phone records by lunch," Brad said, rubbing his hands together.

I pulled my phone from my purse, pissed at myself for not seeing the email. I still was piecing together how I'd operated in the past—how often I checked email, how I dealt with people I worked with, how I got shit done. I quickly came to the conclusion that recreating my life from scratch was about as much fun as…

I heard the crying howl of the wind, and I glanced over Brad's head toward the front door. Two women entered the coffeehouse, chitchatting as if they were walking through a mall in perfect atmospheric conditions.

"As much fun as winter in Boston," I said, finishing my thought aloud. My cohorts gave me strange looks.

"What's as much fun as winter in Boston?" Nick asked.

"Oh, nothing. Just my life, or the house of cards that it's being built upon."

I glanced back up and watched the women move through the line, gabbing away as if no one else existed.

"Damn, they're oblivious." Nick had followed my eyes to the women.

"They're probably plotting to overthrow the government," Brad joked, slouching more in his seat.

Noticing the time on my phone, I grabbed my coat off the chair, but paused before standing up.

"I don't want to muddy up our profile or running theory, but what if two women, maybe more, had formed some type of pact? Brought together by the common bond of their cheating spouses."

"A women's murder club," Nick said, shaking his finger.

"I've heard of crazier shit," Brad said, inching up a bit in his chair.

"To at least dismiss it as a possible theory, can you see if you can find any way that Agatha Barden and Jeanne Lepino might know each other?"

"I'm on it," Brad said, his eyes scanning something on his tablet.

"Didn't mean you had to do it in the next sixty seconds."

"Just making a few notes, that's all."

"Good. I like thoroughness. It will keep you from coming back and asking me questions later." I sounded like a real boss, but with this much on the line, I didn't have the luxury of wasting time because of oversight and disorganization. "We know the Lepinos live in the upscale community of Weston, which is west of the city, while Beverly is north, but see if their kids might play on the same teams. Maybe they go to the same church. Maybe they belong to the same country club, or Bunco club, or whatever."

"Strip club?" Brad said.

Nick and I gave him straight-faced responses.

"What?"

"Here I thought you were all grown up, ready to sit at the adult table." My expression remained stoic.

"Oh, well, I guess it was a tad inappropriate."

Nick bellowed a laugh.

"Dude, we're just yanking your chain," I said.

"Good one. Now I know what it's like."

"You should. You're still wearing the FBI diaper."

Another Nick snicker.

"Funny," Brad said while tapping madly on his tablet.

He seemed to be a natural multitasker, just like the kids. Then I had this thought: Brad might be closer in age to Erin than he was to me. Jesus, I didn't want to go there on about a thousand fronts.

I gave a nod to Nick and stood, knowing we needed to head to the Lepino house for our interview with Jeanne. I glanced down at Brad. "You can hang out here and work. Maybe the president of the *Brad is Awesome* fan club will serve you all day."

"Hold on. One more thing." He raised a finger, then slipped a phone from his pocket and used his thumb to type as his eyes slowly made their way up to me.

I put on my coat. "Yes."

"The Daughters of the Revolution."

"Right, the group of ladies Mr. Trow brought up, said he

thought they might—and I do mean *might*—be connected to the robbery at the museum."

"Yeah, I had some time on my hands last night, and I looked into the three names Trow sent over."

"You must live a boring life."

"All work and no play. That's the FBI way, right?"

"Something like that. You were saying..." I buttoned my trench coat.

"The three ladies—Brandy, Lois, and Trina—recently formed a corporation."

"For what?" Nick asked as I slung my scarf around my neck.

"Their company is called Priceless Artifacts."

"Any revenue or other information?"

"Nothing as of the end of last month."

"Dig more."

"I did, but not on the corporation."

"What else is there?"

"Two of the stolen items were found up for sale on the Dark Web."

"Just two?" I asked.

"The cyber squad is trying to identify the seller."

"Maybe this will finally lead us to the person who ran you off the road. You remember, that was supposed to be our primary mission," Nick said.

"Shit happens. What do you want me to say?" I walked around the table. Brad pulled his stuff together and caught up to us as we walked to the front door. I noticed Nick reading something off his phone.

"Checking to see if you're winning your Candy Crush game?"

He stopped in his tracks, halting Brad and me in ours.

"What is it, Nick? We've got a hundred things to get done today...you know, before another dead body is found floating in another bay."

"There was another killing last night."

Gripping his forearm, I said, "Tell me it wasn't—"

"It wasn't. Just some guy who got whacked overnight. A single GSW to the head. The brass will probably leave that to the Boston cops. As long as it's not on our plate, I'm good," Nick said, pocketing his phone.

"Where?" I asked as a blast of cold air brought water to my eyes.

The wind whipped more snow and ice in our faces as Nick tried to protect himself by putting his nose into his arm. He yelled above the weather, "I don't know. Some bar in Back Bay."

I knew then where we'd start circulating Barden's picture. For now, though, we had to figure out if the "women's murder club" theory had any roots of fact.

Thirty-Three

"**W**hat's your take so far?" Nick whispered as I ambled over to the fireplace, glancing at framed family photos.

"I think Jeanne is holding back."

"But she just broke down and cried right in front of us. Do you think that was all an act? If so, she belongs in Hollywood." Nick craned his neck to look down a wide hallway that led to the kitchen.

"People cry for many reasons. You ever caught a kid lying?" I asked him.

"I do have this one niece who can just turn on the tear faucet at a moment's notice."

I raised an eyebrow. He'd just made my point.

"Okay, the jury's still out," he said.

"I apologize, Agent Giordano and Agent Radowski. I just needed some time to gather myself." Jeanne had swept in from the dining room behind us, startling me. For a brief moment, I wondered if she'd overheard our conversation.

"That's okay. I understand how difficult this must be. No one expects their husband to die at such a young age."

With the grace of a swan, she took a seat on the couch while extending her hand for us to sit in chairs opposite her. "I thought

Gerda was in the process of getting you a refreshment. I'll need to speak with her. She's a little, uh, rough around the edges."

While Gerda had been forced to wear a traditional maid outfit, she had the build of a German tank, or a Patriots linebacker, depending on which you feared most. Her demeanor was stoic, but I could see her displeasure as she looked down her nose at us when we'd arrived. Why exactly, I wasn't sure, unless she just hated her life.

"No sighting of Gerda, but we're fine. Just had our morning shot of coffee."

"Very well," she said, emptying her lungs for at least ten seconds.

I searched her facial structure, looking for a hint of her true thoughts. She pursed her lips, then set her hands in her lap. Her eyes drifted to the fireplace where a simmering fire added a homey vibe to an otherwise stuffy place.

"Please," she said again, offering for us to sit in the chairs. I gave Nick the eye until he got the hint that we needed to oblige her request. He went for the Queen Anne chair on the left at the same time I did, and I almost sat on his lap. It was a nice comedy routine, if we weren't in the middle of a highly sensitive discussion.

Taking the other chair, I said, "Do you have family here with you, maybe upstairs consoling the girls?"

She sniffled, then pulled out a tissue and dabbed her nose. "It's just us. Our families live in California. We've had a few friends come by, drop off food that we'll never eat." Another deep breath. "We're having a contest, the girls and I, to see who can shed the most tears by this weekend." She tried to laugh at herself, but she hardly made a noise.

I took another gander at the mother of twin teenage girls. Time hadn't been kind to Jeanne. Her bio had her age at forty-one, but if it had said fifty-one, I wouldn't have been surprised. Not that she didn't put effort into her looks. Her highlighted hair was set in a neat bun. Her makeup was top dollar, as was her outfit, a flowing, black chiffon number. Jewelry was just south of Gaudy and Overindulgent. She couldn't make a hand gesture without clanging platinum or diamonds.

With all the resources at her disposal, however, she hadn't been able to curb the influx of wrinkles. Given their lavish lifestyle and the likely social pressure to always look thirty, I wondered if nip-and-tuck surgery had been debated between her and Rick. Then again, not all couples shared everything. I was hoping to find out if that was the case with the Lepinos.

"I see lots of happy faces in your family pictures around the living room. How long have you and Rick been married?" I asked casually.

"Just celebrated our nineteenth wedding anniversary."

"Do anything special?"

Jeanne took in a shaky breath. I didn't want to interrupt her thoughts, so I let her take a moment and calm down a bit.

She attempted a smile, then said, "We talked about going to Europe, maybe Ireland, but then Rick changed his mind. Said he was in the middle of so many important deals, he didn't want to leave the country. Then he said we could plan something really special for our twentieth. Maybe take a two-month tour of Europe."

My phone buzzed from inside my purse. I peeked at it and saw Brad's name. Not wanting to seem distracted, I left the text for later and returned my focus to Mrs. Lepino. With a look of stone, she stared straight ahead. I flipped a quick glance over my shoulder, wondering if she'd zeroed in on a memorable picture or memento. The only thing behind us was a set of framed windows outlined by blue, silk curtains.

"Jeanne," I said.

Her eyes didn't blink.

Nick gave me a nod, then pretended to clear his throat, obviously hoping to wake her from this daze.

"Jeanne, do I need to get you a glass of water?" I leaned forward, ready to rise.

Looking beyond her, I wondered if I should try to find Gerda or possibly Jeanne's daughters, someone to bring her back to planet Earth. I just hoped she wasn't having a panic attack, or worse yet, a nervous breakdown.

Nick removed his keys from his pocket and jingled them.

Her eyelids began to droop and just that small change in appearance made her look tired as hell, or drugged up. Maybe both. I hadn't smelled any alcohol on her breath.

"Jeanne, are you okay? Can we call a friend?"

Out of the corner of my eye, I spotted a tank of a woman slipping through the far room.

"Gerda," I called out. But she kept walking.

I looked again at Jeanne and noticed her fingers fidgeting with her tissue. Actually, mauling it. "You're upset, Jeanne. It's completely understandable." My voice was soft and delicate. "We can take a break while you take care of yourself."

"It's not necessary," she said in a loud monotone, her eyes still boring holes through the window.

"Okay." She seemed off kilter. I traded glances with Nick.

"I'm not losing my marbles, and I haven't been popping pills."

I paused for a second, then said, "Glad you're doing okay. You just had a worried—"

"The problem is Rick. Was Rick. And now he's dead."

I had no idea where she was taking this, but I needed to keep her talking. I said, "Husbands, spouses in general, can be difficult. I know that as much as anyone."

"You didn't know Rick."

"True. Only you did. Well, you probably knew him the best. What was he like?"

She turned her head in my direction, resting her open hand on her knee, as if that might help conjure up her words.

"You really want to know what Rick Lepino was like?"

She'd gone from nearly catatonic to animated in just a few seconds. I could practically see lava spilling out of the gurgling volcano.

"Yes, Jeanne. Tell us."

She leaned to her left and yanked a tissue from a decorated box, and then she pushed both hands down into her lap.

"Rick Lepino hasn't been close to me or the girls in years."

"Why do you think that is?"

"His fucking ego, that's why," she said loudly, throwing up a hand.

I scooted back in my chair, since her voice had practically rattled my brains. "I understand he was an insurance salesman."

"Sure as hell was. He wasn't one of those cheesy guys set up in a rundown strip center, chasing a hundred dollars here and there. No, Richard B. Lepino only courted the big corporations. Or, if you got him after a couple of drinks, he might say they begged to do business with him. Why? Because he thought his shit didn't stink. Well, I got news for them, you, and everyone else in this fucked-up world. Richard B. Lepino's shit smelled worse than any shit I have ever smelled. Bar none!" She raised a finger to the sky.

My concerns about her opening up had just been erased, in spades. But I doubted her deep-seated anger had anything to do with his bathroom habits. At least I hoped not.

I ignored the potty talk and focused on her first comment at the higher decibel level. "Jeanne, it's not uncommon for relatives and family members to show anger in a time like this. No one is perfect."

Her cheeks puffed, and a bit of drool flew out of her mouth. She was seething, as if she were a wild animal who'd just been branded.

"Perfect? He was perfect at just one thing."

I paused, but realized I had to ask. "What was that?"

"Fucking up my life."

Nick gave me the sign, and he jumped in. "Jeanne, looking beyond some of this initial emotion you're feeling, can you tell us if Rick, or even you, had been threatened recently, maybe going back the last two years?"

"I threatened him." She fired a fake gun with her fingers and gave Nick a knowing nod.

"Can you please—" Nick started.

"Gerda, please bring us some ice water," she called out, then clapped her hands twice.

I understood why Gerda looked beaten down.

Moving at the same methodical pace as earlier, Gerda walked in carrying a tray with a glass carafe and three glasses. She poured water into each glass and set them on coasters on the table.

"Is that everything, Mrs. Lepino?"

"Yes," Jeanne said, back to staring out the window, then she held up a hand before Gerda could disappear. "Don't call me Mrs. Lepino ever again."

"Very well. What should I call you then?"

"Jeanne. No, that won't work. Call me by my maiden name, Uhew."

"Okay, Mrs.—"

"Ms., thank you."

"Right. Ms. Uhew."

And just like that, she'd changed her name. Nick and I each raised an eyebrow as Gerda plodded out of the living room.

Jeanne took three big gulps of her water, then wiped her mouth with the back of her hand.

Nick said, "Jeanne, as you know, we're here to talk about the murder of your husband. I'm not trying to accuse you of anything, but you did say you threatened him."

"That's an easy one. I threatened him all the time. Threatened to stop cooking, to stop cleaning. Well, I actually followed through on those." She strummed her fingers together while giggling in a nefarious way.

"How so?" I asked.

"I put my foot down and stopped. It was that simple. And then he made a countermove."

"How so?"

"He went out and got Gerda, that's how."

Interesting that Rick Lepino had chosen a German tank over a slinky sports car. For some reason, my mind went to Sydney. I'd forgotten to ask Mark who had hired her and why. I'd been so needing of his attention, I'd let many of my other concerns fall to the wayside. But I couldn't drop it. The collegiate free spirit not only had crossed the line with me, but her actions were impacting our daughter, and not in a positive way.

"Jeanne, do you know of any colleague or neighbor or anyone else who has threatened your husband's life?" I tried to guide her off the revenge soapbox.

Her lips formed a straight line, and she lifted her chin. "It's time."

"Time for what?"

"That I tell you everything," she said, locking her eyes on mine.

I wondered what the last ten minutes had been all about, but I was game.

She gulped more water, then spilled her guts. "About four months ago, at about ten in the evening, the doorbell rang. Gerda had gone home for the night, so I answered the door." She pinched the corners of her eyes and shook her head once.

"And who was there?" I said with a quick glance at Nick, who was watching Jeanne intently.

"A young girl, crying, in hysterics."

"Did you know her?"

"I'd never seen her before in my life."

I looked down at the rug for a second.

"But I had *heard* her before, moaning and yelling in all her glory."

Oh hell. I wasn't sure I wanted to ask a follow-up question, afraid the Jeanne Uhew volcano might erupt.

Nick stepped in front of the speeding locomotive. "Moaning, yelling, crying. Was she on something maybe? I'm assuming she didn't attack you."

"Hell no. She attacked Rick, scratching him and clawing him with her obnoxious fingernails."

"What?" Nick's eyes nearly bulged out of his head as he moved to the edge of his seat.

Jeanne shook her head, apparently annoyed that Nick hadn't caught on.

"Agent Radowski, the little tramp fucked my husband and left her marks on him like a dog pissing on a tree."

He blinked a few times and sat back. "Oh. Sorry."

"I'd found a grainy video he'd taken on his cell phone, a sex tape I guess you'd call it. Can't see much, but oh my, the sounds carved a hole in my chest. That little slut. *Felicia.*" She said the name with notable disgust, then drained her glass. She picked up the glass pitcher and started to pour more water, but changed her mind and returned the pitcher to the tray.

She inhaled a deep breath. "She stood in the doorway that night yelling at me, and then at Rick, claiming he'd made all sorts of promises to her about leaving me and shacking up with her. I was devastated, of course, but I just laughed in her face."

"I bet that didn't go over well," I said.

"She took a swipe at me with those nails. Rick grabbed her by the wrist and asked her to leave. I told her she was nothing more than a Kim Kardashian starter kit. And if she wanted her actual fifteen minutes of fame to become a reality, she needed to find another ugly, half-bald husband."

"I'm confused. You hated him for cheating on you, but then you stood up for him in front of his—"

"It's easy. I signed a pre-nup. If he dumped me, I'd get seventy percent of everything, now and going forward."

"Why would he have signed that?"

"Because he was in love, I guess. Who knows?" She licked her lips. "The sad part was, when we finally closed the door, our daughters were standing at the bottom of the stairs, both with expressions of disbelief. They'd heard everything."

"Must have been rough."

"It was. But it's best for the girls to know what their father was truly like and not some make-believe Superman image."

A quiet calm settled over the living room. I reached for my water, but before my lips touched the glass, Jeanne let it rip.

"Felicia was one of many."

I took a quick sip, then set down the glass. "Jeanne, you don't have to—"

"No, I do need to say it. Everything. There's a method to my emotional madness, I assure you."

"Go ahead," I said.

"I frankly can't tell you all the names, but in the last year I'm aware of Kelly, and Amber, and of course our house visitor, Felicia. Oh, I've heard him having phone sex with a girl named Amanda. I'm not even sure she's in college yet. Can you believe it? He fucked some girl almost as young as his daughter. He's fucking sick!"

After a moment of silence, I ventured with, "Does that help you, getting it off your chest?"

She released a tired breath and rubbed under her eyes. "To a degree, yes. But there's something else I need to tell you."

"What's that?" Nick asked with little enthusiasm. Perhaps he was tired of the histrionics and drama.

"The police detective showed me the pictures of the rings. They are mine."

Now we'd finally hit the meat on the bone.

"Were they recently stolen?" I asked.

"Yes, but I wasn't sure at first. Let me explain." She repositioned herself on the couch and propped a pillow behind her. "About three weeks ago, I went to work out at my gym. As usual, I left my rings in the locker room. When I got back to my locker after my aerobics session, they were gone."

"Did you talk to management?"

"Hell yes, I did. Those rings are worth more than your salaries combined." She froze for a brief moment. "I don't mean to offend you."

"That's okay. We get the picture," I said.

"But I talked to management, and they talked to security, who checked their cameras. Nothing came up, from what I was told several days later. Frankly, I figured one of Rick's little floozies had somehow squirmed her way into the locker, stolen my rings, then seduced someone to keep her identity hidden."

I just stared at her.

"You think I've watched too many *Mission Impossible* movies, don't you?"

"It's a theory."

"But now that we've heard how he died, I have my doubts that any of those bimbos could have pulled it off." A smile cracked her creased face, and then she wagged a finger between me and Nick. "You're wondering if I could have done it." She began to laugh. "Oh, I hated that man so. And I'm in decent shape. But I'm just not that creative or violent."

I wasn't sure about the violent part, but I nodded anyway. "We'd like to look at your cell phone without getting a warrant."

"I have no problem with that. I'm pissed and upset, but I'm ready to move on. I got a nice fat insurance payday ahead of me."

More incentive. I would ask Brad to look into the insurance policy and when it was purchased.

She retrieved her phone, saying she'd be available to talk more if we needed her.

Nick and I shut the house door behind us and walked into the blustery cold.

"This weather beats the weather in there," Nick said, moving quickly to his car.

"It was so cold, it almost got hot. If that makes sense." I gave him a quick glance, wondering if he would think I was off my rocker. He was just hustling to his car door. "And Uhew? What a name."

"You're one to speak."

"So you know about my maiden name too?"

"About your mom teasing you with Pouty Troutty? Yes, sorry." Nick crossed his heart and gave me a sarcastic smile. "But I haven't told a soul, I promise."

My hand touched the door handle as I read Brad's text message.

I called out to Nick through the swirling wind. "Brad and Roy worked together and found a man who fits the profile. Was released from prison six months ago for kidnap and assault. Works at the Cape Ann Marina. According to local police, he went postal on some fishermen on another boat last week and pulled a knife on them. Oh, get this. He was also a sniper in the first Gulf War, dishonorably discharged. A team is on the way to his home."

Seconds later, so were we.

Thirty-Four

Wind-whipped weeds smacked against the metal siding of the trailer we were hiding behind. Avoiding a protruding piece of rusted metal that could have sliced me open like a pig, I peeked around the corner, confirming what I'd seen just two minutes earlier. Robert Earl Dotson's double-wide was wedged between two pine trees about a hundred feet north of our location. The bottom part of the storm door was void of glass.

It appeared his homemade front porch was made of balsa wood. I could see at least two holes in the flooring from my current vantage point. A section of artificial grass, crumpled and stained, nudged against the bottom step. The area just south of his address was empty, giving us a clean look to his front door. We had a pair of agents positioned a hundred feet on the other side of his trailer, and they confirmed his next-door neighbor on that side had left for work.

But not Robert Earl. He hadn't been seen at work in the last week, according to Brad, who had worked with Randy to set up this raid. While we had no direct evidence linking Robert Earl to the murders—at least not yet—we had cause to question him, especially with the rate at which the ring murders were taking place. And casually walking up to Robert Earl as he ambled outside to pick up the morning paper wasn't an option, not when the FBI was involved. Mitigating all risk was priority number one, followed closely by securing the suspect without harm to him or us.

Was it overkill? Possibly, but as I turned to look at my colleagues—including four detectives from the local police department—I could sense the anticipation of action in their movements. Men and women shuffled side to side, apparently trying to curb the flow of adrenaline. Two agents reloaded ammunition in their handguns, while two others with binoculars stood behind a cluster of trees off to my right.

"You got your vest on, Alex?" Randy had just holstered his pistol and sidled up next to me. A bit too close for my liking, but I tried not to make a scene. The timing wasn't right.

I pulled open the standard-issue FBI jacket I'd swapped out for my red trench coat. I might have rolled my eyes just a tad.

He leaned down to my ear. "I like it when you flash me." He blew in my ear, then scooted away before I could jab my elbow in his ribs.

"That mother—"

"Whoa there, Alex," Nick was just a second behind Randy.

"Did you just see what he did? What he said?"

He held up two hands. "I'm right here. No need to shout."

I ran my fingers through my hair, trying to funnel my anger at Randy into a compartment that would allow my temperament to fall below the boiling point. Taking a few deep breaths, I watched a rat scurry from under the trailer into a pile of wood. I walked a few steps away from the trailer and let the wind sober up my emotions.

"Better now?" Nick asked from behind me.

"Only because I'm trying to pretend it didn't happen."

"What did he say to you?"

I repeated the words verbatim.

"Bastard," Nick said.

"Perverted bastard," I countered then blew out a breath. "But I know now isn't the right time to confront him."

"That could be why he did it. Either that, or he can't control himself around you."

I turned to ensure Nick could see me rolling my eyes.

"You don't think I'm serious?" he said, leaning in closer to keep from being overheard.

"I don't know. I'm too angry to read him. He's just a—"

"Perverted bastard. We agree on that one. No offense, but if he's harassing you, I bet he's done it to others."

I glanced over Nick's shoulder and watched Randy place his hands on the shoulders of two male agents, acting like the concerned parent.

"What a piece of work." The rush of adrenaline had ignited a flurry of images from the past that included Randy. Mostly work-related scenes, but a few in a casual setting. One stood out, where he was sitting with his arm around me in a booth, his hand moving up my thigh. And then...

I started giggling.

Nick's eyes found mine. "Alex, are you losing it on me?"

"What? No, I'm fine."

He pursed his lips and glanced over his shoulder. "You're laughing, though. Twenty seconds ago, you were ready to cut off Randy's dick."

"And stuff it down his throat," I added, followed by another spurt of giggles.

Nick's face began to soften. "You're not going to share the gossip from that brain of yours?"

"I just had a few more memories zap my mind. And one that, well..."

"It involved Randy?"

"I don't know where we were, but he essentially tried to seduce me in a public place. And then I racked him."

Nick put a hand over his mouth and winced. "I think we know why he's toying with you now."

"Maybe. Didn't think he was smart enough to toy with anyone."

"True," Nick said. "But I think you should probably go to HR. This isn't the 1940s, you know."

"I thought it was the 1980s, given his porno mustache."

We shared another quick chuckle at Randy's expense.

"Nick, I can tell I'm not a big bureaucratic person."

"You got that right," he said.

"HR will just make me fill out forms, then ruin my reputation. Everyone will think I'm weak. Well, I'm not fucking weak." Nick watched my jabbing finger like a dog following a tennis ball. "At the right time in the very near future, Randy is going to understand that if he screws with me one more time, I'm going to use his balls as target practice for my Glock."

Even with temperatures in the twenties and a cold, blustery wind, I could feel perspiration gather just above my lip. I wiped it clear.

Nick held up a hand to make a point. "Let's change the topic please. We've potentially got a killer sitting in his double-wide a hundred feet from us. Catching this creep now could be big."

I motioned for him to follow me, and we moved back toward the rest of the group, where Randy's phone was being passed around. The circle of agents opened up just in time for us to have our turn looking at Robert Earl's mug shot.

"Damn, he's ugly," Nick said.

The picture wasn't flattering. Unkempt dark hair draped down his forehead just above tiny, charcoal eyes. His face looked like the surface of the moon, and he had more missing teeth than a two-year-old.

"Bad DNA in that family tree," I said.

"Apparently, this guy's lucky to be alive," Randy said as he slipped his phone in his pocket. He then stuck his thumbs in his pants, his feet wider than his shoulders. Even at his best, he was an awkward leader. "According to his parole officer, Robert Earl has been in and out of rehab for cocaine addiction. OD'd at least twice, and doctors brought him back to life."

"Everyone makes mistakes, including doctors," I said.

Randy just stared at me for a moment. Then he turned away from me and kept talking. "He's owned guns in the past, so we can't be sure he doesn't have any in '*la casa*.'" He made quote marks in the air. "On top of his addiction, he's got anger-management issues."

"So we've heard," Nick said.

"How old is he again?" I asked.

"Uh…" Randy pointed at another agent, who said, "Fifty-three."

I nodded. "Never killed anyone that we know of?"

"Not as a civilian. Remember, this guy is a trained sharpshooter, which is why we need to be extra careful approaching his residence."

"A guy who loves to shoot. Hmm. What would motivate him to tie down middle-aged men and flaunt their infidelities?"

"He's fucked up, Alex. Fucked-up people do fucked-up things. You should know that, given your experience with the Bureau."

"Is he married?"

"Once, when he was young, before the war. Got a divorce just after returning."

"Do we know if he's attached to anyone else?"

"Can't say for sure, but all indications are no. More of an angry loner type."

"Who was his vic for the kidnap and assault convictions?"

"Don't know the name, but supposedly a female. Taught at the local elementary school."

Twisting my lips, my sights wandered over to the two agents still holding vigil with their binoculars.

"Don't you think that, if anything, this guy would have some type of vendetta against women, not middle-aged men who can't keep their dicks in their pants?"

A few snickers from the circle. Maybe they were either embarrassed or thought I was just cracking a joke. But I was serious.

Randy huffed out a breath and crossed his arms. Then he stroked his mustache a couple of times while trying to stare me down.

I didn't flinch.

"Alex, are you trying to say this isn't the right guy? From what I understand, Brad and Roy based their profile on what you gave them." He cocked his head and continued to glare at me.

"The profile isn't perfect, first of all. But we've overlooked a key factor here. This guy isn't naïve or young. It doesn't sound like he's got any connection to a woman."

"Why the hell are you so fixated on a woman? No way a woman could pull off a murder like the two we've seen. Well, I have known a couple of military bitches who could kick ass, but outside of a handful, it just isn't possible."

I could feel the penetrating stares of my colleagues.

"Look, Randy, I don't have a crystal ball. I can't say for certain Robert Earl Dotson isn't involved. But I'm just saying it doesn't feel right."

"Fucking A," he said, clapping mockingly. "No one can ride the fence better than Special Agent Alexandra Giordano."

No one moved or made a noise. Or maybe I couldn't hear them because of the roar in my head. I was about ready to leap across the circle and gouge out Randy's eyes. Instead, I counted to five, attempting to take the high road.

I said, "We're only going to find out for sure if we pick him up and question him. So let's stop talking and get his ass into custody." With that, I left the group and walked to the edge of our cover trailer.

Thirty-Five

The agents took position, and I heard Randy give orders to engage the Dotson's trailer, just after saying, "Alex, you have no weapon, so pull up the rear."

I'd yet to find time to bullshit my way past the doctor in order for Jerry to reissue me my weapon, so I didn't push back. Not yet.

Staying low to the ground, I followed behind Nick, who had his Glock drawn and aimed at the trailer. The contingent met at the trailer from all four sides. Randy gave one of the guys the signal to knock on the door.

"Robert Earl Dotson, FBI. Open up, sir."

We waited for a good ten seconds but heard no response. Quick glances all around.

The agent repeated himself, but I didn't hear anything from inside, just wind whipping in my ear.

"Dammit," Randy said, gritting his teeth. He licked his lips, maybe his mustache, then pointed at the agent. "See if it's open."

"But, sir, technically I'm not—"

"Do it, or you're working the desk for the next year."

The agent pulled open the rickety storm door, creating a pig-like squeal. That just added another level of anxiety. I wondered if Robert Earl might be on the other side, getting his jollies while sitting on a stained couch, pointing a shotgun at the door. Seeing a lot of hard swallows around me, I guessed others were thinking the same thing.

The agent twisted the doorknob and nodded—the door wasn't locked. Then he pulled his gun up. Three agents were right behind him.

I saw him mouth, *One, two, three*. He and three other agents flew into the trailer, everyone yelling, "FBI, hands up where we can see them!"

Not thirty seconds later, the agent walked back onto the wobbly porch and shook his head.

"Crap," Randy said. "Turn this place upside down. Look for anything that might give us a lead on where he went. We've got to find him."

Wanting to get a better sense of Robert Earl's life, I went inside to inspect the trailer. Porn magazine pictures took up nearly every inch of available wall space, although it was difficult to see much detail. Aside from two dim lamps glowing in each corner, aluminum foil kept any outside light from seeping into the trailer. I moved out of the way of another agent walking by, then shuffled past a chewed-up ottoman.

"Any sign of a dog or any other animal?" I asked a passing agent.

"*Nada.* Not sure the conditions in this place are conducive to anything living."

Two more steps, then I tripped and had to catch myself on the La-Z-Boy. "What the hell?" I raised my hand, now coated with something sticky and brown.

"Nasty," a female agent said, walking behind me. "Kitchen sink is around the corner. But proceed with caution."

Holding my hand at shoulder level, I nodded and headed for the kitchen, more closely looking at the floor. The fatigue-green shag carpet was covered with clothes—men's T-shirts, socks, boxers, dark pants—and trash, mostly fast-food wrappers and food remnants.

Three steps from the kitchen, a wretched stench hit me like a freight train. Just then another agent ran by with a hand over his mouth. "I'm going to throw up."

Must have a weak gag reflex.

Holding my breath, I walked to the sink and flipped on the water. The faucet spit out something that had a green tint, and I turned it off. I knew I'd have to use a more primitive method to clean my hand, so I walked back through the living room. My eyes spotted a notebook sticking out from under the La-Z-Boy. Using one hand, I opened it and found pages and pages of disgusting drawings of women being killed or raped, with hateful words scratched next to the pictures.

I walked outside and approached Nick and Randy.

"Our alleged perp has been busy drawing when he wasn't decorating his home." I handed the notebook to Nick.

Randy looked on as Nick thumbed through the pages.

"This guy has more than a few anger-management issues." Nick stopped on a single page and held it out for me to see. "He seems rather obsessed with this name."

The name "Nancy" and a flurry of cuss words were etched on the paper.

"Who knows how many people he's killed?" Randy added.

"I'm not sure he's killed any," I said, suddenly noticing a strange vehicle parked under two low-hanging trees just across the way.

"What the hell are you talking about, Alex?" Randy exclaimed.

Distracted for a second, I knew I had to wipe off my hand. "Randy, it's been a pleasure learning from you on this case," I said, extending my hand.

He gave me an oddball look, paused a second, then shook it. "Eww," he called out. "What is this crap?" He held up his hand.

"It won't kill you, but it will give you an STD."

He muttered something as I popped him on the back and moved around him to get a better view of the car. "A hearse," I said while nudging my head in that direction. "Not exactly your everyday car. Anyone check this out?" The black car looked to be twenty years old and had the coating of dust to prove it.

"I don't think so," Nick said.

Spotting a bumper sticker on the back window, I walked closer and read it out loud: "Don't ask me where the dead bodies are."

"Someone is either into dark humor or…" Nick didn't finish.

I completed the thought. "Or hiding their obsession with dead bodies with dark humor." Cupping my hands, I looked through the murky glass of the back window, and my heart skipped a beat.

"What, Alex?"

"A body, or a live person, I don't know."

Nick drew his Glock as I took hold of the handle.

"What did you guys find?" Randy shouted.

Ignoring him, I nodded at Nick. "One, two, three." I popped the handle and pulled while I jumped back a step.

The man didn't move. He had a mask covering his face, his arms draped over his chest.

"Is he dead?" Randy had just jogged over.

Nick nudged the man's bare feet with the barrel of his gun. No movement. I then noticed his feet were shaded blue, the shape of bricks.

"Who's going to check his pulse?" Nick asked, his breathing suddenly rapid.

I did a double-take on my partner and then glanced at Randy. Two stool pigeons. Moving around Randy, I lifted a knee into the back of the hearse—wincing a bit from the broken-glass wounds from the day before—and took in a waft of what smelled like bleach. I paused a moment, looking for movement of the man's chest. Nothing I could see. In glancing at his face, I saw pictures of skulls painted on the mask, one over each eye. The artwork was rudimentary, like something a first-grader might create. Even with the cover, I could see his scraggly hair.

"I think it's Dotson," I yelled to the boys while on my hands and knees.

"Do you see any weapons?" Randy asked.

I glanced around every part of the hearse I could see, inside a nook next to me, and around the rim of the back area. "Nothing visible from here. Could be something up front, though. If he's…"

"Hurry up, check his pulse. I need to know whether to call paramedics or the ME's office," Randy said.

I didn't bother replying. Leaning forward, I brought my hand up, still searching for any sign of life…or death. If he was dead, it hadn't been long. I pressed two fingers against the side of his neck coated with prickly hair and pockmarks, paused, and then slid my hand an inch to the left, then back the other way another inch.

I flipped a glance over my shoulder. "The only thing I feel is his nasty neck—"

I heard the moan and felt the tug on my wrist at the exact same moment. I nearly swallowed my tongue. The man was alive. Swinging around, I pulled back, trying to pry my arm loose, but he'd locked on with his gorilla fingers. Releasing a guttural moan, he leveraged his weight off mine to pull himself up. His mask slipped off, and I stared into beady eyes spinning out of control.

"FBI," I called out through clenched teeth. "Let. Go."

His grip only grew stronger, his eyes more intense. He was higher than a kite.

Off to my right, I could see Randy step onto the bumper then crack his head on the frame of the car and fall back. Nick yelled at Robert Earl to stand down, but he wasn't in a listening mood.

He grabbed a fistful of my hair, and my neck snapped back. I called out as my pulse skyrocketed. I was fucking pissed.

Using all of my weight, I leaned away from the asshole, then sling-shotted back toward him with a closed fist ramming into his nose.

He fell back to the floor, covering his face, although I could already see red liquid squirting between his hairy fingers.

"Alex, are you okay?" Nick asked, now with one foot in the back of the hearse.

"I'm fine," I said, hopping onto the gravel, inspecting my arm. I found four fingerprints. "What happened?" I looked at both men.

Randy had just gotten to his feet. "I slipped, dammit."

"Yeah, right."

Ten minutes later, a female medic with spiked hair urged a handcuffed Robert Earl to hold some gauze pads against his nose.

"You do it, bitch. I don't care if I bleed all over the back of your truck. We're all going to die anyway."

Randy stepped over to Robert Earl and put his cheesy 'stache about an inch from the man's enlarged and crooked schnoz. "Listen, you piece of garbage. Do as she says, or I'll ram that nose into what's left of your fried brain."

I was almost shocked to see Randy come to the defense of the girl.

Robert Earl rolled his eyes, then raised his arms and pressed the gauze against his nose.

Randy walked back to me and Nick. "Fuckin' maggot."

"And you were expecting anything different?" I swung my head around and glanced at the hearse. I spotted the metal hood ornament in the shape of a girl with wings. Was that supposed to be an angel on the vehicle of the man who appeared to have a fascination with death?

"When he's not defying orders, he's ranting and raving about death," Randy said with a frustrated tone. "The CSI guy found cocaine residue on the floor of the hearse."

I rubbed my arm where I knew some bruises would soon form. "Is he the owner of this morose mobile, or just a squatter?"

Randy said, "We confirmed it's his."

"Have you found out if he has a Nancy in his past?"

"He won't answer a straight question. Just keeps rambling."

"Have we checked the records to verify the name of his ex-wife?"

"Uh…" Randy said, his chin suddenly rigid. He called to the agent who had nearly puked inside the trailer and spoke to him quietly while they both looked at a tablet.

I pulled out my phone, wondering if I'd received a text from one of the kids, or even from Mark. I felt a need for us to pick up where we'd left off last night. I allowed myself to at least partially think ahead to tonight's interaction. Maybe we could add in a glass of wine, kick off our shoes, so to speak, or anything else that might need kicking off. I blew out a breath. Dammit, I needed to get laid by the man who's loved me for the last seventeen years.

"You frustrated about something?" Nick asked.

I arched an eyebrow. "It's nothing you can do anything about."

"Got it. TMI, by the way."

I could hear Robert Earl rambling about wanting to go back to sleep in his death box.

"Hey, what happened back there?" I asked.

Nick took in a full dose of chilled air. "I just froze."

"That's not like you."

"No offense, but how would you remember? I could be the worst federal agent since the beginning of time."

"For whatever reason, I've recalled more about your

mannerisms and even a few flashes of moments we've worked together than about anyone else."

"I'm flattered. I think."

"So, you going to share, *partner*?"

"You won't let this go, will you?"

"Who, me?" I brought a hand to my chin and shot him a wink.

He did a full three-sixty, perhaps looking for a way out. Then he looked me in the eye. "It goes back to when I was a teenager. A friend and I were creeping around a cemetery. We came upon this crypt and found it open. We walked around to the other side and found a man lying on the grass."

"Holy shit."

"We just about did. I got close to the body and…" He scratched the back of his head while shuffling his feet.

"And?"

"The damn thing woke up and grabbed my wrist, just like with you and Robert Earl Dracula over there."

"Was that the same person who'd been in the crypt, buried alive?"

"Who the hell knows? I peed my pants and managed to wiggle away from the guy. We hauled ass out of that cemetery. Never went back, never told anyone else. Anyway, this crazy setup sent me back about twenty-five years."

"You ever think about trying out for a part in the *Walking Dead*?"

Nick's jaw dropped open to speak, but Randy cut in, having just rejoined us.

"Fuckin' A, his ex-wife's name is Nancy."

I felt certain I was the least surprised in the group. "He's not our guy, is he?"

Randy looked off into the gray sky. "We still need to take him in, question him under the lights. But probably not."

Shaking my head in frustration, I turned and spotted a plastic sign flapping against a chain-link fence. It read: *$99 Move-In Special. You Pay, You Stay.*

I tapped Nick on the shoulder and headed for the car. "We're going bar hopping."

Thirty-Six

Just as I cut hard off the brick pavers to avoid an older man and his three-pronged cane, my right foot slipped on an invisible sheet of ice. I threw out my arms for balance, hoping to grab hold of Nick, but he was nowhere to be found. I landed hard on my ass.

"Jesus, Alex," Nick said, trying to pick me up.

Resting my elbows on my knees, I said, "Give me a minute. Need to make sure I'm still in one piece."

In reality, besides a bruised ego for showing my athleticism was not at optimum level, the only pain was in my brain—again.

I closed my eyes and felt snow flurries sticking to my face.

"If Jerry were here, he'd ask if you're falling asleep on the job, or why you're such a klutz."

"But Jerry isn't here," I said, pushing off the ground to get to my feet. Now looking directly at Nick, I added, "And by the way, a real klutz would have knocked the old man to the ground." I tapped him on the chest and glanced up at a neon sign. "Monty's, let's go." I grabbed the brass door handle.

"Alex, we've been to, what, seventeen bars and restaurants in and around Back Bay? I'm tired and I'm hungry."

"We can catch a bite in Monty's. I'll even pay."

"More cheap burgers or nachos? No thanks. I'm getting old,

Alex. All this walking and crap food will do me in by the time I'm fifty-five."

I took a step in his direction. "If Jerry were here, he might say you're wimping out on me."

Nick removed a pack of gum from his pocket and offered me a piece. As usual, I waved him off. He tossed a piece in his mouth and started smacking away.

"What's up, Nick? You normally don't whine like a sixth-grader being fed chicken mushroom casserole."

"It's, uh, a special day for Antonio and me. Been together twenty-three years today. He's made a surprise meal for me. Home-cooked food. The guy is one hell of a chef."

"You should have said something. Go home. I'll dig around in Monty's and then get a cab."

He took out his keys and tossed them at me. I snatched them out of the air.

"You still got it, Alex. You just drive yourself home, then pick me up in the morning. I'll take the cab."

I wasn't going to argue my newly bestowed privilege. "Sure thing. Enjoy your evening, at least what's left of it."

Walking into Monty's at almost nine-thirty, I felt a longing to be at home myself. Earlier, when Mark hadn't responded to my text messages, I reluctantly called Sydney and asked her to stay late. After the fiasco with Robert Earl Dotson, I knew we couldn't waste another night of chasing FBI theories. While I still awaited Brad's research on Agatha Darden, old-fashioned investigative work seemed like it might get us there just as fast, or at least confirm our suspicions—Agatha was partnering with a younger man, and possibly other women, to exact revenge on philandering husbands.

"You waiting on anybody?"

Swiping off a mixture of sludge and mud from the back of my

trench coat, I glanced up to see an attractive thirty-something man with perfect hair and a warm smile sifting through menus.

"Uh, no. Just me, myself, and I."

His grin widened. I wasn't sure why he found my statement that witty, but dealing with anyone pleasant and genuine—the antithesis of Randy—was a welcomed change.

He turned his back for a moment. "Outside of our quiet side room that's usually reserved for more discreet couples, it will be probably ten or fifteen minutes until a table is ready. Unless you'd like to sit at the bar."

"The bar it is."

He showed me the way, even pulling out the barstool for me.

"Thanks," I said, sliding onto the stool while I pulled my phone out of my purse.

"Dad here will help you when you're ready to order."

Just as I turned back to ask the host a quick question, I heard a gruff voice behind me.

"Junior's busy running this place. What can I get ya?"

Flipping around to face the bar, I saw a napkin with the Monty's name on it, and I asked, "That's his name? Junior?"

"That's what I call him. What's it to ya?" He was in his sixties with two chins and a Jimmy Durante nose. He planted two sausage-like hands on the rim of the wooden bar.

I looked more closely at his eyes. "If he's Junior, are you the senior Monty?"

His eyebrow twitched, but he didn't crack a smile. "Like I said, what's it to ya?"

Inching a little taller in my seat, I rested both arms on the bar and locked eyes with the senior Monty. "I suppose I could ask you just as well as I could ask him."

He held up a hand. "Not sure who you are, but before you ask anything, you gotta place your order. Food, drink, whatever."

My headache had subsided, and the day had been hellaciously long. Just a little nip would take the edge off before I headed home to deal with any drama from Sydney or Erin. "A glass of your house chardonnay."

"Got it." He clanged bottles behind the bar, then unsealed a cork and poured me a generous glass.

Someone called out Monty's name, and he set the glass in front of me so quickly a bit of the wine sloshed over the rim. He held up a finger and plodded over to another customer.

"But—"

He held up the finger again without even looking at me.

Glancing around the main area, the décor was slightly dated, but very clean. A few tables had larger crowds, but the booths were understated with low lighting and high backs, probably made for intimate moments.

Just then, Junior walked by, and I reached out and tapped his shoulder. "Can I borrow you—"

"He's not a blow-up doll, lady."

Senior had snuck up behind me.

I could feel a laser beam of heat light up my face. With my canines showing, I turned back to Senior, my finger extended. "Listen, I'm not—"

"I know what you're going to say."

"And what do you think that is?"

"You're just here to get a drink and people watch."

"And if I was, then what's your problem with that?"

"Junior is, you know, not interested."

"I didn't know he was fifteen and needed Daddy's permission."

"Damn, you're feisty. I kind of expected it. You have that look."

I was about to go across the bar after this guy. "What look is that, Monty Senior?"

"You know, short hair, kind of athletic."

I started to rise out of my stool. "Listen, Monty Senior, I've got more—"

"Hey, hey, everyone." A man behind me was trying to intercede. A hand touched my arm. It took every bit of me not to make an aggressive countermove.

"Excuse me," I said through gritted teeth. I turned and saw a calm, but concerned Monty Junior.

"Dad, are you harassing our customers again? Jeez," he said, wiping his face. "I apologize, Miss…"

"Giordano. Just call me Alex."

Junior gave his dad a go-to-hell look that would have melted a glacier.

"What? She started it," Senior said, while throwing an arm in my direction. "Just another feminazi."

"Dad!" Junior's face turned red as he stabbed a finger toward the opposite end of the bar. "Down there, now." Senior shrugged then moseyed in that direction.

I blew out a breath. "I didn't need saving, you know."

"But my dad did. Another thirty seconds, and I think you would have leaped across the bar and broken his nose with one punch."

He tried to smile, but I could see this wasn't his first attempt to rope in Mr. Progressive.

"How did you know?" I asked.

He slid onto the barstool next to me. "Know what?"

"That I could take him out in one punch."

"You have that…athletic look." He broke out in laughter and tapped my hand softly a couple of times.

"Like father, like son," I said, arching an eyebrow.

"I'll take any compliment but that one. I know he's just a

grumpy bigot. But until he's six feet under, he'll be here every day and night, chasing customers away."

"And then you'll spend all of your time trying to win them back. Am I right?"

"So right," he said.

I sipped my wine, then opened the camera roll on my phone. "I need to ask if you've seen either of these two men in this bar."

He nodded, releasing a sly grin. "I knew something had to be up. An attractive lady dressed more for business than fun."

I first showed him a picture of Christopher Barden. It was actually a picture of him and his wife Agatha.

Junior tapped his chin, then lifted his eyes, a glowing amber. "This is official, isn't it?"

"Do you want to see my credentials?"

"Not really, although you'll probably impress me more if you show me."

I discreetly pulled out my creds and opened the leather pouch to where only he could see them.

He whispered, "Fuckin' FBI? Who robbed the bank?"

"No one. Beyond that, I ask the questions."

A slow nod of his head.

I stowed my creds and pointed to my phone. "Seen him around Monty's?"

He pressed his lips against his teeth, the whitest I'd ever seen. Had this guy been a model?

"I see so many businessmen in and out of here, they all start to look the same."

"Okay, how about this guy?" Rick Lepino's picture came straight off his company's website. A cheesy grin with a hand propping up his chin.

Junior held up a finger to me, then looked around the restaurant. He spotted his dad and shook his head. "He won't help us any." Then he continued scanning the room.

"Wait," he finally said, hopping off his barstool and disappearing into the kitchen. A minute later he returned, accompanied by a short, frumpy man with baggy pants.

"Alex, this is my brother, Lonnie. He has a better memory for customers than I do."

"Your brother?" I almost thought it was a joke. Then I recalled dear old dad's appearance, and Lonnie's look suddenly didn't seem so farfetched.

"Lonnie. That's my name," he said with little enthusiasm.

I showed him Lepino's pic first. "Looks kind of familiar, I think." His droopy eyes looked up at me, as if awaiting my approval.

"This isn't a test. I just need an honest answer."

"Try the other guy," Junior said.

I thumbed to the picture of Christopher Barden, realizing this was another lost cause. Lonnie stuck out his neck and then put a finger on the phone. "Damn. I'm usually pretty good at this game."

"It's no game, Lonnie, but if they don't look familiar—"

"I know that scumbag." An ultra-thin woman with cropped red hair had sidled up to Lonnie and Junior while balancing a tray of food and glasses of wine.

I jumped out of my stool. "Tell me more."

"Hold on." She ran off and served the food, then walked back to the bar. "I'm not sure if the food servings are getting larger or I'm just getting weaker. I was shaking. Did you see that?" She flipped her extra-long fingernails against Lonnie's shoulder.

"Eh," he said.

"Tess is one of our longest-tenured waitresses at Monty's," Junior said.

"He's trying to say that I'm old as dirt." She let out a high-pitched giggle.

I stuck the phone in the middle of our space, Barden's face still on the screen. "So, you know this man?"

"Sure as hell do. Saw him here just the other night. He's one of those…" She looked around, then leaned in closer. "Players. You know, the guys who have all the money, think they can land any girl who walks through the door. Typically, though, the guy is married, and the girls they bed are half their age."

"Is that the case with him?"

"His name is Christopher. Don't recall his last name. He always paid in cash. Gave me a handsome tip, especially if he thought he was getting lucky that night."

"So, the other night, did you get a good tip?"

"Sure as hell did, sweet pea."

"What about this guy here?" I swapped out Christopher's picture for Rick's.

"This guy here…oh yeah. Can't forget him. Name's Rick something. He really threw his money around. Heard him sweet-talking some young girl. Practically undressing her in the middle of the restaurant."

I bit my lip, knowing we'd finally found a common thread between the two victims. Now, the tough part.

"This is going to sound odd, but do you recall if anyone was watching either of these two when they were here?"

"You mean, in a creepy way?" Her neck tensed, bones and ligament appearing as though they might break the skin.

"In any way."

Tess flipped on her heels to look around, then turned her head back to Junior. "Have you seen Peacoat tonight?"

"Uh, don't think so. It's been busy. I can't say for sure."

"Who's Peacoat?" I asked.

"A peculiar fella, always wears one of those Navy peacoats."

An image of Mark's coat of the same type came to mind. "Go

on."

"He was really shy, a little awkward. But I could see he had an eye on that table the other night. I thought he was checking out the pretty girl. He seemed closer to her age than that Rick prick."

"Tess," Junior said.

"Did I say that?" she said, pretending innocence.

"So," I said, swinging her attention back to me. "Do you recall if this same man in the peacoat was here when Christopher was here?"

"He's here all the time. I'd bet money he's seen both of those guys."

I asked, "Junior, do you have cameras in the restaurant?"

"Only at the front and back door."

"I need to see the video from the last month. But start out by giving me just two nights. Wednesday night and Tuesday night."

"Sure thing. It'll take a few hours. Might be in the morning."

"As soon as you can. Tess, do you know Peacoat's real name?"

"He always paid in cash. Not sure he had a credit card. He just seemed like a real simple guy."

I nodded, thinking more about what type of person we were dealing with. "Can you give me a good description?"

"Dark, thick, wavy hair. His peacoat was old. His hands were large and had callouses on them. Good-looking guy. Wore some scruff on his face each time I saw him. I thought he'd be a real charmer, but he was strange. Maybe, uh, what do you call it…OCD?"

"Obsessive-compulsive?"

"Always had to repeat the same routine every time. Got pissed when it didn't happen. One time, I took a peek over his shoulder, and he was staring at a bunch of numbers on his phone, mouthing the numbers, it seemed like. Not violent, just strange."

Junior touched my elbow to get my attention. "Can you tell us what you think this Peacoat fella did?"

"Rick Lepino and Christopher Barden were killed on separate nights. We're looking for anyone who has knowledge of their murders."

"Holy shit, Alex. Would have been nice to know that up front."

"Would have been nice to know your dad was an asshole, but I had to find that out the hard way, didn't I?"

Thirty-Seven

$\rule{2cm}{0pt}$⟨⊙⟨⊙⟨⊙⟩$\rule{2cm}{0pt}$

I pulled Nick's Impala up behind a row of cars parked along the side of Dartmouth Street, about half a block down and across the street from Monty's. Walking the streets, asking questions had finally paid dividends. The Barden-Lepino overlap had been established. And, thanks to Tess, we had a real suspect.

Outside of a vague description, we still didn't know Peacoat's name or any other information about him. And, frankly, we had no reason to think he had any involvement or knowledge of the murders, only an observation by a waitress that he appeared to be watching the two men who had later been killed. And, of course, he seemed "different." OCD was the term Tess had used.

With the off chance Peacoat would still show his face that night, I decided to give myself just one more hour outside Monty's. I cracked the driver's-side window so I wouldn't fog up the windshield, then killed the engine. These older FBI-issued cars had a tendency to overheat. How I knew that was beyond me, but it was still a trivial revelation when compared to the many gaps that remained in my memory.

It only took a couple of minutes for the nighttime chill to invade the inside of the car. As my eyes drifted down to the dust-covered dashboard, I could feel my shoulders tense up so much that the pain seeped up my neck into the base of my skull. Damn, I felt like a wimp, and all of this crap came from a fender bender. Okay, it might have been slightly more than that. But still, part of me knew that Alex Giordano was no wimp, in any sense of the word.

There weren't many people out on this night, which allowed me to eye each one that passed on each side of the street. A woman in red leather pants and five-inch heels clipped past my window, then jogged across the street. Talented.

Lots of pairs roamed the sidewalks. Older couples, buddies, lady friends. I could overhear snippets of their conversation. Most either complaining about their job or their significant other. It made me appreciate my life, despite my frustration from not truly connecting with my family members. Mark especially. Maybe something would change later tonight.

I lifted my sights to the front door at Monty's. A fireplug of a man wearing a Red Sox baseball cap exited and held open the door for a nicely dressed couple merged at the hip. They stepped onto the sidewalk—and my heart stopped.

Grabbing the steering wheel, I pulled myself closer to the windshield as the couple turned and walked west, away from my location. I forced out a breath, but my chest felt like a two-ton weight had just been dropped on it.

I said to no one, "What in the hell is Mark doing with that woman?"

Thirty-Eight

—⟨ɐ⁄ɐ⁄ɐ⟩—

Was it really Mark? I rubbed my eyes and refocused. The well-coiffed hair, his confident gait, even the ritzy Burberry cashmere trench coat.

Fuck! It's him, my husband. Practically molded to that woman.

A mane of dark hair flowed over her coat and down her back. I could see her tight calves slope down to black heels, professional, but sexy at the same time. They had to be Jimmy Choo, or a cheap knockoff.

Working late—that had been his excuse. Was there any way this was a late working dinner?

With my hands crushing the steering wheel, I looked closer, my eyes unblinking. The woman nuzzled her head inside Mark's comforting arm. Her arms enveloped his waist. Turning toward her, he appeared to tell her something. They kissed.

They fucking kissed!

"Fucking two-timing asshole!" With blood flooding my veins, I threw open the car door and jumped to the curb. Instantly, I lost my balance and fell against the open door. The dark sky was spinning, and I couldn't get my bearings. My breathing was erratic. Leaning down, I put two hands on my knees and focused on slowing my gasps. I kept looking over my shoulder, trying to find Mark and that woman.

"Get it together, Alex!" I demanded of myself.

Using the car door for balance, I pushed myself upright and spotted them sauntering down the sidewalk. I slammed the door shut, then took off in their direction. I only got three steps. They'd stopped next to a car. They hugged. Not like coworkers or even family. More like a couple who was in...

I couldn't even think the L word.

They kissed again, pausing for an extra second. Emotion engulfed my body, and I could feel each thud in my chest chip away at my heart. It didn't just ache; it was a stabbing, writhing pain. Was I having a frickin' heart attack on top of everything else?

I closed my eyes and, for a brief moment, forced my thoughts back to when I was a kid. I could feel the warm sunrays against my skin as I swayed this way and that on a small float in the ocean. Freedom, not a worry in the world.

I blinked and took in a couple of deep breaths to steady my pulse.

Opening my eyes again, Mark opened the back door of the older model Lexus and the woman got in, and then he joined her in the back seat. Who was driving the car? As I turned to get in Nick's car, my eyes spotted a man in the alley next to Monty's. He held something against his eye in the direction of Mark and the slut.

Wait. That was a camera.

Squeezing my eyes, I strained to get a better view. I could only make out a silhouette. Dark features, dark coat.

Was he wearing a peacoat?

I jerked my head back to the Lexus.

Red taillights came on.

Back to the man in the alley. He brought the camera down for a second. Then he turned his head my way. I wanted to call out, to ask him what the hell he was doing. But I thought I knew, so I withheld the urge. Had he seen me?

Then he faded into the blackness of the alley and was gone.

Which one should I go after? My cheating husband and his floozy, or the man who might be involved in the brutal slayings of…two cheating husbands?

Bile tickled the back of my throat. My hands were flat on the hood, my feet set, ready to dart in one direction or the other.

Suddenly, red lights flashed to life in the alley. There was a roar of an engine, a sports car of some kind. Then I heard rubber squealing off the pavement.

I turned back to Mark, and the Lexus's rear lights turned white—the car was going in reverse, pulling out of its parking position at the curb. I picked up two letters off the license plate. S and P—maybe.

Fuck! Which one should I follow? No time to call for help. I smacked my hands on the hood and jumped into Nick's car just as the Lexus surged forward. Throwing the gearshift into drive, I punched it, then slammed the brakes.

"What the fuck you lookin' at, woman?"

It was the fireplug wearing the Red Sox cap, the guy who'd held the door open for my cheating husband and his gal. He stood there in front of the car with his arms wide, his eyes even wider. An older woman was using a walker to cross the street.

I held up a hand and yelled through the crack in my window, "Sorry. Didn't see you."

"You tryin' to kill someone?"

"Come on, dammit." I pounded the steering wheel.

"Everyone's in a rush, I tell ya," he said, still standing guard in front of my hunk of metal as the woman, possibly his mother, inched across the street.

Craning my neck, I could see the Lexus coast under a

streetlamp. The car was navy blue, a gold stripe down the side. It turned left onto Beacon and vanished out of my sight.

"It's a damn shame. No one cares about slowin' down, enjoying life," the fireplug continued.

The old woman finally made it to the curb. He looked at her, then at me. Was he deciding whether to help her up the curb or to continue his rant against me?

Finally, he held up a hand and shuffled over to the woman. I gunned it, although I didn't intend on tires squeaking. A hundred feet, and I pushed through a yellow light onto Beacon. This road had more traffic. I wove around cars as fast as possible, hoping the Lexus hadn't turned down another side street.

Just ahead, I saw a Lexus turn left. I surged forward, then hit the brakes hard to execute the turn. I then spotted the Lexus parked against the curb—it was black with no stripes and a new model.

Wrong car. Crap!

I hit the brakes again. Car horns blared all around me. Twisting the steering wheel back to my right, the symphony of horns only increased. I saluted everyone who could see me with my middle finger and forced myself back into the traffic moving west on Beacon.

"I lost them, dammit," I said to myself.

For a brief second, I thought about the choice I'd made: Mark over the man in the peacoat. I couldn't let someone else die, not like that.

"Just call Nick." Apparently, I liked talking to myself.

Leaning left, I found my purse while my eyes remained focused on the street. I fumbled through the purse, but my fingers couldn't find anything thin and metal.

"Crap. Where is it?"

I was so fucking pissed at the world I could have punched a hole in the window. But that wouldn't help me find my phone or the Lexus that held my husband and his…whatever she was to him.

A momentary lapse of focus. If someone else was driving the Lexus, what were Mark and the woman doing in the back seat? A quick snippet of another time came to mind. I was younger, in my twenties, and I recalled a passionate kiss with Mark in the back of a limousine. We lost ourselves in each other. Suddenly, I was on top of him, rocking his world, and mine too.

Tears bubbled at the corners of my eyes. I slammed a fist off the steering wheel. "Stop it, Alex. Get your shit together, dammit!"

With my eyes focused well ahead of me as I drove, it wasn't until the last second that I saw the brake lights. But that second counted. I jammed the brakes and rocked to a stop about an inch behind a Hummer. I could hear a deafening bass as it rattled the Impala. I cursed the Hummer, if for no other reason than it was in my way, but it gave me a quick moment to reach over and grabbed my purse.

I tossed out anything and everything that wasn't a cell phone. The streetlight turned green, and I punched it just as I dumped the contents of my purse on the seat next to me. Trading glances between the road and my purse, I still couldn't find my cell phone.

"Fuck, fuck, fuck." That made me feel better, at least for a few seconds.

My eyes scanned up ahead. *There!*

I spotted a car zipping by on the upcoming cross street. I was almost certain it was a blue Lexus. Nudging the nose of the Impala into the opposite lane of traffic, I gave a quick glance around and then gunned it.

Lights were headed right for me, about four-feet high off the pavement. It was a huge truck. Horns filled the air, and I yelled out, pressing my arms against the steering wheel. Sweat bubbled on my forehead as I jerked the car back into my lane just before impact. I emptied my lungs, feeling like I'd just played a three-set match.

Seconds later, I bothered to obey the law a little bit and flipped my blinker. The fact the light was red didn't go unnoticed, but I didn't have a choice. I had to find Mark, to confront him for what he'd done, or was about to do.

I turned right and realized I was on a bridge, driving north across the Charles River. The illuminated water rippled with whites and yellows and a smattering of red. I pressed the gas and reached fifty in no time. I could see ahead to the other side of the bridge, where a Lexus disappeared around a tree-lined curve.

Or had my eyes deceived me? I couldn't turn back at this juncture, so I forged ahead. I rolled off the bridge, but moved at a pedestrian thirty-five miles per hour. Within the time it took to cross the bridge, snow flurries now poured from the sky as if the lid to a salt shaker had fallen off. Visibility was cut in half, and despite living north of the Mason-Dixon Line, the folks driving the four or five cars in front of me had this notion of playing it safe.

Playing safe didn't register in my mind. Not with my life seemingly cracking at the edges right before my eyes.

Just as I was considering another dangerous passing maneuver, I felt something heavy jostle against my leg. I patted my coat. It was my cell phone.

Of course. I'd left it in there after my visit with the crowd at Monty's. Had the FBI not thought about getting Bluetooth for all its vehicles? Safer, more efficient...ah crap, who was I kidding? It would never happen.

I refocused my energy on the here and now. One of the cars in the procession slowed down and completed a turtle-like turn. One down, four to go. I was almost certain I could see the Lexus up ahead, moving at a sane speed, probably not thinking they were being tailed. I realized these cars between us were actually good cover, allowing me to follow without being noticed.

I tried to separate my personal self from my professional self for just a moment. I pulled out my phone and punched up Nick's line. It rang four times then went to voicemail.

"Nick, Alex here. I'm in pursuit of…well, forget that part for now. I need you to call me back. We might have a lead on Peacoat."

I tapped the phone dead. Then it hit me. Nick had no idea who or what Peacoat was. "Dammit!" I was acting like a frickin' rookie. Actually, more like a college freshman chasing after my man.

Fuck him!

But here I was, tailing him and a woman, and some mysterious driver, to…where the hell were they going? We'd just passed Cambridge, where I'd met Nick and Brad at the Starbucks earlier in the day. Now I was seeing signs for Arlington. Thanks to the thick, wet snow, the cars ahead of me had slowed to thirty miles per hour. Still, every time we hit a bend in the road, I could see the Lexus, although it was almost a quarter mile in front.

Toying with the phone in my right hand, an idea hit me. What if I called the player himself? I could ask him what was up, all casual-like, tell him I was heading home after a long day of work. What if I had the gall, or guts, to ask him if he wanted to stop at a hotel and have crazy sex?

The thought sent a shot of acid into my throat. I couldn't fool myself. I'd been searching for that seed of a connection with Mark, and I thought I'd found it. Felt it. But why did I have to try so hard? He'd seemed distant, and that only made me wonder what our life was really like pre-crash. Maybe this was it—secrets, lies, and fucking other women.

A quick thought zapped my brain. Was there any way I'd learned about Mark's indiscretions before I lost my memory?

My eyes saw red a split second before my brain recognized it. And it almost cost me. Jerking the car left, it fishtailed on the slick surface. But I released the brake at the precise moment needed to miss the truck stopped in the middle of the road. I ended up with two front tires off the road, but not far enough where I needed a tow. I caught my breath for a moment, then put the car in reverse. I could hear the tires spinning against the pavement. The conditions were growing worse by the minute.

But I couldn't stop until I figured out where Mark was going. What I would do when we met up? I couldn't predict.

Once back on the road, through the thick snow, I saw a set of car lights moving over the upcoming hill at an accelerated rate of speed.

Had they somehow figured out they were being followed?

With my fingers gripping the wheel, I picked up the pace—as much as I could. I squinted and realized the numbnut behind me had his brights on. Flipping the switch on the rearview mirror to block the lights, I refocused my sights on the Lexus, now almost a half mile in front of me.

For a quick second, I flashed back to Peacoat and wondered where he'd gone. Why had he been taking pictures of Mark and the woman? I almost didn't want to go there. If he was the ring killer, was he gathering intel on his next victim…Mark, my husband?

I could feel my pulse begin to labor. The thought of Mark being tortured like that brought back another dose of emotions. Maybe he was a lying, cheating asshole. But he was my asshole, at least for now. And no one deserved that type of punishment.

Then again, the anger and resentment stirred inside of me like a boiling pot of water, ready to burn anyone who touched it.

My phone buzzed. I kept one eye on the road, then quickly read a text from Nick.

What or who is pcoat?????

Not surprising. He needed more context. In a few minutes,

once I reached my destination, I'd call him back.

Pressing harder on the gas pedal, I almost caught air descending down a hill, and for a second, I thought I'd lose control. The tires gripped the snow and kept a straight path, but then there was a quick curve. I leaned right. The back end slipped just a tad.

Then I felt a bump. I glanced in my rearview mirror. The car behind me had rammed the right rear panel. And it didn't stop. My car started spinning.

I could hear myself scream as I tried turning violently left and then right. But I had no control over the two tons of metal, or my fate. On one of my rotations, I saw more lights heading right for me. I held my breath. Then the Impala slid off the road, my face was smashed, and everything went black.

Thirty-Nine

Herb honked his horn just as his brakes squealed to a stop in front of One Center Plaza, FBI's main office in Boston's West End.

"Appreciate the drop-off. You ought to apply for Uber. Make some money on the side."

"Uber, my ass. I tow what no one else can, cars and trucks." The man who looked like a grizzly bear tapped his greasy fingers on the dash of his growling tow truck. "And Old Betsy here is the best. Hasn't let me down yet. I just did this as a favor to you and the FBI. You know, to serve my country and all. I couldn't let you freeze to death, get buried in the snow. Hell, you look like you got in a fight with a Chinese star. No offense."

Looking out the windshield of Old Betsy, I spotted Nick, Jerry, and Brad converging just outside the front door. I'd updated all three on a quick conference call earlier while I waited for Herb to clean out his front seat to make room for me.

I climbed out and threw a twenty-dollar bill on the center console. "That's all I got. You can bill me later."

He coughed out a laugh and stuffed the bill in his gray jacket. "No worries. This ride was free. I'll put this toward the car tow. That will cost ya."

I slammed the heavy door shut as he choked out another laugh.

Trudging through snow that felt more like packed quicksand, I joined the boys. Nick and Brad were shivering shamelessly while Jerry, wearing nothing more than a brown sports coat that probably fit him back in college, seemed like he was out for a casual evening stroll…except for the scowl on his face.

"After this is all over, we've got lots to talk about," he said, opening the door to the building for all of us.

Nick put his arm on my shoulder. "You don't need to go to the hospital?"

I'd eaten eggs less scrambled than my brain felt, but every other body part was intact. "I'm fine."

Nick turned me around as we all dusted snow off our coats. "You always say that. And your face is…"

"I could think of a couple of comebacks, but now's not the right time. The airbag went off, and that's a good thing."

"That explains some of the cuts and burn marks on your face, but you have a pretty deep gash on the side of your head. Did you bang your head against the glass?"

I wasn't sure of anything at this stage, but I did suddenly remember something. I held up the middle finger of my left hand. "Don't make fun of me, but I tried to experiment with fake nails this morning." The nail on that finger was gone.

Nick looked closer at my cut. "I think the fingernail is still embedded in your head."

"Later. We'll deal with it later. We don't have much time." I walked from the group. "Someone going to show me the way?"

"Forgot you didn't know where you were going," Jerry muttered.

Nick pulled up beside me. "You never liked this office even before the crash. I mean the first crash."

"Funny."

We took the elevator up to the fourth floor where a team was already assembled, and we gathered in a huge, open area labeled "War Room 1."

I threw my coat over a chair and walked to a table as Jerry pulled out his cell phone and took a call.

"What do we have on the Lexus, or on Peacoat? Give me something," I said, tilting my head to lay eyes on an enormous flat-screen showing a digital map of the area west of Boston. I looked around and noticed I'd been abandoned. Nick was huddling with Jerry, who still had the phone to his ear. Brad had peeled off and was speaking with a female colleague, who had a laptop in front of her. I saw four other people about the same age anchored behind their computers, all angled toward the front of the room, where I stood.

When Brad walked back over, I pointed to the group of five. "Who are they?"

"My team of analysts."

"You have a team?"

"I'm a team lead during critical situations like this. More of a liaison between the investigators and research analysts who are brought in. If we don't know it, we'll find it. Legally, of course."

"Of course."

I glanced back over my shoulder and saw the older guys getting animated. Not a good sign.

"Do you know if they, or anyone here, has been able to locate the Lexus?"

He shook his head. "Haven't seen or heard anything, but it's only been an hour since the team has been assembled. Jerry could be getting an update right now."

We turned to look at the map. Brad said, "I know it's none of my business, but your husband Mark was reportedly in this older model Lexus?"

"There are no suppositions. It's true. I saw him with my own eyes." I swallowed back a hint of emotion and some pride. "Brad, it is your business. Mark left that bar with another woman I've never seen, and it's obvious they weren't bowling partners. He got into the back seat of the Lexus, and someone drove it northwest out of Boston. I tailed him all the way up until I had the wreck."

A quick loop replayed in my mind. While I pondered what it meant, Brad was muttering something.

"Alex, did you hear me?"

"What?"

"Are you sure you didn't suffer a worse head injury?"

"Hell no. I'm fine." My eyes shifted to the screen, but it only served as the backdrop for that same video playing in my mind. I gripped Brad's forearm and looked him in the eyes. "Brad, I just remembered something important."

Forty

Brad glanced at my hand on his arm, and then up to my gaze.

"I got clipped by another car."

"I heard that's what you believed, yes."

I paused, wondering if he and the others thought less of not only my opinion, but also my ability to recall basic facts.

"I'm not bullshitting you." A few heads turned my way.

"Sorry. I don't mean to doubt you. Go on."

"Two things. First, when I was spinning out of control, I now remember seeing a brown sedan pass me. That was the car that hit me."

He motioned for me to follow him as he walked up to the same girl he was speaking to before. "Describe the car."

I closed my eyes for a brief moment.

"Just your first thoughts. Anything."

"It was light brown. Tan, four doors."

"Foreign or domestic?"

"Domestic. I think."

"You're getting this?" he asked the girl.

"Yes, Brad," she said calmly as she typed faster than I knew was possible.

"Anything else about the car?"

"Had a prominent grill. Oh, and the wheels were a simple, smooth metal, no design."

He nodded and then looked over the analyst's shoulder.

"Sorry I don't have a plate or a specific make or model."

"That's okay," he said, glancing down to get the analyst's confirmation.

She said, "I'll tap into the DMV database and start trying to put a net around a subset of vehicles, then overlap that with owners living in the five counties immediately in or around Boston."

Brad held up a hand, looking like he was about to add something, but the attractive girl spoke up first. "And, I'll ask Landon back here to start pulling camera feeds from around the Monty's location."

I said, "Good, thanks. We don't have much time. We need a lead. Quickly, uh…"

"Bianca," she said through tight lips.

Brad turned back to me. "What's the second thing?"

"Right." I quickly replayed the few seconds when the Impala took the curve and then feeling the loss of control, wondering if I was going to be blasted into oblivion by the large truck.

"The person who did this had training. They executed the PIT maneuver to precision."

Nick had just marched over. "You said you thought you were bumped?" he asked.

I nodded.

"Not just a hit-and-run?"

"It was a hit-and-run, but by someone who is or has been in law enforcement."

Brad shuffled a couple of steps and shared the information with his pretty little assistant, and I turned my attention to crisis number two.

"Nick, tell me you got something on Peacoat."

He smacked his gums just once. "Nothing. Not yet. Looking through mug shots won't help, right? You didn't really see his face."

"Not really, no."

"Are you sure he was taking pictures of Mark and this…?"

"Woman, Nick. He was with a woman. It makes me want to bite a hole through my lip, but from what I saw, they hadn't just met. That's right. He's having an affair with another woman."

I sucked in deep breaths, doing everything in my power to keep it together. I laid my hand on Nick's shoulder. "He might be a two-timing asshole, but I can't let anything happen to him. Not until I get my hands on him."

"I understand completely. And once we find him, I'll be the second in line to kick his ass from here to Back Bay."

I snapped my fingers and said, "Nick, remember seeing the gold paint on the other car I crashed? Well, the one that clipped me tonight was tan. Tan, gold, similar colors. It could be the same car."

I put both hands over my face and tried to think. "I need a whiteboard. Now."

Within seconds, Brad rolled one up from the corner and handed me a red marker.

I nodded, then uncapped the pen and wrote *Profile* across the top. "Tess told us the Peacoat she knew was awkward. OCD, even." I wrote down *OCD* and underlined it. "What does that sound like to you, guys?"

"Like the guy has social issues," Nick said. "He's probably most awkward around women."

"To the point where, what? Maybe he was trying to prove something to a woman." I fidgeted with the pen cap. "Brad, did you ever find anything on Agatha Barden?"

"Dammit, I forgot to send that to you. I have it right here." He grabbed his tablet off a desk and tapped the screen about a dozen times, then he held up a finger. "We found numerous Facebook posts with her complaining that she wasn't getting any at home. She actually said, quote, 'If Christopher thinks he's the only one who knows how to lure another person to bed, then he's got another thing coming.'"

I nodded. "Any mention of retribution?"

"Not on Facebook. But we found an interesting recent text conversation between her and her brother-in-law."

"Trent?" I was a bit surprised, given the history with Christopher's brother-in-law. "Why was it interesting?"

"It was in code, essentially. We deciphered it this afternoon. It was mostly fluff, but there were references to the size of certain appendages and something about them dancing in the sheets that Christopher owned."

"Around us, she had acted like Trent was scum. I wonder if she acted that way so we wouldn't suspect the two of them working together. Where's the reference to payback against Christopher?"

"That was it. Basically having sex in his house, his bed."

I tapped the marker in my hand. "Now that I think about it, it all makes sense."

"What? What makes sense?" Nick asked while removing a piece of gum from its package and curling it into his mouth.

"Trent's a mess, but he's not awkward around women. And we didn't see anything to indicate he's OCD or anything. So I think that might rule out the team of Agatha and Trent."

"So what are you thinking?"

"Nothing concrete yet. Tess mentioned Peacoat had this strange fascination with numbers and repeating behaviors. Add that to the awkward social skills."

Nick snapped his fingers. "*Good Will Hunting!*"

I turned and wrote *Math Whiz* on the board with two arrows

pointing to *social skills* and *number fixation*. When I flipped around, Brad's mouth was half open, ready to add something. But I beat him to it. "This also means he's probably smarter than all three of us put together."

Nick scratched his chin. "But are all math geniuses socially awkward? Think about the Matt Damon character. He had some decent moves for Minnie Driver's character."

I heard Bianca clear her throat, and I glanced her way. She appeared to shift her eyes. Maybe she thought she was the bomb. I gave Brad the look. He moved over to Bianca, and they spoke briefly. She stood up and stepped toward me.

"My brother is..." She tilted her head. "Kind of shy. Well, actually, he's really awkward. No social skills whatsoever. But he's also pretty smart."

"Are you saying you think he's a suspect?" I asked.

"No, no. I just wanted to say that your description was pretty accurate. But it was tough growing up with him. Not every kid is like this, but my brother had episodes where he just lost it. I think he was lashing just because he knew he was different and didn't know what to do about it."

I thought about the two murder scenes, the attention to detail to not only torture the men, but also shame them.

"Thank you," I said calmly, even though my gut was churning like a blender.

She nodded and started to turn back to her computer. Then she flipped back around and said, "I didn't give my brother justice. He's smart as hell. There is nothing he can't do, especially with numbers and computers. Brilliant."

Brad practically jumped at me. "Alex, Nick, check this shit out. The items stolen from the museum? I have their catalog numbers. There's something about the combination or sequence that stands out, but I can't figure it out. None of us can. Not yet."

I wrote *Museum Catalog Numbers* on the board and underlined it three times. "So we're basically saying that the tan car that clipped me tonight could be the same car that made me crash when I left the museum almost a week ago, right? And we're also theorizing that this Peacoat fella robbed the museum?"

"Do you remember Mr. Trow pointing out the randomness of the items stolen?" Nick asked.

"Exactly. But, in hearing Brad here, maybe the historical collectibles weren't his target. Follow the number trail." I tapped my pen again. "The museum had its video footage erased. Someone hacked into their computer system. Someone damn smart was behind that."

We all nodded.

"Is there any possibility this same guy was the sniper on your second visit?" Brad asked.

I turned and wrote *Sniper????* on the board. "Doesn't fit the profile, but we'll keep it up there."

"I've waited long enough, dammit. Give me the confirmation I need to do my job," Jerry yelled into his phone. He was across the room, and we could hear him loud and clear. I ignored his grumpiness as more pictures of the ocean crossed my mind. I looked back up at the big screen with the map. "I think I recall my dad, Nick."

"Damn, Alex. Freaky timing, but that's great."

I could see my dad's pointer finger showing me things on a map. I must have been ten or eleven years old. I recalled a logo on his shirt.

"He was in the Coast Guard," I said. "And he was really into maps. Every place on Earth could be identified as an intersection of longitude and latitude."

The three of us traded stares, then I turned and popped the pen off the white board. "We're looking for a white male, dark features, who wears a Peacoat, could be a computer genius, has awkward social skills, and likely needed some prodding or incentive from someone. I'm guessing a woman, an older woman. Not sure about the law-enforcement connection, though."

"Yes…" Nick rolled his arms in a *keep-it-coming* motion.

"It's got to be in the numbers. Can we pull up a map of the longitudes and latitudes of both murder scenes?"

Brad scooted over to one of his team members. "Can you bring that up?"

The guy nodded.

Then he got the attention of his team and pointed to my red scribble on the whiteboard. "Get this down and start to identify a list of suspects."

"How quickly do you need it?" Bianca asked.

"An hour ago."

I looked at Nick and lifted an eyebrow. Who would have thought that pretty boy Brad could bring the heat when he had to. I was impressed.

Forty-One

The map went dark, dropping shadows on the room, then it came back to life with a grid placed over the eastern part of Massachusetts. Two red balloons appeared on the map.

"Darla, give us the long-lat of the murder at Choate Island," Brad said to one of the other gals on his team.

I looked up and read the screen: 42.66408 / -70.744.293.

"What does the negative number mean? I know, I'm not Coast Guard material," Nick said.

"Anything south of the equator is considered a negative latitude, anything west of the prime meridian is considered a negative longitude," I said. "In case you're wondering, the prime meridian is in Greenwich, England."

We studied the numbers, and I calculated in my head. "If you add those numbers together, you get a negative 28 point something."

The complete number flashed on the screen and it read: -28.080245.

"What about the murder in Sandy Bay?"

"Give me one second," Bianca said, her perfect complexion now with a trench between her round eyes.

About five seconds later, we saw the following equation:

42.664770 / -70.619849 = -27.955079.

Three of the analysts lifted their heads and began to study the numbers along with Brad, Nick, and me. Jerry was still in a heated phone conversation across the room.

Seconds turned into minutes, and the only thing that could be heard was an occasional rattle of a keyboard and the associated hum of the laptops. But no one had a theory.

"I don't have a fucking clue. Anyone?" I scanned all faces, but came up empty.

Brad looked at me over his shoulder. "I still have to show you the catalog numbers from the museum. Later, once we figure this long-lat puzzle."

"Put them up on the screen here," I said.

Brad paused for a moment.

"Look, a numbers savant could do any one of a million things with these numbers. While I'm guessing the longitude and latitude are part of it, maybe there's an overlap with other numbers. The stolen artifacts' catalog numbers are a good place to start."

Five minutes later, seventeen catalog numbers were listed vertically on the right side of the screen.

Biting my lip, I tried to think what these numbers represented together that they didn't represent individually.

"Add up all those numbers in the column," I said to the team.

A moment passed, then the girl said, "Here we go."

The first two numbers were eighty-four.

"Wait," Brad said. "Remember, we found two of those items on the Dark Web. There's a possibility that Peacoat didn't steal those." He walked over to the table where his team sat, and a minute later, only fifteen items remained with a new total. The first two numbers were eighty-two.

My mind could suddenly see how this all added up.

"Cool. Now, add the longitude and latitude together for both locations. Then, ignore the negatives and add them together, and then subtract that number from your eighty-two. What do you get?"

A moment passed, and Nick walked over next to me.

"Who's the Rain Man…I mean, Rain Woman?"

"Let's see."

Brad ran his long fingers through his hair as he and Bianca worked the grid from her computer.

I forced myself to breathe, then tried to rock side to side. Seconds felt like minutes—no, hours. I could feel my shoulders tense up again, but not from the cold. The stress of finding a killer, finding my husband, wondering if the two events were connected.

The silence was finally broken by Brad.

"Holy shit."

I looked up at the big screen, which showed the updated numbers and a third balloon.

Brad said, "We're left with the coordinates of a third location." He pointed to a location up the coast near Lynn. "It's in Nahant Bay."

Jerry had just walked up, his eyes boring holes in me.

"Jerry, this might be a bit of a stretch, but we need a team to go to this location at Nahant Bay."

"Alex," he said somberly.

"Jerry, you're not moving. What's going on?" I paused a moment, a cork in my mind plugging my emotional bucket. "It's about the Lexus and Mark, isn't it?"

He nodded and tried to reach for me. I took a step back.

"Alex, state police found the Lexus in a hotel parking lot about ten miles north of where you went off the road."

"And Mark?"

"He wasn't in the car. The driver had a bullet in the back of his head, and the woman had been knocked unconscious."

I closed my eyes for a second. My blood ran cold, and a fog began to coat my brain. I wondered if my body might completely shut down. I bit my lip hard, which ignited my senses.

"Have they searched the area? Maybe he's hurt, looking for help."

"According to the sergeant I spoke with, his officers said there's no sign of blood outside the car. But they've called out more officers and are conducting a broader search."

I turned and squeezed Nick's arm. "Peacoat. It's him. He targeted Mark for being the lying piece of shit that he is. He must have seen me, maybe knew who I was, and tried to take me out, then hunted down the Lexus and took Mark."

Brad stepped over. "It's just crazy to think that he wouldn't ensure you were dead, or for that matter…" His blue eyes shifted to the floor.

"You mean the other woman," I said, turning back to my boss. "Jerry, we need an agent at this woman's bedside the moment she wakes up."

"Makes sense. I'll call Kowalski. He lives out that way." Jerry got on the phone.

I took in a jittery breath, and when I turned around, Brad was standing there with a bottled Diet Coke.

"You used to drink this stuff when we worked late on a case."

"Thanks, Brad." I cracked the top and chugged two mouthfuls.

Jerry turned back to me. "Kowalski is on his way to the hospital to talk to the woman. I reached Mason and Silvagni and told them to head to Nahant Bay. And I included Randy on a quick three-way call just to keep him in the loop."

I muttered a four-letter word under my breath.

"I know," Jerry said. "We'll deal with that later as well. Brad, send Mason and Silvagni the exact coordinates."

"Will do."

"The road conditions aren't getting any better," Jerry said. "So, even if Mason and Silvagni make it that far, who's to say this Peacoat guy will go through with his whole macabre scene?"

I let Jerry's words play in my mind, and I tried to think like the person we'd conjured up in our profile.

Jerry shuffled a couple of steps closer to the big screen. "So we're basing our theory on catalog numbers from the museum theft along with the longitude and latitude of the previous murder scenes?" He pulled at his face like it was made of rubber.

"We think Peacoat is some type of socially-challenged genius. It appears he's fascinated with patterns."

"Why the hell would he steal those items from the museum to begin with?"

"Maybe he's just a colonial buff? Or maybe he did it for someone else?"

"I've read all the case notes. I know you considered partner theories when you thought a woman might be pulling the strings, but you seem pretty certain about this Peacoat guy. The guy you saw outside of Monty's, did he look strong enough to pull this off?"

"Absolutely."

Nick chimed in. "Like you said, Jerry, Peacoat might break his routine because of the weather or because he knows we're on to him. Who knows where he is? Or who he is? Given what we think we know, he might not have a regular job. Needle in a haystack."

"With a foot of snow on top," Brad added.

I chugged some Diet Coke, letting the sizzling carbonation penetrate my senses. Then a lightning bolt shot through my skull.

"Hey, you." I marched five steps and tapped the pretty girl with the raven-black hair on the shoulder.

She practically jumped out of her seat, jostling her long locks into her face. "Bianca, remember?"

"Sorry. How did parents deal with your brother's habits and awkwardness?"

Her button eyes looked down for a moment, then she scooted up in her chair. "Now that I think about it, they enrolled him in this group of like-minded kids hoping he'd relate better to people like him. I think it ended up being more of a support group for my parents. My brother just didn't have a desire to socialize. And when you think about it, this current digital environment makes it even easier for kids to hide behind a computer screen."

"Do you recall the name of the support group?"

"Math Wizards Extraordinaire. MWE. I think my parents are still involved to a degree."

"We need access to their database. We need to find a historical list of males living in this area. Guys in their twenties and thirties. Can you do that for me?"

"Uh…" Her eyes shifted to Brad, then Jerry.

I spoke up again. "We don't have time for negotiation with them, and we sure as hell don't have time to get a warrant. I need you to make it happen. Talk to your parents, call the president of the organization."

"At one in the morning?" she asked.

"Does that make a difference if someone is going to die?"

"No, ma'am."

She pulled out her phone and was talking to someone in less than twenty seconds. I walked back over to Nick and Brad.

"Nick, I think I need to go to Nahant Bay."

"What? That's not a good idea, Alex."

Jerry stuck his belly in the middle of our conversation. "The weather sucks, Alex. Just leave it to Mason and Silvagni." He tilted his head as if he'd just made a compelling closing argument. I gave him nothing, so he continued.

"Who knows if you can even make it up there? And we know

it's just a random theory anyway. It could be a waste of your time. You're better off here, helping us try to find real leads."

I went over and grabbed my coat, then turned back to the group, wagging my cell phone. "New technology. You can actually call me even when I'm not near a landline."

I turned to Bianca and opened my arms. She was on the phone, but covered it and said, "I'm working on it."

Facing my colleagues in the room, I upped my volume to make sure everyone heard me. "I need a list of possible suspects in twenty minutes. Call me to review each one. Is that clear?"

The men and women either nodded or said yes, then quickly got back to work.

I then walked up to Jerry with my hand extended. "I need my gun."

"You can't have it."

"Why not?"

He smacked one beefy hand into the other. "I need the doctor's note," he said in perfect rhythm.

"What you really need to see is that my brain is functioning properly. Haven't you just seen that here, tonight?"

He scratched the back of his head and shuffled in place.

"If you don't give me my Glock, I'm going to the closest pawn shop and buying the biggest gun I can find."

Nick had just pulled up next to me. "At least she's not asking to borrow my backup piece."

"Crap." Jerry walked out of the room and returned a minute later with the Glock in my shoulder holster.

I grabbed it, but he didn't let go. "You're close to this one, Alex. Too close. They'll have my ass for breakfast if you fuck this up."

"Yes sir."

He stabbed a finger at Nick. "And you don't let her fuck this up."

I jogged out of the room, pulling Nick along. Then I yelled back to everyone. "A list of suspects in sixteen minutes and counting."

Forty-Two

All I could hear were windshield wipers squeaking against the glass. And voices too. But they were indecipherable. I focused on the repetitive screech and even found myself counting them out loud. Anything to drown out the piercing agony.

The metal edge of my cell phone dug into my fingers. Then a hand touched mine.

Glancing up, I saw Nick's green eyes. His compassionate, concerned eyes.

Rocking in my seat, I could feel a swelling pressure in my chest, trying to bury the news we'd just heard from Mason and Silvagni: Mark's dead body had just been found floating in the shallow waters of Nahant Bay.

Just like Barden. Just like Lepino.

But he wasn't just like Barden and Lepino. He'd been a man I'd married fifteen years ago, and I now knew what he'd meant to me.

The father to our two beautiful children. A patient, kind person. A fun-loving jokester. A best friend and an even better lover. A partner for life, or so I'd thought for the last fifteen years.

My chin quivered like a jackhammer. I tried to speak, but nothing came out. There were no words to define the blade twisting in my gut.

And there was no way to describe how I felt about Mark's unconscionable betrayal.

I must have known about it before my first crash. The sense of separation had been festering for months, maybe longer. I couldn't recall all the details, but I knew he'd emotionally checked out on me and the family long ago. For this other woman, I assumed. Maybe there was more than just one. I wasn't sure I'd ever find out. I wasn't sure I really wanted to know.

I hated Mark. But I loved him too. It made no sense. We were destined for divorce. And what about Erin and Luke?

A blast of cold air invaded my wet eyes.

"Alex." A pat on my hand.

I focused my eyes. Nick was trying to ask me a question. Over his shoulder someone was at his window, as snow fell like ashes from an inferno.

"Are you sure you want to go to the murder scene? According to the officer here, they've closed off the roads to pedestrian traffic. They'll let us by, though… Only if you feel like you have to do it."

I couldn't say no.

I nodded, then Nick turned his head and said something to the officer. My phone buzzed. I punched it up and put it on speaker.

"Alex, we've got the suspect list." It was Brad, his voice on hyper-drive.

I wiped my eyes and tried to break free from the emotional fog of despair. "Tell me."

I could hear the suction of the windows closing as Nick put the car in drive. We turned right off 107 and headed east.

"Bianca's dad got the president of the support group on the phone and convinced her to give us temporary access to the database. Bianca ran some queries, and we've got a few who fit our profile. Here they are."

Brad cleared his throat and then I heard a mumbled voice and footsteps. During those few seconds, I could feel Nick's stare. I said, "If you don't watch the road, I'll experience my third crash in the last week."

"But—"

"Nick, I'm not made of balsa wood. You focus on driving, I'll focus on the suspects."

"You there?" Brad asked for clarification.

"Yes. How many?"

"We've been able to most likely narrow the list down to five."

"Most likely?"

"You gave us twenty minutes. If we have more time, we could vet the top twenty or much deeper."

"Vet tomorrow. I want to catch this maniac tonight. Give me your top five."

"Alex, I—"

"I know, I know. It comes with a huge caveat. I got it."

"Yeah, that too. But I just heard from Jerry about…I'm so sorry. I can't imagine what you're feeling right now."

I swallowed hard. "Thanks, Brad. Now give me the damn list."

"Number one is thirty-three years old, a painter. But we believe he's studying at an art school outside of Paris. We just don't have confirmation. Again, with more time, we could verify if he's there or if he used that as a ruse while he stayed here and implemented his demented serial-killing plan."

The age seemed a bit old, and I couldn't see this Peacoat guy as a painter, whether he was in Europe or stateside. "Move on to the next one."

"Number two works in the math department at Boston College. He's twenty-seven and was recently arrested for assaulting two male students for sexually harassing a female student."

Someone with a vendetta mindset. "That could be him. Is he in jail? Do we have an address?"

I heard Brad say something to Bianca. "We're working on that info. Moving on to number three…"

The phone jostled for a few seconds. "Yes, number three. Not much on him, other than he's thirty-six and works at a grocery in Waltham."

Too old again, but some people looked much younger than their age, so I couldn't completely rule him out.

"Do you have mug shots on all of these guys?"

"A few. I'll have Bianca send you what we have. Number four lives in New York City. He works on Wall Street as a financial analyst. He's twenty-nine. Still verifying his attendance at work the last several days."

"Makes sense."

Nick laid on the horn, and I saw a German shepherd galloping across the snow-filled street.

"Damn dog just flew in out of the dark. Who lets their dogs out in weather like this?" Nick muttered.

I stared back toward the phone.

"Alex, Bianca just hit send. You should see the mug shots in a few seconds."

"What about number five? You did say you had five suspects, right?"

"I'm getting there. This last guy is just twenty-four. We actually were able to reach his boss and—"

"Where does he work?"

"The docks in Gloucester. Boss says he's a good kid, stays to himself, works hard, gets along with everyone."

"Hmm."

"Hmm, what?" Brad asked.

"There's got to be more."

"Oh, well, he flunked out of two universities before he turned twenty."

"Which ones?"

"Bunker Hill Community College and…hold on a second."

More mumbled conversations. I looked up at the tree-lined road. The headlights illuminated branches sagging from the weight of the snow.

"Alex," Brad said, bringing my attention back to the phone, "the other university was MIT."

"MIT as in Massachusetts Institute of Technology?"

"I know what you're thinking, but remember he flunked out."

"But he got in. People flunk out for various reasons. Doesn't mean they weren't smart enough. Remember, this guy was part of that MWE group. Getting through college might have been a very challenging social experience."

"True."

"Could have created lots of anxiety, possibly forcing him into very strange behavior."

"But he's been the model employee. And it sounds like he's really into the blue-collar job."

"Has he been at work every day the last week?"

"Perfect attendance."

I volleyed the data points around in my mind, even brought my head down and rested it on my hand.

"Alex, you okay?" Nick asked.

"Fine. Just thinking."

Brad broke my concentration. "Take number two off the list."

"The professor at Boston College? Why?"

"Just found out he was killed in a skiing accident a week ago."

I felt my phone buzz, and I tapped the email from Bianca. It pulled up the camera roll, and I thumbed through mug shots of three guys.

"I looked at the pictures, Brad. My view earlier tonight was quick, across the street and poor lighting, but none of these do it for me. Wish I had the mugs of the other two."

A slight pause. "You only got three?"

"Tres. Three."

"Bianca…" and then his voice trailed off.

"Frickin' weather is making the connection cut in and out," I said to Nick. When I didn't hear anything for a few more seconds, I shouted, "Brad!"

"I'm here. Hold on. She accidently left one out. We don't have anything on the painter. Here comes the last one we have."

I tapped her new email and opened the picture.

I could feel my pulse taking off. "Brad, what's the address on number five?"

"We have them pinned on the map I'm looking at," Brad said. "Number five, a J. L. Cobb, has a small residence in the middle of nowhere in Rockport, north of Gloucester. It's right on the ocean."

Nick locked eyes with mine for a split second, then set his sights back to the road and said, "Do you want to go to see something that will eat at you the rest of your life, or possibly capture the man who did it instead?"

It was an easy choice. I just needed someone less emotionally invested to push me in the right direction. "Brad, we're headed to Rockport."

"Got it. We'll continue vetting all the top suspects, gathering more intel. This was a quick turnaround, so we're not completely sure the perp is even in our top five."

"I am."

Forty-Three

Frozen snow weighed down my eyelashes. It was annoying as hell. Even more so than my toes going numb in the foot-deep snow. I wiped my face and felt a sting on my left temple. That reminded me of my crash just a few hours earlier.

Another reason to take down this demented asshole.

Peering between two trees, I could see light seep around the edges of one window covered by shades. Smoke curled out of the chimney in the center of the gray, weathered structure, no more than fourteen hundred square feet or so.

"Cover the back," I whispered to Nick.

"We need to wait for backup, Alex. It's not just protocol, it's smart. Who knows what kind of traps this guy has set? We could open the door and trigger a bomb, some type of guerilla warfare trap. If this is the right guy, he gets his jollies by torturing people."

"Torturing cheating husbands. Not just everyone. He could have grabbed me, or Mark's bitch, but he didn't. He took Mark."

A swell of emotion surged throughout my body. I reset the Glock in my fingers, and I focused on the end game.

"I'm going in with you or without you."

As I high-stepped it through a cluster of trees, off in the distance I could hear waves lapping against the shore.

"Dammit, Alex." Nick had pulled up beside me, then signaled that he was flanking right.

I watched him pause at the lighted window. He tried to look inside, then dipped his body, waddled past the window, and disappeared to the back of the home.

Eyeing the front porch, I walked ten more steps. I heard something. It sounded like a wounded coyote, or it could have been the wind whistling through the tall trees. Lifting my eyes, the smoke continued to pour from the chimney.

I flinched. Beyond the dilapidated house, lightning splintered the sky over the ocean, illuminating menacing clouds. A few flashes, and then clouds disappeared like a dream.

Or a living nightmare.

Edging closer to the porch, my pulse peppering the side of my neck, I could feel the need to release my anger. Part of me hoped for a physical confrontation. Prayed for it. He might suffer. I might suffer, but someone needed to suffer. Someone *would* suffer.

Heel to toe, I inched across the porch, ensuring I kept my presence muted. I could now see a faint light around the edge of the front window, but it seemed to flash on and off. It had to be the lit fireplace.

Suddenly, I felt vulnerable, and I wondered if I should have listened to Nick. A ball of emotions stirred in my gut, but I didn't have a death wish. I bit down on my lip, engaging my focus even more, and I thought about my options, while keeping my head on swivel. No sound from inside. Not a TV or radio, or footsteps even. Not a ding from a microwave or an electronic sound from a more modern device. Zilch.

I had to move now. Waiting any longer would render my legs useless. One more step forward, and I was a foot from the door. I reached out and gripped the doorknob.

It turned. Raising my Glock to my waist, I slowly nudged the door open. An inch at first, then another two inches. No sign of J. L., but shadows danced on the far wall. I could hear a crackle and took in the familiar scent of burning wood. Readying myself for a surprise attack, I pushed the door open and crouched into a Weaver stance, my finger on the trigger.

My heart skipped a beat once the door opened halfway. A man in a denim shirt with his back to me was crouched in front of the fire.

"Stand up with your hands straight up. Now." My voice quivered, and I fought the shakes to keep my Glock steady.

He stood up as I called back to Nick. I heard the back door bounce off a wall. And then I heard a high-pitched shrill, and I instantly wondered what the hell we'd stumbled upon.

"Can I turn around?" the man said calmly.

Just then I spotted a poker in his right hand.

"Drop the poker."

He did, and it clanged off the wooden floor. He then turned to face me just as Nick came out of the back room holding the arm of a forty-something woman whose hands were tied together. Nick had pulled down the rag that had been in her mouth.

"Thank God you're here. Margaret Turov, State Police. Arrest this…this monster."

I turned my sights back to J. L. He didn't look at her. He stared at me, then glanced at the shadows, or at nothing. It was hard to tell.

"Mrs. Giordano," he said, "I've been expecting you."

Forty-Four

Her arms quaked as she lowered her body until the tip of her nose touched the carpet, made moist from her sweat. She completed her one hundredth pushup, moved to her knees, slipped the weighted backpack off her shoulders, and caught her breath. Her arms glistened from the slick film of perspiration.

But she needed more.

A quick swig of water, then she hopped on her exercise bike, turned up the resistance to a ten, and started pumping her legs. Within ten minutes, she began to feel that familiar burn. It only fueled her adrenaline that much more.

She brushed her hand across her perspiring forehead. Her eyes stopped for a moment at the tools on the kitchen table. Just as quickly she looked away, her mind searching for that zone where she could be focused, driven, yet content.

At least for a little while longer.

While still pumping her legs, she moved her hands to her waist, recalling her online research earlier. She'd stumbled upon two people whose lives had taken very different paths. She remembered that one famous quote from the first Stephen Richards, the guy who wrote so-called self-help books.

"When you connect to the silence within you, that is when you

make sense of the disturbance around you."

She'd laughed out loud when she read it the first time. This guy had no idea. Oh, she knew she was very self-aware. But there was no silence in her mind. Anything but. It was a nonstop, balls-out party taking place. All because she had come up with a new plan. One that didn't rely on others to carry out the twisted acts.

It was all about satisfying her greatest needs, her most primal urges. And then there was that revenge factor. The mere thought gave her goose bumps.

Back to Stephen Richards. Well, Stephen Richards number two. The person with whom she really connected. This guy had been dead since 1879, but his life now served as an inspiration. He'd murdered nine people, most using an ax. His victims were old and young, people who might have even cared about him. But they must have done him wrong. Or maybe he just couldn't resist the ecstasy of splitting each victim with the ax. She knew firsthand what that felt like.

Her body quaked again, and she finished her bike ride. She slipped off the seat, found a chair at the table, picked up one of ten blades, and pressed her finger into the point until it bled. The taste of rust swirled in her mouth.

Blood, sweat, and tears. She would orchestrate a killing spree that would evoke the full spectrum of emotions. Except her tears would be born from joy.

A joy unlike any other.

Forty-Five

Three weeks later

I'd been holding the envelope in my hand for so long it stuck to my fingers.

Peering up, I watched Erin and Luke struggle to get air with their kite. It was heartwarming to see them working together, running around like kids should. Just letting out all of their anxiety and grief after being stuffed inside for most of the last few weeks after their dad's murder.

I flipped a loose strand of hair out of my eyes and turned to face the wind while sitting cross-legged on a blanket on Revere Beach. It was still chilly by my standards, temperatures hovering near fifty with a gusty wind, but to smell the sea salt, sink my cold bare feet into the sand, it was worth it. More than worth it to see Erin and Luke just being normal kids. They had bonded like I could have never imagined a few weeks ago. They even hugged each other goodbye when one would run off to a school event or practice.

Filling my lungs with a sobering dose of salty air, I knew the healing process had just begun for Erin and Luke. They would see reminders of their father—of what they were missing—for months, if not years. They would see friends doing things with their fathers…creating memories. Even thinking of those future heartbreaking experiences, I could feel mini-explosions deep in my gut.

But I could now relate to my kids like I hadn't since the crash. Strangely, my dreams in the last week had been filled with memories of my parents, mostly my mom, and then the feeling of absence after she'd died. The death of a parent. Maybe that was another reason that I'd bonded with my two beautiful children. Mark hadn't bothered to tell me how my mom had died. I knew I still needed to reach out to my father. Lots to share, and even more to learn.

"Are you going to bury the letter in the sand?"

From behind me, Brad came around the blanket, and he wasn't alone. "You remember Bianca?"

"Hey," she said with a tight-lipped smile.

She didn't know what to say to me. No one did.

"Hi there."

Brad turned and saw the kids wrestling with the kite string. He nudged Bianca with his shoulder. "Hey, let's go help them out."

With smiles on their young faces, the couple—and I felt sure they were an item—jogged over to Erin and Luke.

For whatever reason, a quick image of Sydney came to mind, the morning following Mark's death, after Nick and I had taken J. L. Cobb into custody. Standing in the kitchen, she broke down when I told her about Mark. She literally crumbled to the floor and emotionally lost it. With my heart already torn to shreds, I had to listen to her spill her guts, and it wasn't pretty. She lashed out at the world, including me, admitting that she and Mark had slept together on and off since she'd been hired six months earlier. She claimed they'd "banged each other until they had nothing left" two nights earlier in the utility room before I'd gotten home. Nothing says romance and true love like "banging" on a tiled floor coated with cat litter.

I'd asked her to leave that night. Forever. Thankfully, she didn't show up at Mark's funeral. Otherwise, we might have had to make it a two-for-one special.

I'd yet to speak to the "other woman" who'd been tied to Mark's hip when he left Monty's that night. I wasn't sure I wanted to tear that wound open. On the surface, I knew people looked at me similar to how they looked at Agatha Barden and Jeanne Lepino. I couldn't change people's perception. I just held my head high and took one tiny step each day. To put the betrayal behind me, to let the anger fade and allow me to live an authentic life with my two kids.

I was due back at One Center Plaza in two days. I hadn't figured out how I would juggle being a single parent of two active kids with the responsibilities of being a federal agent. In fact, I hadn't told anyone, but I wasn't sure the FBI was for me anymore.

With all the drama and grief, it hadn't been difficult to shove the details of the case out of my mind, at least temporarily. From what Nick told me, J. L. hadn't shared much about his escapades, but he didn't deny anything either. When asked if he targeted cheating husbands, he just smiled. Fortunately, law enforcement officials found all but two of the stolen museum artifacts in his cottage. It must have had something to do with his fascination with the catalog numbers. As for the state police officer he'd kidnapped, she was shaken but not injured. Apparently, she'd tried to pull him over and found blood. A scuffle occurred, and then he took her hostage.

I still had questions, even with J. L. in custody. Was J. L. the one who'd used his car to push me off the road both times? And then there was the sniper shooting. Authorities found no weapon at his home, nor did he have any history of owning a weapon. To me, it just didn't fit with his persona, and I'd shared as much with

Nick and Jerry. They knew they had their killer, but they weren't ready to completely close the investigation—at least not when we'd last spoken a couple of weeks back.

I was quickly learning that a burning need to know was a part of me. Always questioning, always pushing to find the truth. I was no lawyer, so phrases like "beyond a reasonable doubt" didn't mean a damn thing to me. It was more about guilt or innocence. How or why I ended up going to law school was something I'd yet to be able to answer about myself. Maybe my father would know.

A flurry of sand sprayed my face. "Whoa!"

"Hey, Mom, I'm freezing," Luke said, plopping down next to me.

Erin jogged up behind her brother and huddled close to me on the other side. They didn't say anything. Nothing needed to be said. I could hear the quick cadence of their breaths, and that alone let me know they were making an effort to move forward with their lives.

"Hey, check it out!" Luke pointed up.

Brad and Bianca maneuvered the string, and the kite soared across the vast sky. I could hear red and blue streamers flutter against the wind.

"You guys want to take control now?" Brad called out.

"Come on, Mom," Luke said, jumping up and running off.

With a smile on her face, Erin lifted to her feet and jogged over to join everyone. "You can do it too, Mom," she said, calling back to me.

I got to my feet, dusted sand off my pants, then noticed the letter on the blanket. I ripped it open and read the commendation I'd received for apprehending J. L. Cobb, serial killer. But that wasn't why I'd opened the letter. I'd noticed who it was addressed to: Alex Troutt. The first step toward taking my life back.

"Mom, check this out!" Luke said as he arched his back,

making the kite dip and then soar back into the sky.

I ran over to join my kids. To enjoy my life today. It was one step, but one I would remember forever.

John W. Mefford Bibliography

The Alex Troutt Thrillers (Redemption Thriller Collection)
AT BAY (Book 1)
AT LARGE (Book 2)
AT ONCE (Book 3)
AT DAWN (Book 4)
AT DUSK (Book 5)
AT LAST (Book 6)
AT STAKE (Book 7)
AT ANY COST (Book 8)
BACK AT YOU (Book 9)
AT EVERY TURN (Book 10)
AT DEATH'S DOOR (Book 11)
AT FULL TILT (Book 12)

The Ivy Nash Thrillers (Redemption Thriller Collection)
IN DEFIANCE (Book 1)
IN PURSUIT (Book 2)
IN DOUBT (Book 3)
BREAK IN (Book 4)
IN CONTROL (Book 5)
IN THE END (Book 6)

The Ozzie Novak Thrillers (Redemption Thriller Collection)
ON EDGE (Book 1)

GAME ON (Book 2)
ON THE ROCKS (Book 3)
SHAME ON YOU (Book 4)
ON FIRE (Book 5)
ON THE RUN (Book 6)

The Ball & Chain Thrillers
MERCY (Book 1)
FEAR (Book 2)
BURY (Book 3)
LURE (Book 4)
PREY (Book 5)
VANISH (Book 6)
ESCAPE (Book 7)
TRAP (Book 8)

The Booker Thrillers
BOOKER – Streets of Mayhem (Book 1)
BOOKER – Tap That (Book 2)
BOOKER – Hate City (Book 3)
BOOKER – Blood Ring (Book 4)
BOOKER – No Más (Book 5)
BOOKER – Dead Heat (Book 6)

The Greed Thrillers
FATAL GREED (Book 1)
LETHAL GREED (Book 2)
WICKED GREED (Book 3)
GREED MANIFESTO (Book 4)

To stay updated on John's latest releases, visit:
JohnWMefford.com

Made in the USA
Monee, IL
14 August 2023

41035495R00177